An Orkney Murder

An Orkney Murder

A Rose McQuinn Mystery

ALANNA KNIGHT

This edition first published in Great Britain in 2006 by
Allison & Busby Limited
13 Charlotte Mews
London W1T 4EJ
www.allisonandbusby.com

A catalogue record for this book is available from
the British Library.

10 9 8 7 6 5 4 3 2 1

ISBN 0 7490 8181 3
978-0-7490-8181-2

Printed and bound in Great Britain by
Bookmarque Ltd, Croydon, Surrey

ALANNA KNIGHT has written more than fifty novels, (including fourteen in the successful Inspector Faro series), four works of non-fiction, numerous short stories and two plays since the publication of her first book in 1969. Born and educated in Tyneside, she now lives in Edinburgh. She is a founding member of the Scottish Association of Writers, Honorary President of the Edinburgh Writers' Club, and Convener of the Scottish Chapter of the Crime Writers' Association.

Find our more about Alanna Knight by visiting her website at *www.alannaknight.com*

Dedication:

To ORKNEY
and in memory of
George Mackay Brown

Chapter One

Murder only happens in other families.

So we all pretend to believe. But domestic murder is more widespread than one might imagine.

According to James Payn, editor of *Cornhill*: '*One person in every five hundred is an undiscovered murderer. This gives us all hope, almost a certainty, that we may reckon on one such person at least among our acquaintances.*'

When he expounded his theory to three members of his London club, they were able to name six persons of their various acquaintance who were, or had been suspected of being, successful murderers. To read such sensational opinions in popular magazines is one matter, but as I was soon to discover for myself, the face of murder hides behind many benign masks.

The idea that the family of my father, Chief Inspector Jeremy Faro, lately retired from the Edinburgh City Police, might harbour an undetected murderer was as unlikely as his proud boast that his grandmother was a seal woman.

Having laid aside for the immediate future the mantle of Rose McQuinn née Faro, Lady Investigator, Discretion

Guaranteed, I stepped off the steamer in Stromness that August day of 1896 with no thought of anything more violent than the certainty that I would have cheerfully killed for a cup of tea after a somewhat stormy crossing from Leith.

This was the prelude to a long-awaited visit to my younger sister Emily. We had been close as children and now I was looking forward to seeing her after a separation of more than a decade.

Emily had been content to remain in Orkney. After I left to become a schoolteacher in Glasgow, she settled down and married Erland Yesnaby, a widower of ancient lineage, somewhat her senior. The intervening years since that event had been inexpertly bridged by a succession of vague communications, a weakness shared, I might add, with the majority of the Faro family. As I learned to my cost while I was in America, letter-writing is sadly not one of our finest accomplishments.

Happily anticipating a joyful family reunion, I made my way gratefully along a static quayside, on terra firma once more, first checking that my luggage was safely anchored on the back of my bicycle in a container artfully designed for that purpose by Jack Macmerry.

The machine had aroused some interest among my fellow passengers for such equipages were still regarded with cautious amusement despite the emergence of an occasional horseless carriage on the streets of Edinburgh – an event assuring those citizens of a lugubrious nature that this was a mere whim, a passing phase. There was no future in such outlandish, noisy, smelly means of travel, beyond a clear indication that the world was going to the dogs.

Bicycles? Yes, perhaps, but they were still deemed undignified, a little *outré* if not downright improper as a means of transport for ladies, displaying to the general public their lower limbs. Quite disgraceful.

As I disdained to include myself in society's definition of a lady, I cared little for such opinions. Years of pioneering life in the American West had set at naught the notion of behaving according to the conventions of middle-class Edinburgh.

To return to more practical matters. As Hopescarth lay some distance to the north-west of Stromness, I considered the advantages of a bicycle where only the fortunate few owned carriages and most folk still travelled by cart, on foot or on horseback.

Prepared for the worst, I pictured a bleaker, more remote and less populated area than Kirkwall, our home with grandmother Mary Faro after Mamma died in Edinburgh with our stillborn baby brother, leaving Pappa grief-stricken and at his wits' end about the future of two small daughters.

As for dear Emily, her worst fault over the years had been an irritating habit of ignoring what I regarded as urgent family matters. Her one-page replies to my letters contained little information beyond stressing that she was well (which was not always true as I was to discover) and ended as speedily as possible on a cheerful note in the hope that this also found me in good health and spirits (often a far from accurate assessment).

I tried to stir her interest from time to time by laying claim to a more dramatic existence in Arizona, mentioning occasional Indian raids, cattle lifted and property burnt. All of which failed to arouse any comment from Emily in her eventual replies.

After Danny's disappearance and the loss of our baby son, I kept my promise to him that if one day he walked out and failed to return, I was to wait for six months and then, presuming some fate had befallen him in the course of his employment with the Pinkerton Detective Agency, I was to return home to Edinburgh.

Ever since I arrived in May 1895, I had been confidently expecting an invitation to Orkney, perhaps even the suggestion that I make my home with them at Yesnaby House. The distant tone of Emily's infrequent letters, hinting that our grandmother, frail and needing extra care, was now living with them, made me suspect that only a sense of duty directed her to reply at all. Indeed in moments of depression and doubt, of which there were many in those early days, I felt that she wished to banish memory of the tragic circumstances of her only sister's return to Scotland.

As time passed, I often asked myself if it was unreasonable of me to expect an immediate invitation to Hopescarth, and I believe I could be forgiven for nursing bitter disap-pointment at not even the suggestion of some future visit.

Reluctant to think Emily heartless, I gave her the benefit of the doubt and assumed a total inability to express her emotions in letters of some pressing domestic anxiety of her own – which indeed proved to be the case.

To my anxious requests for more details regarding our grandmother's health her replies were carefully veiled.

There was no mention of yet another relative, older even than Gran. A great-grandmother, whose existence had never been mentioned in our Orkney days.

Certainly, had I given the matter of Sibella Scarth considered thought, a simple calculation based on Gran's eighty-four years would have set her own mother's age at past a century, her bones presumably laid peacefully to rest long since in the local kirkyard.

But to return to Emily's eagerly awaited invitation.

It had arrived at long last, at what seemed the most opportune of moments. In Edinburgh, an indifferent summer had already given up in despair, rain and cold winds sought out every crevice in the stone walls of my ancient home in Solomon's Tower at the base of Arthur's Seat. Already there was a touch of mellow autumn in the slanting sunlight on harvest fields, an air of melancholy bringing with it the stealthy return of bitter memories.

This was the second anniversary of Danny's disappearance and I was not yet reconciled to the inevitable conclusion. I still hoped – with faith undying – that somewhere he was still alive.

So many deep-rooted scars were miraculously healed in dreams. There was one where a door opened. Danny was there smiling, holding out his arms awaiting our rapturous reunion.

The dream faded rapidly into a sad reality as, once again, I opened my eyes to an empty room, an empty heart and a door obstinately closed against the one person I longed to resurrect, totally ignoring what common sense screamed at me.

That I was willing back to life a dead man.

True, I had found another love. Detective Sergeant Jack Macmerry of the Edinburgh City Police. And Jack was growing impatient. His practical, logical mind could not accept that my desire not to commit myself was due to my deep-seated faith in Danny's return. Jack wanted marriage – now – and children – before it was too late. Reminding me that I was thirty-one years old, he believed that I was making an excuse.

Lately he had accused me of not wanting to settle down

and be a policeman's wife. Perhaps he had guessed my secret, knew me better that I did myself, for I enjoyed my detective role as a lady investigator.

I now had a logbook of domestic mysteries and hotel robberies which had called for utmost discretion. All had been successfully solved without calling in the police and losing the desired anonymity of the victims: in most cases, a wealthy bored married woman with a young lover or a well-kenned gentleman with a mistress or a taste for the seamy side of Edinburgh life, for whom disclosure and scandal would mean ruin.

There had also been two very alarming and dangerous encounters with murderers where my own life had been in deadly peril and I had narrowly survived, in part due to Jack's intervention.

However, as I have already remarked, Emily's letter was opportune. I needed an escape clause. I was between cases. With no clients for the past three months, I had begun to despair of unfaithful husbands, indiscreet wives, thieving domestics and fraudsters.

How Jack gloated over my lack of business, certain that this would persuade me to set the date for our wedding, heartily sick of our 'on-off' arrangement, for I was neither mistress nor wife. It was all too casual, too unconventional for him. He – and his parents, whom I had yet to meet – had set their hearts on a Christmas wedding.

And what was more important, it seemed that a wife would strengthen his chances of promotion. For some reason he believed that the Board would look kindly upon the non-flighty, well-settled family man.

No wonder I fled! Too cowardly for a definite 'No' – for I did not want to lose Jack. I loved him in my way, and as Gran was to point out when we talked later, I had every intention of having my cake and eating it! In that she was quite correct, without my adding 'as long as I can!'

But I did not doubt Jack's determination to bring the issue to a conclusion. When I returned from Orkney, Jack must have his answer one way or the other.

As we said our goodbyes, in the prickly manner of one who feels himself ill-used, Jack said: 'You're not concerned about Thane, I trust.'

I smiled. The deerhound Thane, my strange companion for the past year, was the least of my problems. He needed no human carer. He had his own life. Long before we met – how long I had not the least idea – he had survived and would continue to do so, returning to the existence he had always known in the wild secret haunts, the hidden caves of Arthur's Seat.

'Three weeks and we'll be together again,' Jack had sighed as he kissed me and added in a quite unnecessary tone of consolation, 'Don't worry, it will soon pass.'

I forbore to mention that this was a holiday, one I was greatly looking forward to, as he continued: 'You'll be back home in plenty of time to plan everything. Everything, Rose.' The firm set of his jaw left me in no doubt of what he had in mind: our wedding date.

And so I closed the door of the Tower behind me, confident of my return, with not the remotest idea on that sunny morning of how a family visit to a beloved sister might erupt into danger greater than that involved in any of my Edinburgh cases.

And this time, without Jack or Thane in a last-minute rescue bid, delivering me from evil.

Or death.

Chapter Two

As I bicycled down the road to Hopescarth, my progress assisted by a stiff seaward breeze, I realised that this terrain was different to Kirkwall, the town where I had grown up.

This was a new land, a foreign soil. I had forgotten there would be no trees, at least none worthy of comment or sheltering charm, like sturdy oak, horse chestnut and elm. The only trees bold enough to inhabit these cold northwest isles were timid sycamore and melancholy willow. Offering no airs of protection and benevolence, they hugged close to house walls in a manner suggesting despair if not downright apprehension, their continual fight for survival clearly visible in twisted and distorted limbs.

Orkney may lack trees or mountains and display little of the grandeur of the Scottish highlands or the tamed splendours of shady glens in suburban Edinburgh, but there is adequate compensation in wild beauty and an atmosphere which is unique. Infinite space, the great sweeping confluence of sky, sea and rolling landscape, undulating hills in a sea-bitten, wind-torn pastiche of greens, greys and peat browns, interrupted here and there by a patchwork of scattered crofts, few out of sight or sound of the sea.

As I puffed up hills and soared down them again, the wine-clear air, so bracing and familiar, seemed to hold out a promise of recapturing the nostalgia of youthful days. Of returning to sunlight and long golden beaches from Edinburgh's close-packed smoky city, rightfully termed Auld Reekie.

That confused blur of excitement tinged with sadness. Goodbyes to Pappa and beloved stepbrother Vince, clutching my memory of Mamma, a smiling photo, that last bedside farewell. The disbelief that she would not open her eyes when I kissed her. Or that the little wax doll at her side was the baby brother who would never grow to run out into the street to play with Emily and me.

A fate, at the time mercifully concealed from me, that one day would also befall me: I too was to have a waxen baby of my own, that now lays in a lonely unmarked grave, lost for ever in the Arizonian desert.

Here in Orkney, home of my carefree child- and girlhood, I was confident that I would again find the surroundings healing, for Edinburgh still pressed hard upon me, scarred with memories of Danny unfolding at every street corner. This island was different, part of my world before Danny McQuinn.

Now Stromness lay a mile or two behind and fragments of that happier past returned as I sailed effortlessly downhill. Eventually I stopped to wipe my nose, with a wry smile, for cool breezes always had that effect. That little matter taken care of, putting away my handkerchief, I set off with an increasing sense of pleasurable anticipation that I would enjoy every moment of the weeks ahead, that

Orkney's magic of old would work for me, and a change of scene would be followed by a clear sense of purpose and faith in the future.

On my return to Edinburgh, I would give Jack his answer. Already I had to confess to missing him just a little and imagining us returning together and introducing him to the places of my early life.

At that moment I had no doubts about the future. I could hear myself saying, 'Yes, I will marry you. And we will honeymoon in Orkney.'

For suddenly it was all easy, simple. Too simple. I was brought down to earth with a grinding wobble on my front wheel.

I had picked up a stone in the spokes.

Perhaps that was an omen, the first of many I should have heeded.

There was worse to come.

Removing the offending stone I discovered that the front tyre was punctured. Cursing under my breath in a very unladylike fashion, I took out the tin box containing the repair kit and stared at it blankly, never previously having had any reason to use it with Jack always at hand.

At that moment I wished most heartily that I had him here now to make soothing noises, allowing me to stand by and marvel at his skill and dexterity, assuring him that he was so good at such things and I was all fingers and thumbs.

As I set to work, to crown all the rain began. Where was that lovely sunlit sky? Even the skylarks had taken cover in disgust. Wishing I could do the same, I took out my rain cape.

Then suddenly from the direction I had travelled, the road, hidden by the top of the hill, began to vibrate. Straightening up, I stared at the sky.

Thunder? And at that moment the most splendid sight in the world. Wheels and the blunt nose of a snorting asthmatic monster appeared over the brow of the hill, quickly reassembling itself into a motor car.

Wonder of wonders! The horseless carriage had found its way across the sea to Orkney.

Scrambling well aside, overwhelmed by smoke and fumes, I gave it ample room to pass on the narrow road.

The driver, goggled and helmeted, looked down and saluted me gravely. Then, with a squeal of brakes, the gleaming machine slid a few yards forward. A series of groans announced some misgivings as it came to a standstill and puffed more blue smoke in my face.

The driver jumped down.

'Having trouble, Miss?' he asked, as if kneeling on the side of the road with a bicycle's wheel in the air was not sufficient evidence for even a mildly observant eye.

However, the question was encouraging; it suggested that help might be at hand. So I smiled sadly and decided to become very feminine. Men, Jack told me, liked that. And although nature decreed that I should be small with a cloud of yellow curls, appearances are deceptive. The role of helpless female does not come naturally, as many males, gentlemen and otherwise, have found to their cost.

On this occasion, however, I decided that a measure of innocent deception would never have more reason to be called upon.

'I am indeed. I haven't had to deal with a puncture before.' I made a desperate bid at fluttering eyelashes in a helpless fashion. They are glossy black and thick, like my eyebrows, inherited from Pappa. Completely at variance with yellow curls, the continual despair of my sister-in-law, Olivia, who considers such eyebrows not only unfashionable but rather coarse and unladylike.

Shaking his head, the driver gazed down on me from his lofty height of six foot-something. Frowning, he gloomily contemplated the bicycle with its injured wheel whirring gently.

'It's these infernal roads, Miss, they're a menace. Nothing more than sheep tracks in places.'

I had hoped for more than this dejected appraisal but his tone warned me sadly that he was helpless to deal with a punctured tyre. And at that moment what I needed most was a man of action.

Of swift action, I thought anxiously, if I am to see Hopescarth, still six miles distant, before dark.

'Know anything about bicycles?' I asked hopefully while he continued watching the prostrate machine very cautiously as if it had just dropped mortally wounded at his feet.

'Never had the pleasure, I'm afraid.' Another shake of the head, a sigh. Had it been a horse at that moment, he would have undoubtedly advised shooting it, a mercy killing, to end its misery.

Another regretful sigh and holding out a leather-gauntleted hand palm upwards: 'The rain's getting heavier.' A slight bow. 'Permit me to give you a lift to where it is you're going – you'll do better under cover.'

A gallant offer. But were we going in the same direction? I presumed so as I didn't expect there would be more than this one main road, winding purposefully over the landscape and eventually leading to Hopescarth. I didn't want to discourage him at that stage or to give him a chance to regret his offer, so with a breathless 'Thank you' I watched him seize the bicycle and anchor it firmly on to the luggage grid at the back of the motor car.

Then with an air of triumph, handing me up the step and into the passenger seat, he unfurled a gigantic umbrella.

'There you are. Where now?'

He could hardly throw me back on to the road after all that. And he did sound like a gentleman.

'I'm heading for Hopescarth. Do you know it?'

He laughed delightedly. 'Certainly do. I'm going there myself.'

Here was fortune indeed! 'To Yesnaby House?'

He shook his head. 'Nothing so grand. Just as far as the village. Hold on.'

A great roar and the monster shot forward. We were away.

'Excellent! Excellent,' he chuckled. 'Thanks be that you were downshill or I'd have had to rush past and leave you there, I'm afraid. Daren't stop on an upgrade or it's sheer hell – begging your pardon, Miss. It's the very devil to get the old girl going again.'

He grinned at me. 'Let me introduce myself. Craig—'

I lost the rest as the engine went into a furious performance of moving forward. Noise, blue smoke, rattle and shake of every conceivable bolt and screw. All rather unnerving although the driver seemed happy, indeed positively glowing with pride. I gasped out my name and in return received information suggesting that he was in charge of an archaeological dig. From Inverness, I gathered that the motor car was on loan, the easiest way, he explained, to transport delicate artefacts to the Leith steamer, which would take them to Edinburgh, where, I was given to understand, eager antiquarians waited to classify them.

At least I think that was what he said; I couldn't be certain of anything since conversation was severely limited and carried on at the tops of our voices, competing with engine sounds suggesting the middle of a pack of baying hounds heading for the kill.

After a couple of noisy miles the rain stopped and the sky, blue to the horizon, was occupied by a few cumulus clouds, the ones known romantically to us children as 'angels' pillows'.

Skylarks were all around us, soaring into the blue to be seen, but alas not heard. 'Our Lady's Hens,' the Orcadians called them. How Jack loved that! Thinking of him brought back home and Arthur's Seat vividly again and running through the heather with Thane.

As we sped along the road, this land north of Stromness was a new experience. All my Orkney years had been spent in the vicinity of Kirkwall. We had rarely travelled west with Gran, who regarded such ventures with suspicion worthy of darkest Africa and head hunters. Now I realised I had not been quite prepared for the emptiness, wild and bleak, the increasing glimpses of a harsh seascape.

A land whose waiting was measured not in passing centuries but in the darker millenia beyond the ken of God-fearing, churchgoing Presbyterians.

'The isles at the world's end,' mariners called them, to be feared as the home of wreckers and the legendary seal people, as well as mermaids and trolls. Here and there, man had been bold and, turning a blind eye on the vagaries of an unreliable climate, had planted houses perched uneasily as summer flies on hillsides and a boulder-strewn terrain stretching to the horizons.

As I considered whether these new tokens of man's optimism were prepared to defy and withstand centuries of winter winds, the scene before us darkened, the rain began again, heavier this time.

I put up the umbrella. We were going to be very wet by the time Hopescarth came in sight.

A signpost loomed into view. 'Skailholm', followed by a street of newly built stone houses.

Craig Whatever-His-Name shouted: 'The local inn. We'll shelter until the rain stops. Lenny's also the blacksmith. He'll know what to do – fix that tyre in no time.' And patting the steering wheel affectionately, 'The old girl here doesn't care too much for this heaving up and down hills in the rain.'

Neither did I. And his next words stole my heart for ever. 'Fancy a cup of tea?'

I grinned from ear to ear. 'What a brilliant suggestion.'

The old girl, as he called her, seemed pleased too. She stopped with a minimum of braking and what, in human terms, might be credited as a sigh of pleasure.

Craig obviously knew Lenny well and the bicycle was handed over to a man of immense dimensions in every direction. Here was the blacksmith of legend, straight from Wagnerian opera, a modern-day Thor, hurling his lightning shafts across the sky. Through a thick hatch of black beard, a gleam of teeth became visible, a broad grin assuring me of care and instant success, as he lifted the bicycle into the air as if it weighed no more than a pot of ale.

Once inside the inn, I realised by the smacking kiss bestowed on the rather shrill lady who greeted us that Craig was also on excellent terms with Lenny's wife.

Introduced as Maud, she seemed an incongrous addition to my image of female Orkney. Her ample bosom, swaying hips, vivid complexion and elaborate coiffeur fairly reeked of the city and, indeed, would not have come amiss on the stage of one of Edinburgh's variety theatres.

Tea, bere bannocks and cheese were ordered as Craig helped me out of my rain cape. Removal of his gloves revealed a rather grubby hand with broken nails. This indicated a close acquaintance with the soil and a lack of personal vanity as well as soap, which I found quite endearing, thoroughly at odds with the handsome motor car.

'The old girl', his pride and joy I guessed, was still much of a novelty especially as I had seen only an occasional Benz snorting its way along Princes Street and severely frightening the horse-drawn traffic, as well as sending young children and nursemaids with perambulators into hysterics.

The bosomy Maud set our order before us, hovering closer to Craig than was strictly necessary and eyeing me sharply in that 'who-is-this-woman?' manner. I was intrigued to know what had set her down to waste her over-abundant charms on Orkney's desert air and Lenny, the local blacksmith. Despite those narrow-eyed glances in my direction, she didn't scare me in the least. At that moment, hungry and cold, overcome by the prospects of a warm fire, the sight and smell of a teapot made me all emotional and I wouldn't have cared in the slightest if Maud had possessed two heads.

'I didn't get all of your name back there,' Craig apologised.

'Mrs McQuinn – Rose.'

He smiled. 'Pleased to make your acquaintance, Mrs McQuinn. I'm Craig Denmore.'

I was impressed as suddenly Denmore and Inverness clicked into place. The 'Denmore' was Pappa's favourite whisky and a certain addition to every elegant middle-class sideboard in Edinburgh. His father Sir Miles, the local laird, owned the distillery and, doubtless, the borrowed motor car.

And as the lad I presumed to be his son removed helmet and goggles, I was in for the greatest surprise of all.

In that instant he was no stranger. I knew him. Of that I was certain. We had met somewhere before.

But where?

Chapter Three

Craig Denmore was no stranger.

Later I was to tell myself that was just a feeble excuse, wishful thinking on my part. An attractive, above-average handsome man. Tall, with the black hair, white skin and dark eyes of the Highlander, his age hard to place – between twenty-five and thirty-five. His looks seemed to improve at every meeting as did that weird idea that we had met before.

This notion became an obsession which was to remain with me until I learned the truth. I have an excellent memory for faces, but Craig didn't fit in anywhere. A passing acquaintance perhaps, the friend of a friend, but I would surely have remembered this particular Highlander's striking looks.

And what was more, I was sure that it had been in Edinburgh. Completely baffled, I had met this man, or someone very like him, but not quite identical. Memory threw out a message, a face slightly out of focus. Something different. A beard perhaps that he had shaved off. I would ask when I knew him better.

Oh yes, of that I was quite sure, that I was going to know him better, and what more opportune time than now to ask that burning question. Had we met before?

He looked puzzled, taken aback. For a moment his eyes narrowed then he recovered, said heartily: 'You know, Mrs McQuinn, I've been thinking the very same thing.'

'Edinburgh, was it?' I asked helpfully.

He seized that eagerly. 'Some academic society meeting, of course.'

I was flattered but honest. 'Alas, I don't belong to any.'

A frown. 'What about the antiquarian lectures? They're very popular.'

'You give lectures?'

A modest nod. 'Occasionally, I am asked to do so.'

But that didn't fit either. Lectures weren't my thing at all. I shook my head sadly.

'Some gathering of mutual friends then?'

I looked at him hopefully. 'That must be it. Perhaps you had a beard then?'

That idea seemed to startle him. His eyes widened, a hand wavering to his chin, then he laughed. 'A beard? Not I!'

So we skipped through a series of names and drew a blank there too. At last, laughing at the absurdity of it all, he took my hand and said, in a voice that made my knees go suddenly weak: 'It must be Fate intended us to meet.'

His mocking tone warned that he wasn't to be taken seriously and, frowning impishly, he added: 'Do you by any chance believe in reincarnation? Perhaps we both lived here in Orkney before. Maybe I came and carried you off in a Viking raid. All part of the rape and pillage programme.'

Certainly the idea of ourselves as the ghosts of long-dead lovers had a romantic appeal and, as my heart raced, that particular vision, prompted the thought that there could be much worse fates than being carried off anywhere by Craig Denmore. Common sense, however, sternly rejected such absurdity. Reincarnation was all too pat for the practical mind I had inherted from Pappa. There had to be an answer to everything, a purpose. And if this wasn't immediately obvious then it was sure to exist somewhere. One had merely to search diligently to be justly rewarded for one's patience.

So although I pretended and wanted to believe Craig's theory, I knew that deep down I wasn't fooled. The logical explanation was there swirling about in memory's depths and one day it would surface...

There was some mystery about Craig Denmore and solving mysteries was my business. But realisation came when it seemed too late, a sledgehammer blow from a future still mercifully veiled.

Meanwhile, over a second pot of tea while the rain continued to stream down the windows, holding us captive in this cosy parlour cut off from the rest of Orkney, I answered his questions about Edinburgh.

Oh, how he envied me all those exciting facilities – theatres, concerts, parks. I gathered life on a dig was mostly very dull.

'Surely you've found some exciting things?'

'Not really. Just a few beads, some coins and a brooch. But they are valuable – everything fits together and eventually a picture will emerge.'

'Do you know whose grave it is?'

'We're not absolutely sure. A lot of burials in this area, but from the artefacts we know that this one is relatively modern. Almost certainly thirteenth century from the coins.'

That didn't sound relatively modern to me, however the exciting suggestion of the coins hinted at treasure trove.

Criag laughed and shook his head. 'Don't fall into the trap like most of the crofters hereabouts. These islands are full of undiscovered stone cists, remains of Pictish houses, Iron Age cairns, stone circles, brochs. Reason is that there are no trees.' Pausing, he smiled. 'Can you guess why?'

I knew enough about Orkney to answer that one. 'Trees are wood and timber rots.'

'Correct!' An approving laugh, exactly the kind he would give a promising student. 'And with no wood for coffins, bodies were placed in cairns. Some cairns in this area are too delicate to excavate because of the occasional peat-bog burial.' He paused. 'Like Hopescarth, you must have heard about that one.'

And when I shook my head, he said, 'Don't you remember, the woman who had fallen in by accident on her way home ten years ago and lain there undiscovered until last year. October it was. Just before we packed up the dig for the winter.'

He looked at me. 'Surely that was big news for the Edinburgh newspapers.'

I shook my head. 'I must have missed that one.'

I didn't add that I relied on Jack, an avid reader of newspapers, to keep me in touch with any important items or exciting local news. And Orkney was important. Jack would never have missed it. I felt a sudden chill, a cold shaft of dread as if someone had walked over my grave, a footfall I knew well. It was called premonition.

'Mostly they are old bones we find,' Craig continued, 'animals from a litchen midden and once in a blue moon, a coin, the hint of treasure trove. A bag of coins, hastily buried by some departing resident or invader, hoping to return and collect it, but unable to keep that particular date with destiny,' he added ruefully.

I knew what he meant. Fifty years ago, near Kirkwall, a silver hoard was found by an unsuspecting crofter ploughing his field and unearthing a burial chamber with rich pickings. 'A queen's ransom' was how the newspapers described it.

Ever since that day, every crofter went out, hopeful that when his plough struck the next long stone or boulder, this would be the hidden entrance to another cairn with grave treasure intact, the burial place of some long-dead chief, unplundered by the Vikings who, according to the runic symbols they left behind, sometimes took six days to remove all the treasure they found.

The archaeologists were eternally hopeful. The slightest signal of success and they moved in. While the poor crofter watched eagle-eyed from his window dreaming of a life of luxury and untold wealth. The only rewards for the diggers were sore backs and blistered hands, with treasures for the academics confined to another learned paper and another item of knowledge unearthed regarding the ancients.

I continued to shiver. All this talk about burials.

Maybe I was taking a chill. Or had the dreaded footfall of premonition already aroused the demon that lurked hidden deep within the confines of memory?

Chapter Four

Craig was warming to his subject: 'Iron Age and Picts are really exciting, but the thirteenth century is just like yesterday to us.' He sighed. 'But there's always the next one. That's what keeps us going, the hopes of some historic burial site.'

'Even at Hopescarth?'

'Something like that. Have you heard of the Maid of Norway, by any chance?'

I had indeed. And so had everyone else in Orkney. Legends had been built on the heiress to the throne of Scotland, the seven-year old princess who died on board a ship in a storm on Orkney's inhospitable shore. Buried in 1290 in an unmarked grave, her dowry was certainly a queen's ransom, long sought but never found.

Lenny, our genial host, popped his head round the door. 'The lass's bicycle is fixed now.'

Thanking him profusely, I suggested suitable recompense. Brushing that aside with a curt nod, he said: 'Don't worry about that, Miss, it'll all go on the gentleman's slate.'

Craig laughed genially and I had no further excuse to

linger especially as the voluptuous Maud was now alarmingly evident, feverishly polishing nearby tables and keeping a sharp eye on Craig.

For her special benefit, I gave him my most charming smile, my most lingering glance. 'Thank you. You have been most kind—'

He looked at the window. 'Wait until the rain stops, you have quite a bit to go.'

That was true. Grateful for his observation, I sat back and asked: 'Tell me, what makes you think that you've discovered the Maid of Norway's grave? Wouldn't they have been likely to choose an existing burial chamber for her? There are lots of them about.'

'Put her besides the remains of some pagan chieftain, you mean?' he said in shocked tones. 'Never. The Church would never have allowed that. They were very particular – masses would have to be said for her. Remember, she wouldn't have been making that voyage alone or with just a few close members of her household. The entourage would include high officials and priests.'

He shook his head. 'No question of a burial in unhallowed ground. And unless there was already a holy building within sight of the shore, my guess would be that they gave her temporary burial, intending to return and deliver her remains to Iona, the resting place of the Scottish kings.' Pausing he looked at me. 'Know much about the background, the politics of the time?'

'No. Mostly legend based on rumour or the other way round.'

He was dying to tell me. It was pouring down outside. I was in no desperate hurry so I let him have his head:

'In 1284, Alexander the Third of Scotland's only son and heir died on his twentieth birthday. The year before, the king's only daughter, Margaret of Norway, had died giving birth to a daughter – also named Margaret, the Maid of Norway, and in the absence of a claimant this made her heiress-apparent to the Scottish throne. When she was three years old, the King of Scots remarried Yolande de Dreux. Six months later he was dead, thrown from his horse as he tried to ride out a storm and reach his young wife waiting for him at Kinghorn, in Fife. There was no heir forthcoming from that brief marriage and no enthusiasm for a Scotland ruled by a child and a jealous regency.

'So it was decided that Margaret should marry King Edward of England's son, a year her junior, and so unite the two kingdoms. Infant marriages were very popular among medieval royal houses, with consummation delayed until the children matured. After a series of negotiations, arguments and false starts, Margaret set forth in the autumn of 1290.

'All we know after that is that she died from the rigours of a stormy crossing, but there have been more sinister hints that various factions did not want her as Queen of Scotland or were outraged that there was to be a connection with the hated enemy England. There were also the usual hints of poison, a favourite way of getting rid of unwanted royalty in those days.'

'What about her dowry you mentioned – the fabled treasure trove?'

Craig shook his head. 'Who knows? It certainly existed. Some very illustrious persons have long been intrigued by the question of what happened to the contents of the treasure ship that set sail with her from Norway but, according to rumour, never returned.

'After her death it vanished without trace. Very easy in those days for a ship to do just that, go down with all hands in a storm in uncharted seas, disappear off the face of the earth or become the victim of pirates who were very good at disposing of all signs of their ill-gotten gains.'

'What do you think happened?' I asked.

He sighed. 'I'm in favour of shipwreck as the most logical reason. Think of it – the autumn weather which had blown up the storm that changed the face of Scotland's history, could have been equally wild and the seas equally treacherous on the way back to Bergen. That is the way historians see it. But they are orderly folk,' he added wryly, 'and they do like to smooth out the unruly times they are recording, and wherever possible draw neat lines under events.'

He paused to refill his cup from a now tepid teapot.

'Less trusting souls have put forward the theory that someone in authority secretly stowed away the dowry on the island intending to return and collect it. So what really happened is anyone's guess. Maybe the ship went down and the secret died with the plotter – or plotters – abroad. Maybe someone lived to tell the tale, because wind of that treasure has persisted, handed down through the ages.'

I looked at him. 'Do you think the story is just a romantic legend, the tale of a tragic young princess?'

He shrugged. 'I keep an open mind, that's what I'm trained to do but I've learned through the years that behind every legend there are a few grains of truth. And a few more grains for a treasure. All we know for sure, from the records of one Huw Scarth, who lived here in the sixteenth century, is the rather improbable story that he pursued a rainbow across his field and at its end he found a pot of gold. With it, he was able to persuade Black Pate, the notorious Stuart Earl who ruled Orkney at that time, to let him remain here—'

'Wait a moment,' I interrupted. 'So you think this pot of

gold he found might have been the missing treasure – the Maid's dowry?'

He shrugged. 'Very likely part of it – who knows? It certainly bought the poor crofter Huw Scarth peace in his time as well as the lands of Hopescarth. Do you realise that eight generations of Scarths must have lived continuously in the palace he bought from Black Pate? Until Edwin Yesnaby tore it down a hundred years ago—'

'Yesnaby?' I interrupted. 'What happened to the Scarths?'

'The last one was childless. It went to the only remaining member of the family on the distaff side. Under Scots law females inherit, as you know. If Erland Yesnaby has no children, it will pass to the next nearest kin.'

That wry smile again. 'Fortunately he took the precaution of marrying his heiress cousin Thora, now deceased.'

'Will you be wanting anything else – sir?' Maud was now very busy polishing the table next to us and showing a keen interest in our conversation, or was it the very presentable archaeologist?

Craig gave her his most endearing smile. 'The lady and I are just leaving.' And turning to me: 'Where was I?'

'The Yesnabys.'

'Oh yes. Your present destination, is it not? Well, the present rather dull house was built by his grandfather.'

'What a shame. I'm rather sentimental about old castles, however ruinous.'

He grinned at that. 'Me too. But some parts of the original buildings are there to this day.'

My interest quickened again. 'Such as?'

'Well, there's a moat. Couldn't do much about that. Before the castle was built, it had surrounded a broch and now remains several centuries later as bogland, a treacherous place for the unwary. As I told you, a woman fell in and her body lay there for years.' He sighed. 'Peat has marvellous preservative qualities. She looked as if she'd just died.'

Again that shiver went through me, as he continued:

'Quite a sensation for the Hopescarth policeman, who had never encountered anything like that before. His mind immediately turned to murder, especially as she was a local woman—'

'Lenny wants a word.'

Just as the conversation was getting really interesting and I wanted to know more, the interruption was from Maud again, pointing to the massive shape of her husband framing the door.

As Craig excused himself, Maud still lingered, trying to decide what to make of me.

'Thanks for the tea. It was delicious,' I said, my smile of appreciation rewarded by a dour sniff.

'You're heading to Hopescarth, are you?' I said yes and watching Craig go across the room, she said: 'They're a rum lot up there. I'd go careful if I was you. And I wouldn't bargain on staying too long. It's a dangerous place for strangers in the dark.'

A tingle of unease which I tried to set aside. She might just be jealous and hoping to sound casual, I asked: 'In what way dangerous?'

She leaned closer. 'Bad things happen. People fall into peat-bogs and all that sort of thing. You just watch your step too.'

I looked round and had a glimpse of Craig and Lenny in earnest conversation with a newcomer at the door. The man, whom I couldn't see clearly as he was dwarfed by Lenny's massive shape, was obviously agitated. Occasionally a raised arm was discernible.

They were too far away for me to hear what was being said but I could see by Craig's face as he returned that this was some sort of crisis. He was carrying my rain cape and, summoning up a smile, he helped me into it.

Pausing awkwardly, I thanked him for the tea and said, I'd be on my way.

He sounded relieved. 'It isn't far and the rain has stopped. Be a nice ride, most of it is on the flat.'

Despite these assurances, I guessed his mind was elsewhere.

'I could take you in the motor car, of course.'

I heard myself protesting that I wouldn't think of it and he looked even more relieved. 'Something urgent – to do with the dig. I have to see someone sharpish,' he ended lamely.

And escorting me to the door, watched beady-eyed by Maud – I wondered fleetingly where she fitted into all this – he stood by the bicycle, regarding it uneasily. His attitude suggested confusion about what was good manners or expected of a gentleman in this instance. I concluded that he might be adept at handing ladies into carriages or his father's motor car, but I was prepared to bet he had never faced the quandary of handing a member of the female sex on to a bicycle.

'It has been a pleasure talking to you. I do hope to see you again sometime soon.' A very nice warm smile and I was sure at that moment that he meant it. 'Take a walk down to the dig when you have a minute.'

He saluted me gravely as I wobbled unsteadily away on the uneven cobbles, off down the road with a lot of questions that had to go unanswered.

Particularly concerning the identity of the woman in the peat-bog.

Chapter Five

Beyond Skailholm village, where I had left Craig, the landscape was occupied by stones, once human habitations and now shelters for sheep, the bitter record of man's losing battle with the landlords' greed lay in these pathetic skeletons of ancient crofts with sagging roofs and broken windows. Like eyes emptied of hope, each told its own tale of cruel days half a century ago, of clearances and the beggary that still stalked the Northern Isles.

In the bleakness, the peat fields had taken over, stretching with the bog cotton in every direction, my road leading past crofters hard at work. Surrounded by enormous baskets, they stopped their back-breaking toil to shout a greeting, which I returned with a cheery wave as a somewhat wobbly acknowledgement.

Peat workers made me think about the lady in the bog, preserved in peat for ten years. How very nasty, I thought, quite gruesome, and as it had happened in Hopescarth, I expected Emily would have all the details.

The clip-clop of horses' hooves on the steep road I had just negotiated indicated another traveller and I moved aside for a passing carriage whose occupant stared out at me in amazement. I could hear the unspoken thought:

A woman – on a bicycle. What are things coming to?

How did they react to Craig and his motor car? Horseless carriages, my dear, a mere fad. They'll never last.

Happy to have shocked, my departing wave ignored, I remounted and free-wheeled downhill, relishing the ever-changing restless sky which was never the same for more than a few moments. More habitations, scattered widely, secret grey crofts crouched low upon the heath, and well-groomed horses trotting across fields, for pleasure and for labour, signalled evidence that people must be around somewhere.

I hadn't ever had any great success with horses or ponies and remembered falling off and being terrified, much to Emily's amusement, proud that, although younger than I, she was a better rider, fearless and born to the side-saddle.

Now there were fields where black and white cows grazed contentedly and sheep, long past endearing lambhood, hopefully suckled mother ewes short on temper and long dry of milk.

The hedgerow bloomed with cow parsley and ragged robin, garden escapes of cultivated flowers, pansies and lupins. The dark heath was spotted brightly with bogcotton's fluffy tufts, pink sea thrift and the shells of flag irises.

Above all, the constant traffic of seabirds wheeling overhead extended my awareness of the kaleidoscope of colour existing alongside muted shades of grey, blue and green.

I stopped to blow my nose again and took a few deep breaths. Very comforting and rewarding to sniff the air since gentle winds and warm days had brought into being the fragrance of innumerable small plants and wild herbs.

I listened, aware that on every blade of grass and in every ditch an army of stealthy insects winged in rainbow hues filled the air with vibrant music beyond the human ear range. Far into the blue, skylarks, heartened by another burst of sunshine, added their flute notes of joy while flocks of birds, too small to be recognisable, exhausted by the rearing of young, were returning home to a happy celibacy.

Acutely aware of the mystic fulfilment of life, I looked towards the sea and listened to that everlasting sound, night and day, storm and calm, the boom of wave upon rock and shore.

I was not of a religious turn of mind as defined by Sabbath-going Edinburgh folk, but nevertheless I fancied for one brief moment that in the sea's eternal song I was hearing the whisper of creation, beyond time itself.

The sea was far below me. The seals were there, following my progress with almost human intelligence, striking a memory of how they used to follow Emily and me as we raced along the cliff path. Inquisitive, vigilant, with their round shiny bullet heads sleek and grey, and shining eyes that looked strangely human.

Sometimes we were quite scared and Emily, taking my hand, would whisper: 'Do you think they might be able to turn into people – shed their skins like we hear at school?'

'Emily,' I said sternly, consoling her as befits the elder sister, 'it's only a fairy story.'

It was – then. We didn't know about Sibella Scarth then. In our childhood her existence was still a family secret, closely guarded.

Jolted back to the present by a horizon no longer a bleak line drawn against the sea, the headland was occupied by a tall building, stark against the sky.

Yesnaby House and my destination. Less inspiring than I had imagined. Even remembering Craig's warning, something of a disappointment.

The homes of affluent Edinburgh are designed to resemble miniature Balmoral castles but this grey, square, solid-looking house had none of the architectural frills dreamed up by builders eager to please their clients by following the fashion laid down by our dear Queen and her late Consort.

Here the weather dictated fashion and turned its face firmly against exterior ornamentation, adornments which would soon succumb to wild winds and winter storms. Here survival had long been paramount and, in that, nothing had changed.

For centuries past, local architects had learned the lesson of concentration on thick, solid no-nonsense walls, deep set doors and windows turned away from the sea. Buildings offering protection against merciless weather in a style set down by the ancient brochs built by those mysterious early inhabitants, that unrecorded slice of island history.

Before me, the ground dropped sharply across a stretch of bright emerald grass. The bogland I had been warned about, the stone bridge a reminder that once upon a time this house high on the skyline had been a moated fortress against invaders from the sea.

As I crossed the bridge, on my right some twenty metres away, a dingy rubble of broken, untidy stones. Evidence of shovels, wheelbarrows and recently turned earth, plus a warning notice: 'Dangerous peat bog. No entrance without permission. Strictly private.'

So this was Craig's archaeological site. The sniff of

history – but whose old bones would this group unearth in their search? What shards of an ancient cooking pot waited to be excitedly acclaimed, noted and dated, declared 'fragile' and sent importantly to that ultimate destination, a dusty shelf in an Edinburgh or Glasgow museum?

Small pickings indeed and far removed from the hopes and dreams of that legendary long-lost grave of the Maid of Norway, that lure for enthusiastic archaeologists like Craig and the incentive to keep on patiently turning over the soil. A dreary monotonous daily routine even in the best of weather, unimaginable in driving gales and fierce winds.

Beyond the bridge, the approach to Yesnaby House still concealed was softened by a drive of somewhat unwilling trees, offering shelter rather than adornment. Fragments of ruined walls hinted at habitations which had not survived the ongoing battle with the elements.

At last emerging from the replica of a drive and on to a cobbled forecourt, whose antiquity suggested some earlier version of the house, in the interests of preserving my bicycle's newly mended tyre, I dismounted.

As I did so, the front door opened and the next moment Emily had gathered me into her arms.

'Emmy!'

This was my sister at last, she even smelt like Emily, for each of us bears our own distinctive smell, a not unpleasant but recognisable odour that no amount of soap and frequent washing can eradicate.

Now opening my eyes, somewhat misted by emotion, I realised that this Emily was different. Oh, so very different to the Emily I had last set eyes on more than ten years ago.

'Rose – let me look at you.'

Held at arm's length I saw fleeting disappointment

quickly concealed, that this was not the sister either whose image she had clung to through those lost years. For I saw mirrored in her eyes that I too had aged. The woman now past thirty who had married, suffered grief and loss, was not the carefree girl who had abandoned a promising career as a schoolteacher in Glasgow. The girl who had thrown it all away to make real her dream of marrying Danny McQuinn.

'Rose!'

Gran appeared, slower than Emily, of course, carrying with her the familiar kitchen smell of baking bread but lacking none of Emily's warmth of welcome as we hugged and kissed.

In that moment I was overcome by a new emotion. The clock had gone backwards and for the first time in years I felt safe. My anxieties for the past two years had been groundless. Safe with my own kin at last, I sighed with relief, having feared the worst from Emily's vague accounts of our grandmother's frailty and need of extra care.

But with the evidence of my own eyes, Gran looked exactly the same, not one day older, not one white hair seemed different. The same sturdy frame and round rosy face I loved, the same cheerful smile.

As with an arm around me she prepared to lead the way into the house, it seemed that the changes wrought by increasing years obey their own mysterious laws. Youthful beauty is fleeting, soon overtaken and obliterated by middle age. Then there is a period of slowing down, characterised by a less visible and alarming change from elderly to aged.

Suddenly Gran halted. Aware of the bicycle, she pointed with wide-eyed distaste. 'And what do you want done with that thing?' she asked in the same rather contemptuous tone that she might have used towards some dirty disreputable animal I had brought with me, whose presence would be an embarrassment she could not be expected to tolerate in her well-scrubbed kitchen.

That thought, the comparison, so amused me that I exploded into sudden laughter. 'It's not a thing, Gran,' I said proudly, 'it's a bicycle that carries me from place to place. Quite precious.'

She looked surprised, frowned with a sniff of disapproval, while I couldn't explain my amusement to her reaction, so hugging her again, I said I was just happy, very happy just to be here with her and Emily.

Mollified, she listened, but her eyes strayed to that bicycle, regarding it sternly as if it might have a word to say for itself. 'We'll put it in the coach house, beside Storm – he's our carriage horse. I'm sure he won't mind having it for company,' said Emily.

At Gran's sigh of relief for a dangerous situation averted, Emily and I were back in childhood, conspirators once again in a quick glance of suppressed mirth. We seized hands, paused to hug one another again and I thought that not for a very long time had I been as happy as I was at that moment.

Nothing – nothing would ever change it.

I should have waited... Just a little while.

Chapter Six

Up the steps, through the front door and across a handsome marble-tiled hall, and, ignoring a grand oak staircase, we proceeded down a corridor and emerged in a huge kitchen. I looked around in amazement for it could have comfortably accommodated the whole of Gran's Kirkwall cottage in which Emily and I had grown up.

This was Gran's domain. It had her stamp on it. A central table set ready for supper. Bacon, eggs and pancakes and one of her delicious fruit cakes, kept for special celebrations, like the prodigal's return.

As I sat down eagerly, resolved to demolish this rare feast, Erland's absence was explained.

'He's away to Bergen,' said Emily.

'Has some business connections, to do with the shipping,' Gran put with an anxious glance at Emily, as if I might be offended that he was not here to greet me.

'But he'll be back soon,' said Emily cheerfully. 'Any day now. He's looking forward to your visit.'

Then with plates laid aside, appetites satisfied and on to our second or third cup of tea, we loitered by that mammoth kitchen table. The size of a room in a crofter's cottage, it could have seated twenty diners with ease and had obvious associations with a more prolific Scarth, head of a large family and employing a dozen servants.

There was so much to talk about, question upon question, some hardly answered as we skipped on to the next, trying to set bridges over the gaps, the long years apart inexpertly rafted by vague and infrequent letters.

What had brought me back from America alone? Had I really wanted to return? I thought I had made that clear from my letters and got it over as quickly as possible: Danny's disappearance in Arizona, my promise to him that I would come back after six months to Edinburgh.

And the baby? The loss of our baby.

Gran and Emily exchanged glances. I must have given a more moving account than I intended, sitting there with my back straight and my hands tightly clenched under the table.

They both wiped away tears, leaned forward, kissed me gently.

Gran looked at Emily. 'Have you told her your news yet, lass?'

Emily shook her head, smiled. 'I'm having a baby. Next year. In the spring. At last!' she added with a happy sigh.

I was surprised, delighted but a little taken aback. Emily had been married for so long that I had presumed she was to be childless especially as her husband was a middle-aged widower.

'Emmy – I'm so glad. this is wonderful news. Wonderful!'

Gran watched Emily fondly. 'Aye, we think she'll be fine this time. She's past the danger time.' And I learned that Emily had had several miscarriages through the years.

As I had myself. The same pattern, except that the baby I eventually brought into the world, strong and healthy at first, had succumbed to fever on an Indian reservation.

I looked at her. This was a new Emily indeed. All the time I had been aware of some subtle change, as always mildly astonished that we were not in the least alike and that no one had ever taken us for sisters.

I was less than five feet tall, small and rounded. An hourglass figure, small waisted. Emmy was half a head taller with long straight black hair. With never any bosom to speak of, the bane of her life. My very feminine curves and my mass of yellow curls were reasons for sisterly wrath and resentment in girlhood, for moans against Fate and the ladies' magazines who declared that my kind of figure was essential to finding a husband.

However there was consolation. Although Emmy was the younger by two years, people meeting us for the first time presumed that she was the elder. This had pleased her enormously. 'Everyone thinks Rose is the baby, my little sister,' she had bragged, compensation for a sibling with the curls and curves she longed for.

Now there was a new bond between us. That of motherhood, my own so short-lived. But Emmy would be different, I hoped and prayed. For I had wondered often if there was a curse on the Faro women, the dreaded St Ringan's curse that made women barren.

Gran had only one child, Pappa. Had she lost several afterwards? I thought of middle-class Edinburgh families with at least three or four and the poor women in those horrendous High Street closes, raising broods of ten or more in one stinking room. But not for the Faro women the Biblical gift of multiplying exceedingly.

As for Emily and I being so dissimilar, although it

seemed to worry others, it did not seem odd to me. I took after Mamma's side of the family as did our stepbrother Vince, while Emily was what people here called 'a throwback' – meaning she didn't resemble either parent.

But all this was before I met Sibella Scarth, our great-grandmother, the seal woman, and I knew who Emily took after and why Sibella was so devoted to her.

Suddenly my eyes were heavy, fatigue wrapping me in an inescapable cloud.

From far away I heard Gran: 'The poor lass. She's just about asleep.'

The guest bedroom was beautiful, elegant in rosewood and mahogany furniture, fragrant with lavender-scented polish, grand indeed compared to the dormer-windowed attic Emmy and I had shared in Kirkwall.

I was to discover that the interior of the house was a box of delights, far more attractive than could be imagined or expected from its square grey exterior. There was even a bathroom.

A huge mahogany white-pillowed bed invited me to put down my head. I looked at it yearningly. Too tired to get undressed and blaming the crossing and the bicycle ride for my exhaustion, I pulled the covers over and snuggled down into warmth and comfort.

I'd just sample the luxury – for a few minutes – then I'd unpack, have a wash and get into bed properly…

I opened my eyes to birdsong, the room flooded with bright sunshine. Faint sounds from downstairs, a few echoing footfalls.

I sat up. It was morning and I had slept for ten hours.

Guiltily I sprang into action. The water was too cold for a bath, so I had to make do with the stand-up variety and a change of linen. Brushing my curls free of tangles, I stared out of the window with its distant glimpse towards the sea, the peat field and, just visible, the roof of an isolated croft.

Downstairs I ran to warm greetings from Gran and Emily who rose from the breakfast table to bombard me with questions. Had I slept well, been warm enough, was the bed comfortable? Meanwhile I tackled porridge and bere bannocks, and between mouthfuls, provided satisfactory answers.

'That was a long way to come from Stromness,' said Gran eyeing me anxiously. 'You had best take it easy for a day or two, until you recover.'

'I'm fine, Gran. Slept like the proverbial log.' And I smiled, for this was the Gran I knew of old. As one who had never travelled willingly more than a few miles across the island since returning from Edinburgh after my policeman grandfather Magnus Faro was killed, she regarded a sea voyage from Leith as a dangerous and terrifying ordeal. There might be pirates!

Despite my reassurances, she continued to watch me doubtfully. 'Anyway, I was lucky. Didn't I tell you last night? I got a lift in a motor car for quite a bit of the way.'

'A motor car!' Gran and Emily looked a one another and Gran asked suspiciously: 'And who would that be?'

'Craig. Craig Denmore,' I said. 'The archaeologist at the dig over there.'

'Him!' Gran exploded, thumping her fists on the table.

Puzzled, I said: 'He seemed very nice,' in an attempt to placate her. But it was too late. The mention of his name was like waving a red rag at a bull, a not altogether inept simile, for her face had flushed scarlet.

Again she thumped the table. 'I don't hold with them digging on our land.'

I looked at her, thinking it would be inappropriate to

speak my mind that the land wasn't hers after all. It belonged to Emily's husband, in whose house she was a guest.

'Gran!' said Emily firmly as she put an imploring hand on her arm.

'Don't "Gran" me, you know as well as I do that they should leave the dead alone. I don't hold with that sort of thing. It isn't decent. And him a laird's son. Should have more sense. His father's got a title and all that money from the whisky. Getting his hands dirty,' she added contemptuously. 'And he's not even one of us.'

By which I presumed she meant not a born and bred Orcadian.

'What's in it for him?' she demanded. 'He doesn't need buried treasure if the Maid's dowry is what he's after—'

Emily held up her hand. 'Gran – he is a Scarth after all.'

'Only on his mother's side,' was the grudging admission. 'And that was long before your Erland's family took over.'

'Wait a minute,' I interrupted. 'You mean that Craig Denmore's related to us?' Was that the answer? The reason for that feeling of certainty that we had met before, a family resemblance but too fleeting for immediate recognition?

Emily's words changed that idea. 'He might be a remote cousin generations removed since half the folk here are Scarths, don't you remember, Rose?'

I shook my head. It hadn't been important to be one of a clan in my school days. 'I like him,' I said lamely. 'He was very kind. Bought me some tea, as well.'

Gran sniffed disapprovingly and gave me a hard look. A gentleman, I was about to add and then changed my mind. They knew that already, so in his defence I added: 'He seemed very earnest and sincere about the dig, about finding the Maid's grave, I mean.'

'Her dowry, more like,' snapped Gran, through pursed lips.

I let it go. 'There was something else he told me about, far more fascinating than that old mystery. A modern one you must know about.'

Looks were exchanged again. Emily frowned and Gran demanded cautiously:

'And what would that be?'

'A woman's body found last year, in the peat-bog. She'd been there for years and years and yet she looked as if it had just happened yesterday. What did you think about that? Is it true, her being preserved and all that sort of thing?'

My question was met by a sudden cold silence, a stillness as if the two women before me had been turned to stone. Their faces made me shiver as Gran looked at Emily and Emily looked back at Gran.

I saw something else. A mute appeal in that glance...

'Who was she? Did the police ever find out? Missing persons and so forth?' I said eagerly.

They both watched me in stunned silence as I buttered another slice of bread, spreading on the jam.

I blundered on regardless. Now in my element, sniffing out some extraordinary story, a mystery with instant appeal for Rose McQuinn, Lady Investigator, Discretion Guaranteed.

'Well, did they manage to track down her family. Who was she?' I repeated. 'Didn't anyone recognise her?' I flourished the butter knife. 'Surely there must have been someone...'

Emily stood up. She was no longer still. She looked at

me, her lips trembling. Gran's hand was on her arm as she said:

'Yes, Rose. We knew who she was.' Pausing she looked at Gran, who shook her head.

'Well?' I said.

A strangled whisper, so soft I thought I had misheard. 'Thora.'

For a moment I lost the thread. Who was Thora?

Then I was back at Skailholm hearing Craig Denmore saying:

'Erland took the precaution of marrying his heiress cousin Thora, now deceased.'

Horrified, I looked across the table at Gran and Emily staring at me, their faces suddenly white and strained.

'Erland's first wife?' I whispered.

Emily nodded. 'Yes, Rose. That's who it was.'

Chapter Seven

Thora, Erland's first wife!

I leaned across and seized Emily's hands. They were very cold, lifeless. 'Oh, Emmy. I'm sorry – I'm so sorry. How absolutely awful for you. It must have been horrible!'

'It was very upsetting for Erland.' She had regained her calm and smiled sadly. 'You see, she had left home – here – one evening years ago and no one had ever seen her or heard from her again. She just disappeared.'

Like Danny. I remembered how upset Emily had been when I was talking about him. How she seemed so tearful and clutched my hand.

No wonder. Lightning striking twice in the same family. Another odd coincidence.

'We – Erland, that is – thought she had left the island and gone across to the mainland – to Edinburgh or Glasgow. She wasn't very well – in her mind, that is. She didn't like Hopescarth and was always threatening to leave. It was terrible, terrible for Erland—'

And Emily began to cry. Gran put her arm around her.

'There, there, lambie,' she said, meanwhile eyeing me reproachfully as if this was all my fault, bringing up this painful subject. 'Terrible for this poor lass, too. You can imagine what that was like. Married to Erland, and the poor chap had buried someone else in Thora's grave. He thought – we all did – that it must be Thora. A couple of months after she went away, the weather was terrible, dreadful storms and a woman's torso washed up off Marwick Head in the roarsts.'

'The roarsts?'

She paused, frowning at my puzzled expression and Emily said:

'You remember, Rose, the tide-races that beat up on the rocks below the cliffs here at the Troll's Cave. They come up in a spout at high tide. Or in a storm.'

In a voice thin and strained she spoke slowly. 'No man or woman, or boat could survive in those terrible seas, dashed against the rocks. Like giant's teeth, they are.'

She shuddered into silence and Gran said grimly: 'Aye, there wasn't much left of the woman we all thought must be Thora. No arms or legs—'

'Gran! For pity's sake—' Emily put her hands over her face, shutting out that dreadful picture, leaving me to imagine what it had been like for Erland, going down to identify 'what was left' of his missing wife. I shuddered too as Emily straightened her shoulders and tried to regain her calm.

She was very pale as she looked at me and said: 'You know the rest, Rose. We got married.'

'Of course.' But something bothered me. Where had I gotten the idea that Thora was an invalid, that Emily had nursed her until she died? And now I was hearing the real story.

'As Gran said, Thora wasn't well. She was always a little unbalanced.'

'Daft as a brush,' Gran contributed angrily. 'There was a history of it in her family – a couple married not knowing they were brother and sister. Happens all the time in small communities—'

Emily didn't want to be interrupted. 'When the – the body was found, Erland presumed that Thora had committed suicide, jumped off Marwick Head.'

Shock absorbed, my detective instincts were taking over. 'Did he have some reason to believe that she'd take her own life?'

Emily shook her head and Gran said: 'We were told she had rushed out of the house in a furious temper, threatening everyone. So what else could the poor man believe?'

I ignored that. 'What about this other woman? The body they found. Did no one claim her?'

'No.'

'Don't the police here keep a list of missing persons?'

'Apparently not.' And they both frowned at me as if they had never heard of such a thing. Maybe I was expecting too much of a tiny community like Hopescarth with the nearest police station in Stromness.

There wasn't much law to break or much crime either, I was to discover. Nothing more than a little poaching, which hardly seemed to justify paying a policeman's wages.

I studied the little scene across the table. Gran staring bleakly at the scrubbed surface and tracing patterns with a fork. Emily white-faced, touching her stomach as if to reassure the child she carried that all was well.

This kind of event was well beyond my Edinburgh experience of petty crime. It smacked of melodrama. The insane wife on the clifftop, poised above a wild sea, hurling itself against the rocks at Marwick Head.

Poor Emily and poor Erland. And it didn't take any great feat of imagination to hazard a guess that they were already in love with each other long before Thora vanished. One could hardly blame Erland for being relieved to be rid of the domestic hell of an unbalanced wife.

Or his willing eagerness to accept a decomposing limbless corpse as Thora. And who could blame him for suppressing any secret doubts and believing that he had seen the end of a bitter marriage, making sure that he and Emily could have a decent life together at last.

The story of Thora, her disappearance and re-emergence in the peat-bog ten years later, was also the explanation for Emily's vague and infrequent letters, a complete inability to describe in words the happenings at Hopescarth.

We all jumped when the horrified silence of our thoughts was shattered by the Westminster clock's melodi-ous ritual of striking the half-hour.

Gran stood up. 'I'd better make a fresh pot of tea. Sibella will be here any moment, Rose. Takes a walk every day, all weathers – rain, snow, wind or hail.'

Sibella Scarth. And shocks weren't over for the day. This was the first hint of the great-grandmother I had never met and whose existence had been concealed all those years Emily and I had lived in Orkney.

Pappa had proudly boasted that his grandmother was a seal woman, the past tense indicating that she was dead long ago. Logically one would presume so as I made a rapid calculation and said carefully: 'She must be an incredible age.'

Gran smiled sourly. 'Aye, she is that. Past her hundredth birthday.'

'How far past?'

Gran shrugged. ' No one knows exactly. You see, no one knew her date of birth when Hakon Scarth, your great-grandfather carried her into the house. The year it was built, she claims. 1795, that was.'

I did another calculation. That made her at least 102.

'Incredible, isn't it?' said Emily proudly. 'But wait until you see her. You'll find it hard to believe.'

'Aye,' said Gran. 'Hakon picked her up in his fishing nets. They thought she was about two or three, but she could have been older. There was no way of being certain.'

Watching my astonished expression and before I could ask the obvious question of how she got there, Gran went on hurriedly: 'Folks said she must have floated ashore from a Norwegian ship, the 'Sibella', that went down in a storm two nights earlier. So that's what they called her.'

'Poor wee soul. Tragic, wasn't it?' said Emily.

I agreed. 'But that didn't make her a seal woman, surely.'

Gran shook her head. 'Folk here, as you well know, Rose, have always had strange notions about the power of the selkies. The Finn folk, that sort of thing,' she added apologetically, remembering that I had been 'educated' as the local folk would say. Such education supposedly removed me from local superstitions in a society where the schoolteacher joined laird, doctor and minister, elevated to higher ranks of respect and awe.

'What made them think that she wasn't just an ordinary little girl who had been shipwrecked, for heaven's sake?' I asked, my logical mind refusing to accept the absurdities of any other conclusions.

'There was no record of any small child on the ship that went down,' said Gran. 'That was how she became known as a selkie.'

'Perhaps her mother had died and she had been smuggled abroad by her father, one of the crew, who went down with the ship,' I insisted.

Gran shook her head. 'There were a couple of Norwegian sailors who survived and were brought ashore. They didn't have much English but they both swore that they had never set eyes on her before or knew of any wee lass on the ship. So they absolutely refused to take her back to Norway with them. They seemed scared of her, in fact—'

I ignored that. 'What about their shipping line? Surely they had records of the crew, even in those days. For paying them, and so forth.' And clinging to the logical, 'Still sounds as if someone smuggled her aboard.'

Gran smiled grimly. 'Aye, right enough. Perhaps the ship owners didn't pay very close attention to what went on among the crew.

'Sea-going wives, you mean?' I knew about wives and sweethearts who went to sea with their men, unacknow-ledged in merchant ships. 'So it is possible that she had been there on the voyage and no one had taken any notice.'

With a sense of triumph, of problem solved, I added: 'The child could have come aboard with her mother – who went down with the ship.'

Gran nodded. 'True enough. But then a sea-going wife's name would be on the list with the rest of the crew.'

'Not if she wasn't legally married—'

Gran sniffed. 'A lot of those kind of women went to sea and stayed out of sight. The company turned a blind eye on them. They were there for the – er, convenience of the men. Sailors needed female companionship on long voyages.'

Emily chuckled. 'Companionship! Come along, Gran. Rose is a married woman. You can say what you mean to her. That the sailors took their fancy women with them.' And to me, 'It was well known that some of the sailors had a wife and family on shore as well as at sea.'

And thereby lay the answer, I thought. 'In that case it could have been very inconvenient for the child's father, if he happened to be one of the two survivors, to take home a small child to his legitimate spouse. What a predicament!'

'Aye, we've often thought something like that might well have been the reason,' Gran said cautiously. 'But right from the beginning, folks were scared of her. You see, when Hakon pulled her ashore, it was Lammastide – August like now. If it had been any other time, it might well have been different but the seals were on the move.'

'Remember, Rose,' said Emily, 'how we used to watch them, those great colonies of Atlantic seals that move inshore and the racket they made at night.'

I did remember. Night after night we were awakened by the roaring of the bull seals, barking like dogs. An eerie sound echoing on and on with the moonlight streaming through our tiny attic window. How, unable to sleep, two frightened small girls would cling together, scaring one another to death with stories about the seal king. Describing him rising from the waves to snatch a human girl and carry her back to his kingdom of coral and pearl beneath the sea...

To be his wife for a year and a day.

'There are lasses here you still couldn't give a sovereign to, to walk by the cliffs alone at Lammastide, even in this day and age.' Gran sighed. 'I was her only bairn, you know, the only one to survive. Sad, it was. I had a brother, Peter, but he drowned.'

I'd never heard of a great-uncle Peter either and

presumed he must have been a small child when the accident happened.

I shivered again. Sibella Scarth sounded more than a mite strange and I was no longer quite so eager to meet her with my imagination painting weird, sinister pictures.

Scary pictures of the wicked witch who haunted childhood stories now made manifest in a seal woman great-grandmother.

Chapter Eight

As if she read my thoughts, Emily said encouragingly: 'Sibella's sharp and bright as a button, interested in everyone and everything that's new.'

'Aye, she loves young folk about her and is prepared to listen to what they think about it all. Even that Wilma Flitt, Meg-at-the-post-office's bairn who's never out of my kitchen.' Gran's sour tones suggested that this young visitor did not meet with her approval.

'Sibella's a wonderful old lady,' Emily put in proudly.

Gran sniffed. 'That's just because you're the apple of her eye. Different enough with any that cross her.' And Gran's voice managed to hint that she and her strange mother fell into the latter category.

'Oh, you'll get along grand with her, Rose, I just know it,' said Emily. She laughed. 'And I'd like to bet the first thing she'll want to know all about is that bicycle. She loves new inventions, not like some folk here. Another four years and we'll be into a new century and yet they still cling to the Dark Ages. I suppose it's different in Edinburgh,' she added wistfully, picking up her knitting needles.

A shawl, delicate as a spider's web, no doubt for the new baby. I said a silent prayer.

'There are still superstitious people, even in Edinburgh, Emmy, who hold on to strange ideas. You'd be surprised.' And I wondered how they would react to the story of Thane, my strange deerhound companion who roamed the heights of Arthur's Seat.

'So when do I meet Great-Grandmamma?'

'Very soon now. And incidentally she likes to be called Sibella. She doesn't care for the great-grandmamma image,' said Emily with a teasing glance in Gran's direction: 'Doesn't care to be reminded that she has a daughter who is past eighty.'

Gran winced a bit at that. 'Aye, we've gotten used to it over the years, but it does sound a mite disrespectful to folk who don't know her odd ways. She fair dotes on Emily, hardly lets her out of her sight.'

I detected a touch of envy as she added: 'They have a lot in common. Emily takes after her and don't let her hear you calling her Emmy—'

'Oh Gran, that's just because she doesn't like shortened names,' Emily said apologetically.

'Doesn't she want to stay here with you?' I thought of all the rooms in this vast house I had still to explore.

'Not likely,' snapped Gran. Did I hear a suspicion of relief as she went on: 'She lives on the far side of the peat fields over yonder. Has her own peedie croft over the hill. You can just see it from your bedroom window.'

Peedie? I looked up. That word again. How long since I had heard the almost forgotten Orcadian word for 'small', as Gran went on: 'Doesna' want to live in the house with us, but she's never away. That's because of Emily. She hadna' much time for the family before that,' she added, a touch resentfully, I thought.

'What happened, Gran? Why on earth has she been kept such a secret from us all this time? Why did Emily and I never meet her? I can hardly credit it – all those years living here with you and we never knew of her existence.'

I looked at Emily for confirmation and we both turned to Gran. 'Why didn't you tell us?' She gave an uncomfortable shrug. 'Surely Pappa must have known – as a child – about his own granny?'

Gran shook her head. 'No. Especially not my Jeremy. Him most of all. We agreed when he was a bairn that it was best he should think she was – well, no longer with us,' she added delicately.

With a despairing sigh she looked across at Emily who nodded. 'You'd better tell her what happened, Gran.'

In the long pause that followed I thought of the secrets my visit was unearthing and why Emily had been so long in sending that invitation. Now I sympathised.

Not too easy to explain to anyone, Erland's first wife, Thora, preserved for ten years in a peat-bog, a seal woman great-grandmother and a family feud everyone wanted to forget.

'Go on, Gran. Rose'll have to be told sometime. Right from the beginning,' Emily said, and to me: 'You remember how Grandpa went to be a policeman in Edinburgh?'

I knew that story well. How Magnus Faro was killed on duty by a runaway cab and how Pappa, years later, had tried to prove it was murder, connected with the discovery of an infant's body in the wall of Mary, Queen of Scots' apartments in Edinburgh Castle. A tiny mummified corpse wrapped in cloth of gold, who might well have been the real James the Sixth of Scotland, future King James the First of England.

Rumour had it that the Queen had delivered a stillborn Prince and that the Countess of Mar, who was her midwife and pregnant at the same time, had substituted her own son, thereby throwing the entire Stuart succession in jeopardy.

But what I was hearing from Gran had nothing to do with that ancient mystery long ago investigated by Chief Inspector Jeremy Faro.

Gran's story was a familiar tale of squabbles with her mother-in-law. Grandpa Magnus just didn't take to Sibella even before he married Mary Scarth. And his feelings were reciprocated because he laughed at what he called her witches' tales of trolls and hogben and her Finn folk.

Magnus didn't hold with the supernatural or with her alleged nativity. In his opinion she was a Norwegian sailor's bastard, saved from the sinking ship. And what was worst of all, he tried to convince everyone else of the fact.

'He had to explain everything logically, as he called it. He was that kind of man and it made Sibella a liar. Then one day he did prove something – I dinna ken what, but he made her look foolish and shamed her in the face of all these folk who trusted her cures and went to see her for advice as the local white witch.

'But my Magnus was so sensible, honest and down to earth, he just had to tell the truth, come hell or high water, whatever it cost. A terrible row and he threw her out of the house. From then on her name was forbidden. An Edinburgh policeman, hard enough for an Orkney lad, he was in mortal fear of any of his colleagues hearing that he had a silly old mother-in-law pretending to be a seal woman.'

Gran sighed. 'He was ambitious, my Magnus, clever too and determined to succeed. If stories about seal women got around, he'd be laughed to scorn and never get promotion.' Another sigh, a sad shake of the head. 'So I had to choose and I chose my Magnus, so Sibella went away back to South Ronaldsay. Our Jeremy was a peedie bairn at the time. We kept quiet about it, and if he heard rumours about her, we let him believe his granny had died long before he was born.

'And when I brought him back to Orkney after my Magnus was killed, I never got in touch with her. I never wanted to see her again. I know it's awful but I couldna' help it. All those bitter memories.'

'So you never said a word to us either. All those years and never a whisper,' I said reproachfully.

'I know it was wrong, Rose. I should have told you but as far as I was concerned, she was dead. I wanted to believe that. If ever I had a pang of conscience I told myself it's a fair distance to South Ronaldsay and I've never been a good sailor. I'm even sick on the ferry to the mainland.'

She paused to give us both a glance of mute appeal. 'There was only once I felt badly about hating my own mother and being ashamed of her. And that was when I brought the two of you back to live with me after your dear Mamma died and I saw the way you both missed her and wept for her.'

She sighed. 'But then I remembered my loyalty to my Magnus so I went on doing what he would have wished. Then one day just after Emily got married, I heard rumours about Sibella and her marvellous cures. I knew then that she was still alive and I had to make my peace with her. I went to South Ronaldsay and one look told me she was very ill. Neighbours said they were glad I had come because she was dying. I knew then I couldna' let her stay there, let her die alone.

'Erland was so very understanding. He insisted we bring her here to Yesnaby House. He arranged it all and she was too far gone to refuse. Somehow, and without any of her magic remedies either, I managed to nurse her back to life again,' she added proudly.

'Maybe it was just being loved again, being part of the family gave her a reason for wanting to stay alive. And I was glad to be at peace with my conscience at last, when I saw how grateful she was. No reproaches, not one word. It was just as if we had never quarrelled all those years ago. She seemed to have lost her old fire, too, and right from the moment she set eyes on Emily, she took to her, although she was very wary of Erland—'

She stopped sharply, pursed her lips and glancing at Emily, seemed to change her mind about what she was going to say.

Emily looked up from her knitting and smiled. 'I can't think why. Erland is so kind to everyone and to her in particular.'

Gran shrugged. 'The last couple of years have changed her a bit, she has to take it easier these days, take an afternoon rest—'

'Just like me,' said Emily with a laugh.

'And she canna guddle about in the kitchen the way she did before she reached her hundredth,' Gran added with a touch of satisfaction.

I felt Gran would have no time for any female, seal woman or no, who could upstage her in her own domain as she continued: 'Says her feet aren't what they were. But she never had good feet like the rest of us. They were almost more like – like—'

She was cut short by a cough from Emily who interrupted hastily: 'She'll want you to see her croft. First

place she'll take you, Rose. It's fascinating, just like out of
a fairy tale about Red Riding Hood. Crammed with bottles
and books and old birds' nests – just about everything—'

'I've only been there once since she came to live here,'
said Gran. 'I just wanted to tidy up and clean the place for
her. Give her a helping hand. And that set her off. She was
blazing mad at me. I took the hint – I'm no longer
welcome.' She added bitterly, 'That's the privilege of the
very few. Like Emily and that Wilma.'

Emily smiled and touched Gran's arm. 'We like the
house as it is, spiders and all.' And when Gran shuddered,
she looked across at me: 'You'll understand, Rose. You'll
love it too. I know you will.'

As dust and spiders were constant companions in
Solomon's Tower, where my life did not include intense
activity with mop and broom, I had a natural fellow feeling
for weird houses, a bond already formed with Sibella.

'I can't wait until she sees that bicycle,' said Emily.
'She'll probably want to have a go at riding it.'

'You won't let her near it!' said Gran.

An unnecessary warning since imagination defied the
vision of a century old seal woman on a bicycle. I laughed
and Emily said:

'And she'll be delighted to know that you need it to
investigate crimes in a wicked city like Edinburgh.'

I hoped Emily had not exaggerated the humbler version
of my career as Gran sniffed again and gave me a hard look
and a frown, which clearly indicated her rather transparent
thoughts: that such things weren't nice for a young woman
to think about, never mind to get involved with. Crimes
were sordid, dirty and disagreeable. There was something
contaminating about them, too.

And hadn't her own darling Magnus been a murder

victim? That she could never forget, nor would she ever forgive Edinburgh for allowing the death of one of its policemen to go unpunished.

As for her darling Jeremy, our Pappa, she had never understood why he didna' stay in Orkney and take a nice respectable job behind nice solid walls. He had been clever; even as a peedie lad, the teachers said he would go far. Why, he could have worked in a bank in Kirkwall or taught in the local school. Such had been her dreams.

However, I did know that Gran had been placated over the years by a policeman son who had reached the dizzy heights of Chief Inspector in the Edinburgh City Police. Even, it was whispered, being called upon as the Queen's personal detective at Balmoral Castle. Now that was something not many Orkney mothers could boast about.

The Westminster clock's chime reminded us again of time's passing and Gran stood up with a sigh to attend to the teapot and re-set the table for Sibella's imminent arrival.

'She'll take very kindly to you offering to walk with her,' said Emily. 'Instead of me, that is! As long as you don't mind walking a bit slower – but do it tactfully, I know you'll never hint that she needs a helping hand up the banks and the like. Sometimes her feet make her a little unsteady,' she added with a sharp glance at Gran. 'We do worry a bit when she goes out and stays away for hours, without telling us where she's off to. Mostly she just sits on the headland and stares down at the sea but she enjoys tea and a gossip. Folk are like that, remember, Rose.'

I smiled. I did indeed. 'If you're walking past a door and someone sees you, in you go for tea and bannocks. And whatever your urgency, you're never too busy to do likewise to a passing neighbour and offer them a cup of tea.'

Emily smiled, the bond of Orcadian hospitality between us. 'We worry about the hill for Sibella. It's steep and rough enough for the fleet of foot, although she says she's walked rough paths all her life and they don't scare her.'

'She gathers fresh flowers from the hedgerows,' Gran put in. 'Canna' manage the steep steps down to Erland's garden out there now, but most of the arrangements about the house are hers. I havena' the time.' For the first time she sounded grateful.

'She's a great reader,' Emily added. 'Only took to reading glasses when she was ninety – and she can still hear the proverbial pin drop. By the way, if you want to be on her good side,' she said, taking another cup and saucer down from the dresser, 'don't look too surprised at the mittens.'

'Mittens?'

Gran and she exchanged glances and Emily said hurriedly: 'One of her little fads. She always wears them. Otherwise you'll find she's quite normal.'

I may have seemed prejudiced but 'quite normal' wasn't how I would ever have described Sibella Scarrth.

Light footsteps on the path outside. A shadow passed by the window.

'Here she is now. For heaven's sake, don't hint that we were talking about her. And try not to look startled – because she's so old, I mean. We might think it's an incredible age,' Emily added in a whisper, 'but she just hates to be reminded that she's a very old lady.'

Despite their reassuring words, I steeled myself for my great-grandmother's entrance, expecting the saurian, skeletal face of any centenarian fortunate enough to appear in a photograph.

The sunlight was behind her and I was totally

unprepared for the doll-like figure who entered and sat down, dwarfed by the high-backed Orkney chair.

White hair, pink cheeks, bright eyes. At first glance she could well have been Gran's younger sister, a well-preserved seventy.

'So you are Rose. I've heard such a lot about you, my dear.' And as she held out a small mittened hand, her fingers dainty, exquisite as ivory, I was aware of the emanation of some power beyond the ordinary, some magic at work, to be old, to have survived all her contemporaries.

Though she was undoubtedly frail as glass and moved slowly, the miracle of longevity remained. If her eyesight and hearing were as good as Gran and Emily claimed, so too was her memory and I remembered an old saying about first meetings:

'Look well upon the face of friend or foe at first meeting, for you may never see them as clearly again.'

And I knew then that there was something odd about Sibella's appearance. The sloping shoulders, short neck, the very round almost contourless face were something of a shock and I did not wish to consider the image she evoked.

Or what Sibella's shape reminded me of…

Chapter Nine

Our first meeting was brief indeed. We had exchanged no more than a few words before the pleasant domestic scene in Hopescarth's kitchen suddenly dissolved.

The sound of a carriage on the drive. Doors closing, voices.

'Erland!' cried Emily delightedly.

The master of the house had returned. In that moment everything changed and Sibella disappeared as if by magic.

One second it seemed that I was looking at her in the Orkney chair. Then my attention was diverted to Emily and Gran, now on their feet, Gran hastily tidying the table, touching her hair, smoothing her apron.

When I looked back at the chair, Sibella was gone.

In that one instant I had learned something. Either she didn't like Erland or he didn't like her. Or was it mutual, a repetition of Sibella and Magnus Faro?

As for the newcomer, I didn't know quite what to expect. An ogre of some kind perhaps, terrifying children and old ladies.

But the Erland Yesnaby who flung open the kitchen

door and gathered Emily in his arms was undoubtedly one of the most ordinary men I had ever met.

Tall and bony with sandy hair, growing thin. A perpetually quizzical expression and the most benign of blue eyes behind thick glasses. The curious thing was that, having been prepared for an elderly widower, Erland did not look much older than Emily. I was to discover that there were fourteen years between them but the gap looked much less than that. Perhaps the reason was that Emmy didn't look particularly young for her age.

Erland bowed over my hand in an almost old-fashioned gesture and bade me welcome to Yesnaby House. And then I knew his secret. His was one of the most beautiful voices I had ever heard. Deep, musical and tender – it suggested singing rather than speaking. The kind of voice that, had he recited the letters of the alphabet or Bradshaw's timetable, would have sounded like Orpheus and his lyre.

No wonder Emily had fallen in love with him. All she had to do was close her eyes and listen.

'Yes, indeed. I have heard a great deal about Emily's lovely sister,' he was saying. The voice seemed to smile too. 'I do hope these two ladies of mine are making you at home.'

(Mark the omission of great-grandmother Sibella!)

Gran was obviously delighted, she giggled a lot when he talked to her. A new coy, girlish Gran that made me raise my eyebrows. I was to discover that she found it difficult to keep her hands off him too. In passing, she would touch his sleeve, his shoulder.

She adored Erland, in the most maternal way, of course. As if he were a little boy and that was another aspect of his charm. A beautiful voice and the slightly bewildered expression of a small boy who doesn't know quite how to deal with the world or even the day's problems. I could imagine him quite clearly forty years ago, at school with a slate in his hand, frowning as he tried to do his sums. He probably had a fine voice even before it broke, the pride of the church choir.

Suddenly I realised I was sitting there with a silly smile and hardly listening to the conversation which concerned his business trip to Norway.

He was anxious about Emily, I could see that, stroking her hair back from her forehead, his arm about her shoulders in a very nice, protective way.

Then I was being asked about my journey, and how was Edinburgh?

A glowing Emily gave him an adoring look. 'Rose brought her bicycle. Came on it all the way from Stromness.'

He smiled at me and said. 'How very exciting. I've never ridden a bicycle,' he added in such a wistful tone.

I immediately said: 'Please be free to try mine.'

His eyebrows rose over that high clever forehead. 'May I really? That is very good of you.' And rising to his feet. 'Now if you'll excuse me. I have to go to my study. Papers to sort out.'

And in answer to Gran's question, was he hungry, he patted his waistcoat. 'I had a huge breakfast, thank you. Just a sandwich will do nicely.' And turning to Emily, he said gently. 'Time for your rest, love. Off you go.'

I followed her upstairs. No longer used to being with people all day, I needed time on my own, time to relish that lovely bedroom with its glimpse of the sea.

Closing the door I stacked away my few clothes in the depth of the huge wardrobe, its interior smelling of lavender. Then I placed my reading matter on the bedside table. Emily Brontë's *Wuthering Heights*, which I now

But Gran was alone in the kitchen doing the ironing.

'Emily? She's away out with Erland to Kirwall. Business things.'

I was a little put out. I would have loved the chance to go with them, see Kirkwall again. But obviously Emily hadn't given me a second thought.

My face must have shown it all, as Gran said: 'They didn't want to disturb you. Thought you'd be needing your rest.'

And I felt irritated at being treated like some elderly invalid worn out by the exertions of travelling from Edinburgh.

Gran knew me too well not to notice that scowl and patting my hand she said: 'Don't take on, Rose, there's a good lass. Erland likes to have Emily to himself. After all he's been away a week, and that's a long time apart for them. Now they just want to be together for a few hours. On their own,' she added emphatically.

So I swallowed my disappointment along with one of Gran's well-buttered scones. How food does soothe the troubled breast and triggers memories. The sight and smells of Gran's kitchen again carried me straight back to those early days when Orkney had been my home.

From her questions, I realised that she too was rooted in the past, talking of people we used to know whose names I had long forgotten, as well as the faces that fitted them. Gossip about neighbours revealed that I was still 'peedie Rose Faro' and any interest in my present life was sketchy in the extreme.

And Gran, who gossiped about everything, great and small, never once mentioned Thora or referred to our earlier conversation with Emily.

A curious omission I thought at the time. Almost as if

it had never happened, or I had dreamed it – a particularly unpleasant nightmare.

Watching her bustling about the kitchen, absorbed by the normal daily preparation of the evening meal, peeling vegetables, rolling pastry, my offer to help declined, she said: 'You go out, lass. Get some fresh air while the weather holds.'

That sounded like good advice: it was time to explore Hopescarth.

'And if you see Sibella, she'll be glad of your company,' she added with a shrewd glance. 'Neighbours about here will be curious about you. They'll invite you in for a gossip. Remember what it was like in the old days.'

I hadn't forgotten and it was on the tip of my tongue to say that it wasn't quite like that with some neighbours: Craig Denmore, for instance. I couldn't see Gran rushing to the door and asking the laird's handsome son from Inverness and the whisky distillery to come and sit by the fireside for a cup of tea.

Chapter Ten

Half an hour later, with warnings not to get lost, I was sailing down the hill on my bicycle over the stone bridge to Hopescarth.

Not that there was much to explore. A dozen grey stone houses all huddled together and staring into each other's windows across a rather dull winding street. A square grey building enclosed in heavy railings, the entrances carefully segregated into 'Boys' and 'Girls' carved in stone lintels, marked the local school.

The rest of Hopescarth consisted of a few scattered opulent-looking houses keeping themselves very much to themselves behind high walls leading towards the village church. The kirkyard promised a melancholy but interesting study and I decided the first step should be to acquaint myself with some ancestors.

And there they were, Faros and Scarths, all carefully filed away, peacefully resting under stone slabs and crosses, some leaning at curious angles as if the incumbents were, even in death, attempting to carry on conversations with each other.

The graves went right back to the mid-seventeenth century. A memorial to a Faro who had left Orkney to fight for Prince Charles Edward Stuart and had loyally died by his side at Culloden. A large number of 'Perished at Sea', sad indication of the fate of a whole boatload of Scarth sons, while many tiny slabs were for infants under two years. Others tragically mourned young mothers who had died in childbirth or from subsequent complications.

I stood back and surveyed this scene of aggressive mortality, having made one discovery: a family tree of Faros and Scarths. Pappa, of course, had never had either time or interest to indulge such speculations but I was sure stepbrother Vince, now resident in London as junior physician to the royal household, and his wife Olivia, would be fascinated. I decided to continue my quest with a look at the parish register.

My path passed near to the Yesnaby vault, neatly railed off with a memorial tablet: 'Thora, beloved wife of Erland Yesnaby. Died 1885. Interred 1895.'

That inscription would intrigue future generations I thought as I walked away, sadly aware again of the excuse for Emily's lack of communication. Such happenings would be difficult enough to explain and she had enough nightmares to live through every day without a widowed sister in Edinburgh on her conscience.

Suddenly I realised I was not alone. Here was another interested spectator.

'I'm Wilma. You must be Missus Rose.'

So this was the awful child who haunted Gran's kitchen. First glance could have taken her for someone of my own age. A skinny child, tall as myself, with one of those 'born old' plain faces that never manage to look childlike even in infancy.

She pointed to Thora Yesnaby's memorial. 'D'ye ken that Mr Frank who found her is my Ma's lodger,' she said proudly. 'He let me see her.' Her smile waited for comment and gave me a moment to think of some suitable reply. No doubt disappointed that none was forthcoming, she added importantly:

'After they dug her up, ye ken.' And shaking her head in a grown-up manner: 'She didna' look as if she had been lying there for years and years. She wasna' like a skeleton or the bodies they dig up ower yonder.'

A nod took in the archaeology unit. 'She looked awfa' like a real person who had just died.' A solemn pause. 'Like my aunty who had a bairn and died of it. They're both lying ower there. D'ye want to see their grave? I can show you it, if you like,' she added eagerly.

At my non-committal smile she looked disappointed. Biting her lip, she gave me a sidelong glance. 'Bet you've never seen anyone dead.'

To that challenge I replied carefully. 'Not very recently.' Not very true either, but I declined to prolong a morbid conversation with a twelve-year-old, who was revealing a profoundly macabre streak as she continued proudly:

'I have seen lots and lots of dead folk. There's no need to be scared of them,' she added consolingly. 'They canna' touch you. And Ma lets me go and have a look before the coffin's closed.' Narrowing her eyes she held up her fingers. 'I've seen nine,' she counted. 'No, ten. I'd forgotten grandfather. He wasna' pretty like peedie cousin Vera.' She laughed. 'But then I didna' like him much when he was alive either.'

And indicating Thora's memorial, 'But that lady – she was different. Mr Frank, our lodger, was awfa' upset, ye ken. And real scared. He went on and on about it. Ma was fair fed up.'

I had no comment to offer and she added with a quick defensive glance, 'I go and see Doctor Craig sometimes. It's no' for medicine, ye ken, like our doctor. He canna' cure a cold. Ma lets me go and watch them digging up dead folk.'

She gave me a triumphant smile as if I were about to utter some grown-up's objection: an attitude suggesting that most of her requests were greeted by a shrill 'No, you can't!'

'Doctor Craig lets me have a trowel to dig with them.'

Glad of a diversion, I said: 'And have you found anything exciting?'

She nodded eagerly. 'Once he let me hold a skull.' And closing her eyes ecstatically, 'That was really thrilling. Doctor Craig likes me because I see things. I can tell him where to look.'

The words were in a whisper, staring beyond me as if there was something I couldn't see. It reminded me strangely of Sibella.

'You must be a great help to him,' I said carefully.

Wilma smiled, her approving look told me that I was regarded now as on her side, not one of those wearisome adults who said 'no' to everything.

What an extraordinary child. No wonder Gran did not care for her.

I decided to leave the parish register for the moment as I headed towards the gate with Wilma skipping alongside.

She pointed to my bicycle leaning against the railings. 'Everybody knows that's yours. That's how I kenned who you were. Ma told me to watch out for you,' she added, making it sound quite like a warning as she stroked the handlebars, as if this was a particularly nice but not very trustworthy pony. 'I wish I had a bicycle, Missus Rose.'

She sounded so wistful that I took a quick look up and down the road. No one in sight. And a straight broad path bordering the kirkyard.

I had a strange feeling that this particular child didn't have much to celebrate in her life and on an impulse I said: 'I'll teach you how to ride, if you like.'

She clasped her hands, jumped up and down with delight. 'Oh Missus Rose. Would you, would you? I'd do anything—'

'Come along, then. Right. Up you go. One foot here – and the other. Now press down on the pedals. That's it. Off we go!'

I ran alongside – a few wobbles, fewer I have to say than I made the first time I rode back my friend Alice's newly gifted bicycle from the suburbs of Edinburgh across to Arthur's Seat and Solomon's Tower.

'Watch me, watch me,' she shouted. 'I can do it. I can! Leave go – leave go!'

'No! You'll fall—'

'I won't. I won't!'

'All right.' I ran close behind ready to grab her. But the amazing child was wheeling along the path and back to me as if she's been born in the saddle. Stopping and getting off were tricky. I expected trouble but she managed, and quite gracefully too.

'You were wonderful. Congratulations.'

'Oh Missus Rose, that was the most exciting thing I've ever done in my whole life. Can I – can I do it again sometime?' she asked wistfully.

'Of course you can. Come up to Yesnaby House and we'll have another lesson.' Not that she needed it, I thought in amazement at her progress.

'When can I come?'

'Any time I'm there. Tomorrow morning, if you like.'

Again she danced up and down, clapping her hands. 'Lovely, lovely!'

Suddenly her face fell. 'Missus Rose, would you – I mean, can you keep a secret?'

'Cross my heart,' I replied solemnly.

'You won't tell Ma,' she whispered.

I touched her hand. 'I've promised, haven't I? This will be our secret.'

The church clock belled the hour. 'Thank you, thank you. I have to go. I was taking a message for Ma. She'll kill me.'

And she was off, skipping down the road turning occasionally to see if I was still there, as if our encounter had been just another of her childish fantasies. Another wave and she disappeared.

I smiled. It seemed that the bicycle had found me a strange new friend and heading again towards the church, I found it was relatively modern and therefore rather uninteresting from a historic point of view.

Closer inspection revealed that it had been built on an older foundation. Carved stones, grave covers and lintels piled against the walls, materials scavenged and left over no doubt from the ruined castle Erland's grandfather had pulled down, but the interior was bleak despite one stained glass window, donated by the Tesnabys, of course.

I thought I was alone until a shadow moved and a voice called:

'Hello – so we meet again.'

Craig Denmore.

Delighted to see him so unexpectedly when he now

occupied a substantial measure of my thoughts, I felt an inappropriately girlish blush creeping across my cheeks. Telling myself sternly to stop being so foolish, we shook hands while he murmured conventional pleasantries regarding settling down in Yesnaby House and so forth.

'I was watching you give young Wilma a try on your bicycle.' He paused and then said approvingly, 'Well done, the pair of you.' And pointing towards the stained glass window: 'Just looking round, were you?'

It didn't need a reply and he went on: 'I come here often to consult the old records that Yesnaby left regarding the castle. Parish documents are scarce, anything before the 1820s, that is.' And looking round, 'Nothing much of interest architecturally.'

I had to agree and he pointed to the baptismal font. 'Even that's pretty modern. Fifteenth century.'

I was tempted to smile at his description of modernity as he continued: 'Anything I can help you with?'

I shook my head. 'My purpose is the same as yours. Old family records, if they exist.'

He raised an eyebrow. 'Great minds think alike.'

With no excuse to linger, I wandered outside. Following me he said: 'Come and have a look at the dig sometime. I meant that, you know.' And giving the Tesnaby vault a rueful glance, 'I'm afraid I'm not on the visiting list at the big house, persona non grata.' And a gesture towards Thora's memorial tablet. 'There was a terrible furore, as you can imagine. I was away in Edinburgh when Frank and the lads discovered her. They hadn't the slightest idea that she was Yesnaby's missing wife.'

And with a sidelong glance to see how I would take it, 'This discovery was a considerable embarrassment since the poor chap had buried an unknown woman, believing it to be Thora and had taken a second wife shortly after her disappearance ten years earlier.'

Pausing as if expecting comment, he sighed. 'Not quite the ticket to have wife number one appearing from the dead on the scene, no matter how fleetingly. I got a distinct feeling that they blamed us for finding her. That we should have let dead wives lie,' he added ruefully.

'Especially when no one had a clue to the identity of the woman in the first wife's grave,' I said.

He shrugged. 'Well, we'll never know that now. Too many rough seas have flowed past Marwick Head since then.'

'But doesn't it intrigue you? Who she must have been? Her family and so forth.'

Again he shrugged. 'She could have disappeared from home too and drowned anywhere up the coast. Fallen overboard from a ship—'

'Doesn't it bother you?' I asked curiously.

He smiled vaguely. 'Should it? I'm sorry. I'm afraid my interest in corpses, drowned or otherwise, belongs to past centuries.'

That sounded just a mite unfeeling and I said rather sharply. 'You are aware that wife number two, as you describe her, is my sister Emily.'

It was his turn to be embarrassed. 'Is that so? What a coincidence. Do forgive me, I hadn't the least idea. I thought you were – were just – oh, never mind.'

And with a more intent glance. 'Sisters, eh?' A shake of the head and that phrase I always knew to expect: 'Well, well. You're not in the least alike, are you?'

And there the conversation ended abruptly as a man wearing a clerical collar hurried down the path towards us.

'Dr Denmore. I am so sorry to have kept you waiting.'

I was introduced and greeted cordially. Reverend Mullen didn't make the same mistake as Craig since Emily had told him that her sister was coming on a visit.

'I hope we shall have the pleasure of seeing you in church on Sunday, Mrs McQuinn. Have a good holiday with us—'

A final remark about the weather and with a slight bow he turned to Craig. 'I have some papers for you, sir.'

Thus politely dismissed I walked toward my bicycle, suddenly aware of someone waiting under the shadowy trees outside the kirkyard.

It was Sibella.

Chapter Eleven

Sibella walked towards me, holding a tiny bunch of flowers.

She leaned forward, presenting a cheek to kiss. 'You are looking rested, Rose. You slept well last night?'

When I said yes, she smiled. 'I am just about to take a walk back up to the house. I'd be glad of your company.' And glancing apologetically at the bicycle, 'If it wouldn't be too much trouble, that is.'

'Not at all,' I said, relieved that Emily had been wrong and there was no suggestion that Sibella might request lessons as Wilma had.

'A moment – I have to give Hakon his flowers.'

Was Hakon the minister I wondered, following her back into the kirkyard. But when she bent over the Scarth graves, I realised from the dates and 'Drowned at Sea' that this Hakon was her very late husband.

She was smiling, her lips moving in a silent greeting. Stooping down and laying her hands tenderly on the grave, she turned and said: 'I was telling him about you.'

I tried not to look surprised as she straightened up, a

little unsteadily at first, but without requiring assistance. Remembering Gran's warning, I suspected that my help would not be welcomed in any case, as she went on:

'I am so pleased we've met this morning. Out here, Rose, on our own. An opportunity to get to know you.'

The same thought had been in my mind as we walked a few hundred yards down the road. Sibella paused by a grassy bank, obviously a favourite place, with the whole wealth of the islands spread out below in the glory of late afternoon sunshine, the land calm and welcoming. Skylarks soared heavenward on the field behind us, the house dominating the hill, towering high against a cloudless sky.

And there, in a peace older and more serene than any I had experienced since childhood days in Orkney, Sibella seemed eager to tell me her own story.

'I expect they told you where I came from?'

She wasn't expecting a reply and as I wanted her version of Gran's extraordinary story, I smiled eagerly. That seemed to satisfy her.

'I wasna' born here.' A gesture took in the landscape before us. 'I dinna' ken where I came from but they all said I came from the sea ower yonder and the folk hereabouts still dinna' ken quite how to take me, because of that. Because I'm not one of them – even after a hundred years.'

She laughed sharply. 'My long years are seen as witchcraft – black or white magic.' And with a pause to see how I took that: 'Aye, Rose, they think I'm a selkie. In this day, I ask you, can you credit that? Do folk never learn?'

I felt that was for my benefit as she looked at me intently as if expecting a reply, a denial. I shook my head. I didn't care to mention that in many places on both sides of the Atlantic, witchcraft – a belief in the power of the occult, of good and evil – had never gone out of fashion.

People had always wanted to communicate with the dead, even in big cities.

In Edinburgh, spiritualist societies and mediums were doing a roaring trade and making their fortunes. Every afternoon and evening the bereaved, the grief-stricken, crowded into dark rooms and dim halls in the hope that the spirits of their beloved dead might materialise for a brief moment. Longing to hear and pay dearly for a few reassuring words and, I suspected, not only for comfort but in many cases, to sweep away feelings of guilt. The audiences were mostly female – daughters and widows – those kept awake at night, haunted by feelings that they maybe had not done enough, maybe had not loved with all their hearts an ailing parent or spouse.

Desperately lonely for Danny in those early days of my return to Edinburgh, I went to one such highly publicised meeting. 'Yes, your dear husband says he is happy. You are not to worry. It is a lovely place.'

The message was so unlike Danny, I wanted to laugh. But I stayed and listened to the same words, the same pattern being handed out to the bereaved, a panacea for those still raw wounds. Consolation. That's what they came for and handed over often hard-earned money in return.

'I dinna' ken when or where I was born,' Sibella was saying, 'but I was carried into the house up yonder as a peedie girl. Aye, I well remember the day.'

And closing her eyes as if she could still picture that scene clearly: 'So I must be a year or two past one hundred. There are those who sneer and say that someone couldna' do their sums properly. But they canna' deny that the builders were putting the last slate on the roof in 1795 when Hakon Scarth carried me from the sea, wrapped in his coat. Shivering I was, like a half-drowned puppy, he used to tell me. By my size, they reckoned I was no more than two when he asked his Ma, who was housekeeper to the Yesnabys, to take care of me.'

I have a long memory, inherited from Pappa, and I asked: 'Don't you remember anything before that?'

Even as I said the words I realised that very few people do remember their first two years. Most often tales of those very early days are related by parents, so vividly that they are incorporated into memory and a child can grow up believing that was exactly what he or she remembered.

Sibella shook her head. 'I remember nothing before Hakon lifting me out of the boat, and the smell of fish.' Pausing she added: 'They couldna' get me to eat fish. I just sicked it up and I still canna' digest it, even to this day. Isna' that extraordinary? Everyone but me eats fish on Orkney.'

Then she laughed. 'Hakon thought I was one of his catch at first. There was seaweed wrapped all around my legs and he got a terrible shock. Thought he'd caught a mermaid.'

She sighed softly. 'All I recall is that it was like someone lighting up with a searchlight in what had been total darkness. Like being born. That's the only way I can explain. Coming from a dark womb,' she whispered.

'I canna' remember anything about being on that ship they told me about, the one I was named for, that sank – or whether I heard the poor drowning folks shrieking when it hit the rocks and went under the waves. That's what they told me in Hopescarth about the wreck and I tried to remember seeing it, but all I could ever remember was Hakon gathering me, cold and shivering, into his warm arms.'

She smiled at the memory, her arms hugging her breast, her eyes suddenly narrowing as if she saw Hakon there before her.

'I never thought I was different from other bairns. But when I went to the school they all whispered what their fathers, who were fishermen, had told them: that the month before Hakon rescued me, he had found an injured seal pup. Their fathers said it had been caught in his nets and cut badly. It's cruel to keep it alive, suffering like that, they said, and the kindest thing would be to hit it on the head, throw it back into the sea again.

'But my Hakon wouldna' do that. Even as a lad, he has always had a way with animals. They all came to him, ye ken, just like they come to me these days. Wait till you see my croft – I have a barn full of sick creatures.'

She paused, looking round for a moment bewildered, and I had a strange feeling that sometimes past and present joined hands and were one and the same for Sibella Scarth.

'Where was I? Aye, my Hakon cared for the peedie seal and when its wounds were healed, he returned it to the sea. Now, there's a story among the Finn folk that one of their kind spared to the sea is three spared to the land.

'And so it came about, just like that, when he was out fishing with his father and brother. A sudden storm and the roarst dashed their boat to pieces on the rocks, but the three of them swam ashore. A miracle,' she said with a shake of her head. 'No one ever survives a roarst, but they did. And not even a scratch on them. Folk were pleased but they didna' believe in that kind of miracle. They said it was a selkie's magic did it. Because Hakon had rescued a seal lass.'

And gazing towards the ever-moving restless sea, she sighed. It was almost high tide and huge waves streamed towards the rocks. 'I just wanted to be like other lasses, but then it got me respect – and fear from other bairns at the school. Mostly they were terrified of a look from me and when I grew up, where I came from never bothered the lads who came to court me.'

She smiled. 'But I never wanted any but Hakon Scarth. All the lasses wanted him too for he was the handsomest lad on the island. He was fourteen when he took me from the sea and when I was sixteen and him a man of thirty, still unwed, he asked me to marry him. For I was the one he had been waiting for, for all those years. He had saved up and had his own boat and promised me a bonny house in South Ronaldsay. The other lasses were mad jealous!'

She laughed at that, clasping her hands. 'He wouldna' listen to his family or his friends either who said it was dead unlucky to take a seal woman to wife. Had he not read the old stories? That some day Sibella would be called back to the Finn folk. That I'd maybe bring him a bright summer but it would end in a woeful winter.'

She tapped her breast under the shawl. 'But here I am and I never wanted to go back to the sea. I was in mortal fear of it. Why, I wouldna' even paddle my feet in the water like the other bairns, without screaming.'

She shook her head sadly. 'And it was the sea that took my Hakon from me. Maybe the Finn folk were jealous of our happiness.' She was silent, looking at the sky, and as I took the mittened hand in mine, she turned with that lost look as if she'd just returned from a distant place.

'You're a good lass, I can feel your goodness, Rose. You'll be happy and lucky because you love people right.'

And I thought guiltily of poor Jack, waiting for my reply that I'd marry him, as she said: 'Now, where was I? Ah yes, my Hakon. We were happy as the summer was long and we had a long life together. I gave him two bairns, strong and healthy. Peter and Mary, your grandmother.' Again she sighed. 'The sea claimed my bonny Peter; such happiness as mine and Hakon's required a sacrifice and I suppose it was the right of the Finn folk to claim our first-born.

'Hakon was good to me. Folk hereabouts said he should have put me back in the sea long since. Ye ken, although I looked like a real peedie lass, I was dumb as any animal.'

'Dumb?'

She shook her head. 'No voice, not even a whisper. No one heard me speak a single word. Although most bairns two or three can speak, I couldna'. I had to learn to say even simple words and then I just croaked like a frog. Even when I went to the school I wasna' much better but there were people who whispered that in the circumstances that was quite normal – in a selkie.'

She paused dramatically and looked at me. 'They said I had traded my siren's voice, the one mermaids used to lure sailors to their doom, when I took on human form.'

'Your voice sounds fine,' I said, as was expected of me.

'Aye, but I had to work at it. Hakon understood we weren't like other folk. Sometimes we went days and days without saying a word and knew exactly what each other wanted, or what we were both thinking.' Frowning, she added: 'I sometimes worried about Mary when she was a bairn. A late talker, she was too. But she's made up for it since.' She laughed. 'Aye, she has that. Her tongue never stops wagging, except when she's asleep.'

We had reached the stone bridge and I wondered if she would be coming back to the house but she shook her head.

'Off you go, Rose. We'll talk again.' And she took my

hand, held it to her lips briefly, an old-fashioned gesture of farewell.

I watched her go, observing that under the shawl her chest was completely flat, her shoulders narrow and her body long and thin. No surprise in someone past a hundred, where age might be expected to have brought radical changes to the female form.

But Sibella's legs were very short and, remembering what Gran had told me about trouble with her feet, I had noticed that under the trailing skirt she dragged her legs. That too could be mistaken for age, but when she walked, although she moved quite smartly, she slid her feet along the ground, as if...

As if...

No. As I wheeled my bicycle up the drive, I firmly resolved to banish the image Sibella evoked.

It just wasn't logical. Or possible.

Chapter Twelve

Erland and Emily had returned from Kirkwall.

Walking towards the coach house, I could hear Erland talking to the carriage horse. With a smiling greeting, he took the bicycle and set it against the side of the stall. 'Here's your new companion back again, Storm, old chap.'

As the horse nuzzled his shoulder, Erland grinned at me and said: 'It's going to rain soon.' And looking up at the cloudless sky with a countryman's inborn knowledge: 'The trees are waiting for it. See how still they are?'

Giving Storm a final pat, he led the way out. 'Like to see the garden, Rose? The next storm will lay it bare until spring. The last of the summer flowers are just holding on.'

Orpheus and his lute, I thought again. In this case a superb human voice and that beguiling invitation could have led me anywhere.

The garden lay to the east of the house, down a steep flight of stone stairs, invisible from the drive. Signs of earlier habitations were marked by pieces of broken wall and, as we descended, I looked at the vast array of colourful flowers and shrubs. An old walled garden from an ancient painting, carpeted by plants carefully chosen for longevity, resistant to the elements and sheltered by the house.

'Given our climate, it's a marvel that anything survives at all,' Erland said. 'All I need to maintain it is the pattern my grandfather laid down. Do you know there is hardly a day when I can't find some quiet spot out of the wind to smoke my pipe? There's a corner for all seasons, and a windy day in August is quite different from a windy day in April. I've learned a lot from my garden,' he added proudly and pausing to light his pipe, he watched the curl of smoke absorbed by the air.

'Well, Rose, what do you think of it?'

I regarded the scene in amazement. 'Beautiful! Hard to believe that there's a bleak landscape stretching for miles just across the wall.'

My observation pleased him. He laughed. 'There's another reason for the soil's fertility. This land has been inhabited continuously since man first settled on the island thousands of years ago.'

And tapping his foot on the ground: 'In medieval times, this was the kitchen midden. On this exact spot, animal bones, human excrement and waste deposit from countless generations have been poured into the earth to emerge and grow again into the garden you see here.'

As he spoke, I looked around this scene of perfect tranquillity. Timeless indeed, it suggested sunlight and birdsong, flowers radiant in summer glory. 'If ever gardens were haunted, then this one must be,' I said and Erland nodded.

'A very benign kind of haunting. A feeling of comfort, don't you recognise it?'

I said yes and he smiled. 'Think of it, every person who ever lived here, who has laughed and loved and died here through the passing centuries has left some part of themselves. In essence, they are still with us in spirit,' he added gently and as if embarrassed by this display of emotion, he puffed strongly at his pipe and the aroma of excellent tobacco joined the other fragrances.

'I like to think they watch over the present generations and the ones still to come. Pity we can't get tall trees, but we have the birch and alder and the willow.' He pointed. 'And over there, a hornbeam. Hornbeam,' he repeated. 'Now isn't that a grand name for a tree?'

I smiled. He made it sound like music.

'And over yonder, that's the last of our hazels, doesn't produce nuts any more, the poor old thing. Come and look at these.'

I leaned over beside him and looked at the tiny patch of green.

'Here's our little treasure, the *Primula scotica* which would be just as happy growing on the grassy sea cliff a mile away. It rarely survived cultivation so perhaps it was here – like these wild orchids – and firmly established before man invaded.'

As I knelt and touched the tiny petals, he said: 'What does it remind you of – that little face?'

'A tiny monkey.'

'Right. And that's what it's called: *Orchis simia* – the monkey orchid.' He straightened up with a groan. 'We don't advertise our rare flowers, so keep it to yourself. In a few years they will be extinct and there are some collectors who would come all the way from Edinburgh and Glasgow and further afield, to harvest our rare specimens.'

Pausing, he added: 'Can't you just imagine how all this must have looked before the first people came and set down their roots? They must have seen and taken for granted so many plants and delicate flowers which are now only a memory, or have evolved into something tougher and less beautiful in order to survive.'

Shaking his head and knocking out his pipe on the stone wall, he sighed. 'That was long before man knew or cared enough to appreciate and record them. Just think of the perfumes of exotic flowers and plants lost to us for ever.'

And sniffing the air as if some of that elusive fragrance still remained: 'Think of all the bird plumage lost for ever once they had to forgo their brilliant colours and evolve into dun greys and browns to keep them safe from their chief predator – the hunter Man.'

I tried to see it through his eyes, through that beautiful voice, conjuring up greens and yellows and browns into rainbow shades.

'Somewhere in the house, in the attics, I suspect, there are old drawings and I think a watercolour done by my grandmother of the garden. Do you paint, by any chance?'

I said yes, the artist in me aroused, for here was a theme that pleased and challenged. I resolved to take time and record this garden, go back to earlier days when I had painstakingly drawn botanical specimens. It would be an absorbing and rewarding task on a holiday that offered little else but the ability to eat too much and take time to relax.

Or so I thought. So wrongly, I was to discover.

'Over there is the vegetable patch. You'll find the perennials have been name-tagged. The metal tags are still the original ones my grandfather engraved.'

Our path led past another vivid flower bed, bright with the faces of late pansies. With an exclamation, Erland bent down and picked off a head.

'Dratted slugs! At them again!'

I offered my remedy. 'I have a hedgehog in my garden. She polishes off slugs for breakfast. And with a large young family to support, they all troop out after her for a saucer of bread and milk at bedtime.'

I smiled at the memory of Thane watching over this scene. Huge, but ignored by the hedgehogs. Perhaps too large for their vision to encompass, or perhaps another instinctive reason that they knew they need not fear him. He was on their side.

'Hedgehogs are fairly recent incomers to the island. Did you know that, Rose? Introduced by a minister's sons from the mainland just twenty-odd years ago. 1875, it was. They seem to have flourished and multiplied with biblical zeal. I must see if I can lure one, or kidnap one, more like.'

'I think I should warn you that they won't come to anyone's bidding, or stay,' I said. 'They have to do the choosing.'

'Then I'll get Sibella on to it, see what she can magic up for me. She seems to be a magnet for all living creatures.' He looked solemn as he said it, as if he realised her power and he turned suddenly quiet, leading the way back to the stone steps.

Above us rose the house. With sunlight on it, I saw now that some of the stones looked exceedingly ancient. I pointed to them and said: 'There are some carved stones like that I noticed outside the church. Were they from the original castle?'

'Older than that. Some originated from the broch down by the shore. And these stones in the garden walls and on the sills are from the Earl's palace which occupied this spot in the sixteenth century – the garden is built on its foundations.'

I remembered Craig Denmore had told me how

Erland's grandfather had replaced it with the present building, as he said: 'You'll know all about Bad Earl Robert, of course.'

I nodded vaguely and he continued: 'Mary, Queen of Scots' half-brother and a complete disaster. Everything that ever went wrong with this island, past or present, was laid at his door. The palace here belonged to his son, Patrick, the sinister Black Pate as history records him.'

He stopped and smiled down at me. 'Sibella will tell you his ghost still haunts this place, but take no heed of that, Rose. Sibella has an answer for everything,' he grinned.

I wasn't going to let it go at that. 'Tell me more. I'm intrigued. There are ghosts in plenty allegedly haunting Solomon's Tower on Arthur's Seat, where I live. And I have yet to see one.'

He laughed. 'Well, if you should ever find you are being followed by a black-cloaked rider, galloping on a black horse, you just get on that bicycle of yours and ride like the wind.'

We both laughed at such absurdity and Erland said: 'The Stewarts weren't the first to colonise Hopescarth. Before them, it was The Bu, the Norse Earl or Headman's Homestead.'

I remembered tales of The Bu, house of the Wolflord of Orkney, the convivial Viking drinking hall, as he went on: 'I dare say my diligent grandfather uncovered layers and layers of past history in his building operation. If you're interested, there's a stack of dusty papers in the attic that I've never had the time or desire to read. Might be important documents but I expect a lot more went into the rubbish dump. Those lads hadn't arrived on the scene then with their spades and riddles,' he added with a wry nod in the direction of the dig.

'Grandfather was a practical man and when he inherited the estate and decided to become a farmer, he entertained no grand ideas about living in a palace packed with ancient history. After all those years at sea, sailing the oceans of the world, he had dreamed of a modest, comfortable – warm – house to defy the elements, with a sheltered garden.

'As for the palace, it had been nothing but a costly ruin for the past two hundred years and the family had gradually retreated from leaking roofs and falling masonry into one draughty crumbling wing, which every winter rendered more uninhabitable.'

He smiled. 'Even if you are sentimental about old castles, this one would have been hell to live in. But there is a painting of it. Ask Emily. She'll track it down for you. It's in the glory-hole up in the attics somewhere. By rights, belongs in the local museum. However, to give Grandfather his due, he did leave one tiny piece of the original palace, so we can conclude that he had his sentimental moments after all. Come along.'

As I followed him, I asked: 'Talking history, have you any theories about the Maid of Norway's grave?'

He stopped walking, bit his lip and looked thoughtful. Then with a sigh he nodded again in the direction of the unseen dig. 'Not really.'

I followed his gaze. 'You don't think she's buried over there?'

He shook his head, shrugged and said firmly. 'No.' Then holding up his hand. 'Rain! I knew it! My orchids will be grateful. Quickly – over here.' And taking my arm, 'Let's test your powers on my other treasure,' he added, leading the way to a patch of ground near a compost heap: an unlikely place for a tiny orchid reverently framed by chicken wire.

I bent down. 'This one looks like a skull, white with a yellow helmet – reminds me of the ghost of Hamlet's father.'

A triumphant laugh from Erland. 'Good girl, know your Shakespeare too,' he said approvingly. 'That's one thing I miss here in Hopescarth. We have no theatre. Have to take Emily to the mainland for that.'

And touching the tiny flower, 'You were right again. It's the Ghost orchid, because of the skull and those pale translucent flowers and the fact that it lives on decaying matter in the soil surface.'

Sheltering the tiny orchid, an ivy-covered stone wall. Erland pushed back the foliage, which had almost taken over, to reveal a stone seat somewhat inhospitably wedged in a small embrasure, an ancient carving in the lintel.

'You'll see this better in the painting. It belonged in the palace herb garden but I reckon it is much older than that. Most probably Pictish. There used to be a series of stone lintels like this in the garden walls, each with its own coat of arms depicting the various branches of the Stewarts and their royal connections.

'It must have been very grand,' I said, imagination defeated as I tried to envisage the huge palace, vast herb and flower gardens, dovecots, now reduced to one tiny piece of wall, the only evidence of the once massive foundations occasionally erupting as broken fragments of stone walls.

I looked closer at the stone carving. Ancient, storm-weathered despite the protective ivy, its design almost obliterated by the elements: a mermaid wearing a crown and holding a mirror.

A ghost of memory twitched. Somewhere I had seen it before.

'Is this image quite famous?'

Erland shook his head. 'I doubt it. I expect it should be in the museum in Kirkwall too. But we're inclined to be hoarders, as you'll see when Emily takes you on a tour of the attics.'

Again I considered the stone. 'Maybe I have seen a photograph somewhere.'

'I doubt it,' Erland repeated and when I said it seemed so familiar, he smiled. 'You've probably seen the same design on runic stones in museums. Traditional Pictish design and that's about all anyone knows of its origins, belief is that the mermaid was a fertility symbol.'

I looked at him. Was that a wistful note I heard? Was that why the Yesnabys hung on to it?

But as we walked away, the stone bothered me. I was certain I had seen it before, but not in any of Erland's suggestions. I racked my brains. The mermaid on runic stones, yes, but this was different.

The crowned mermaid and her mirror. I had held something like it in my hand. And that meant jewellery.

I have an excellent memory. My one weakness however is a total lack of interest in the normal female acquisition of rings, bracelets, brooches and necklaces. I have never coveted precious stones or desired any adornment but the wedding ring Danny placed on my finger years ago in Arizona.

The crowned mermaid and mirror did not belong anywhere in American Indian culture so if it was jewellery, then it had to be Scottish. And that, for me, also meant Edinburgh.

But when and more important, who and why?

Chapter Thirteen

Erland left me in the hall, retired to his study and closed the door. In the kitchen Gran was bustling about, her hands covered in flour.

'Where's Emily?' I asked.

'Having a rest. Kirkwall tires her out.' Gran made it sound like a day in the big city. Observing my amused expression, she said sharply: 'Erland insists.'

'Is she – well, is she going to be all right this time?' I asked anxiously.

Gran looked at me, smiled reassuringly. 'Of course she is, lass. It's just that with her past history – I think Erland's more scared than she is. Having a son will mean such a lot to him.' She shrugged. 'After so many failures, perhaps they both feel this will be the last time.'

'She's only twenty-nine,' I protested. 'Lots of women get married long after that and produce children.'

Gran paused in her pastry-making to give me a shrewd look. 'What about you, Rose? Isn't it time you married that nice policemen you were telling us about and had some bairns?'

I had hardly mentioned Jack Macmerry but Gran's matchmaking instincts were as acute as ever.

I smiled. 'I don't know. Maybe there are too many policemen in our family – and I've lost one already,' I added bitterly. 'Do they make good husbands, I wonder?'

I was thinking of Pappa, but she bristled. 'My Magnus was the best in the whole world. There was no one like him.'

'I'm sure you're right about that, Gran.' Tactfully I didn't remind her that she and Grandpa had been married only a few years before he was killed. Maybe if, like Pappa, he had gone on to long service and promotion in the Edinburgh City Police there would have been a very different story. Especially, as I guessed from talks with Pappa, that he always felt guilty about having neglected Mamma. Maybe that had put him off a second marriage to his writer companion, Imogen Crowe – of whom Vince, Olivia and I all heartily approved as an excellent choice of stepmother.

'You shouldn't turn your back on a good chance or let a good man go past you, lass.'

How often had I heard Gran's warning words in my girlhood years. Solemnly handing me a fresh-baked scone, she added with an impish smile: 'Here you are, lass. But remember you can't have your cake and eat it.'

Eager to change the subject, I asked if there was anything I could do to help, my offer again firmly declined: I was here on holiday, to enjoy myself, not to work.

Advised to go out and get some fresh air, I had a feeling I was going to be very replete with that particular commodity by the time I returned to Edinburgh.

'Erland had been showing me the garden.'

Gran beamed. 'Aye, he has right green fingers,'

'I saw the mermaid stone.'

Gran concentrated on the pastry. 'Well?'

'Maybe you can help.'

'How's that, lass?' she asked cautiously.

'I'm puzzled, that's what. Could I – could I have ever seen it before? I mean, when we lived in Kirkwall?'

She sighed, shook her head. 'We never came to Yesnaby, did we?'

'What about school outings?'

'Never as I mind, as far away as here.'

I thought for a moment. 'Maybe you had something like the mermaid stone in the house. An ornament or a picture that I remember,' I persisted.

'I never did. I only had pictures that were decent and had clothes on them, not women with naked bosoms, like that,' she said firmly, returning to the pastry. With a swift change of subject: 'What did you think of Hopescarth?'

So I told her about the church and the family graves, omitting any mention of the memorial to Thora Yesnaby and wondering why she was so edgy about the mermaid stone. Could her prim over-reaction to 'naked bosoms' be the only reason?

'Next time you go down past the village shop you could bring me a packet of salt, if that's no trouble. And some more butter. It's a fair trail for me these days,' she grumbled. 'All that way down the drive is bad enough without that hill up to the shops and back again. It seems to get longer as I get older.'

And suddenly I remembered that Gran was past eighty, a matter of reverence and awe in city life where age is a matter of importance. To country folk, however, as long as one had good health and was able to obey the dictates of the four agricultural seasons, increasing age went by unnoticed and unworthy of comment.

'I'd love to do your shopping, just keep a list handy – so easy with the bicycle.'

At the word 'bicycle' she gave me a doubtful glance as if her groceries might be contaminated, their fate imperilled by association with that alien monster. However, I was soon to discover that mere mention of going to Hopescarth was an unmissable opportunity and brought forth an arm's-length list of urgent requirements.

'I met Wilma wandering about the kirkyard. She's very interested in the dig.'

'Spends every spare minute there,' said Gran. 'Isna' natural for a child her age. What did you think of her?'

'She's certainly a strange child.' I wasn't going to mention the bicycle episode, having made my promise to Wilma, but I hoped I would be around when she came for the offered riding practice.

I said I had walked back with Sibella.

'And I suppose she told you her whole life story. Likes to impress folks, ye ken,' said Gran, her disapproval hardly suppressed.

I laughed. 'I do like her, Gran. She's absolutely fascinating.'

'Hmph,' Gran responded sourly, indicating that the subject was closed. As she rushed back and forward to the oven, my presence was no longer needed and, looking out of the window I saw that Erland's promised rain had come to naught. With the mystery of the mermaid stone still weighing heavily on my thoughts, I came to a sudden decision.

Craig Denmore, of course. He was the most likely authority on the subject.

Walking back down the drive and over the bridge I came upon a busy scene of scratching and scraping.

Craig's fellow diggers looked up curiously. There followed a rapid series of shouted introductions, polite smiles and then all returned to their trowelling and digging.

All except Frank Breck, who I had gathered was Wilma's mother's lodger. He looked as grey and dry as the ground he was working on.

'Good to see you, Rose,' said Craig cheerfully. 'You've come at a great time for us. We've just made a discovery,' he added proudly, with a smile at Frank who did not respond.

'The Maid's grave?' I asked eagerly

'Not this time, but we're very hopeful,' was Frank's earnest reply, watching Craig put a grimy hand into his pocket where, with an air of triumph, he drew out a coin and handed it to me.

Most of the soil had been removed but it was still undecipherable. 'Roman?' I queried and Craig shook his head.

I tried again. 'Viking?'

He laughed. 'No. Not nearly as early as that. Probably thirteenth century Scandinavian. When we have the antique coin experts have a look at it we'll know if it's genuine. Never want to set our hopes too high but finding it right on this spot has great possibilities.'

'You think that it might be part of that missing dowry?' I said.

Craig nodded and looked at Frank, who forced a dour smile. 'If so, then it almost certainly suggests that she was buried in this area.'

I could understand their enthusiasm when I said: 'But weren't there other travellers from Scandinavia at that time – I mean just ordinary sailors trading with Orkney? I imagine they'd been doing that long before the Middle Ages.'

Frank's heavenward glance failed to hide his disgust that here was a Miss Know-all and with a curt nod to Craig he went back to his digging. I watched him go. I had upset him but surely archaeologists were used to this sort of thing, to examining all finds logically, and of having to convince others.

Craig looked quite crestfallen. With a sigh he pocketed the coin and indicating a fragment of ancient wall he said: 'Won't you take a seat? It's all we can offer in the way of hospitality, I'm afraid.' And with a groan as I made room for him, he added: 'Thanks. My back's breaking.'

He smiled. 'You know, you may be right about the sailors. But I hope you're wrong and that the next find will be something that indicates the Maid's grave is right here,' he added, tapping the ground with his foot.

'And Huw Scarth's pot of gold too,' I said and he knew I was laughing at him.

'Maybe. We've already found some coins of Earl Robert Stewart's personal denomination. Not content with a reign of terror by sword, fire and torture, he changed the old laws of the island guaranteed by the Scots Parliament and put through some new enactments, including his own currency. Free lieges of the monarch were banished and their property confiscated, or they were allowed to remain on condition they yielded up their heritages to him. When these two methods of piracy failed, they were left to rot in prison without trial.'

Pausing, he gave me an apologetic grin. 'Is that enough for you to go on with? Or do you want more? First thing about any archaeology project is a thorough knowledge of the area's history. Every record, every happening before you came along, to be minutely examined.'

Without waiting for my reply, he went on:

'Earl Robert compelled lairds and liefs to entertain him and his household in a royal progress, I quote: '*to the number of six and seven score persons with adequate and great cheer at their own expense*'. As he had nineteen children of his own, each with a private army of retainers, even a short visit led to their host's immediate penury and the inevitable transfer of their property into the earl's hands or to one of his brood who had cast a greedy eye on it.

'He also claimed rights to all common moors and pastures and forbade the burgesses to trade except by his leave and licence. Even churches weren't exempt as they had to hand over their benefices to him. The most sinister form of subtle oppression was the increase of *bismer and pundler* to his own specification.'

He stopped and looked at me. 'Bismer and pundler – the ancient Orkney weights?' I asked.

A smile. 'And a bit before your time at the school here. There was no escape from Earl Robert by death either, since by his law, dead men could be charged with old crimes. Condemned in effigy and their goods confiscated, which left a neat margin for appropriating anything that took his fancy. And he showed an amazing depth of imagination, we must give him credit for that.

'As for the live inhabitants, another law: None should leave Orkney and Zetland in order to make complaint against himself. And so all ferries were stopped and passengers required to produce a licence to leave.

'When I looked into Earl Robert's tyrannous rule, I realised that the activities of the wreckers, always regarded as such a discreditable part of Orkney's history, now shone by comparison, a virtual necessity for survival.'

I said: 'Now I begin to see the significance of Huw Scarth's rainbow and the pot of gold.'

'Good girl! One thing stands out like a sore thumb in this story and that is how Huw's pot of gold brought him peace in his time. Think about it, how this one man managed to achieve wealth and security as well as Black Pate's blessing. And he was allowed to remain here – in a Stewart palace.'

Pausing, he rubbed his chin thoughtfully. 'What intrigues us is could this pot of gold be in actual fact, the Maid's missing dowry? If so, I'd hazard a guess that it vanished without trace into the Stewart Earldom long ago. We'll never know, except that there was already interest in the dowry even before Earl Robert came on the scene.

'The Stewart kings were always short of cash and when Robert's father, King James the Fifth, visited Orkney, the hint was that he had heard of "monies" there. Someone certainly passed the word down to Edinburgh because Queen Mary's gift to her half-brother was not quite as altruistic as it sounded. Robert Stewart, you see, was a great crony of that sinister young man, her second husband Lord Henry Darnley. We gather it was at his insistence that Robert was given the preferment of Orkney. As the records tell us – I quote: *that there was much to be gained thereby*.

'When Mary's reign ended disastrously with Darnley's murder and Bothwell's flight to Orkney, Mary wrote to Gilbert Balfour who was then Governor and lived at Nordland Castle, beseeching him to do what he could to help to: *raise monies and treasyrs in particular the Maid's dowry*.

I knew the rest of that sorry tale. Bothwell wasn't

allowed to land and outlawed, went to his end eight years later, mad and chained to a pillar in a Denmark jail.

I still wasn't convinced that the pot of gold had been squandered long ago. Perhaps Craig read my thoughts as he said:

'A pipe dream maybe, but no one on Orkney can resist the thought of buried treasure even if our main concern as archaeologists is finding the Maid's grave. Anything else, we tell ourselves, is just a bonus.'

And then with a change of subject: 'How are you enjoying your holiday?'

About to mention the mermaid stone, there was a shout from the dig.

'Craig!' It was Frank. He rushed over, holding up his hand, shouting:

'There's something else!'

Chapter Fourteen

'One of the lads has found another coin!'

Craig sprang to his feet. 'Excellent, Frank, excellent!' And to me triumphantly, 'You see, I really think we are on to something.'

I smiled. 'Then I'll leave you to it. But can I ask you both something – it may be important for your discoveries.'

That got their full attention.

'Erland was showing me their garden. Have you seen the mermaid and mirror stone in the little arbour?'

Frank looked at Craig who shook his head. 'The garden is strictly out of bounds to us, I'm afraid.'

'Too many precious plants and flowers we might trample over with our muddy boots,' said Frank contemptuously.

'What about this mermaid stone?' asked Craig. There was an exchanged glance between them, an air of suppressed excitement.

'I thought you might know its origins. A carved stone on a little embrasure beside one of his orchids. He hinted at runic stones.'

They were both watching me as I spoke, listening intently now.

Craig said cautiously: 'Yes, that could be it.' And Frank echoed: 'Yes, indeed.'

'You obviously were impressed, Rose. Was it important?' asked Craig smiling.

'It is to me. You see, I am sure I've seen something very like it before.'

'Oh, and where would that be?' asked Craig gently, still smiling.

'That's the problem. I don't know where. I thought maybe you would be able to help. That you might have some ideas. In a museum collection, for instance.'

They both looked disappointed. Perceptible shrugs of dismissal left me feeling suddenly very foolish as Craig said: 'If it's runic then that's too early to have any significance for us.'

'But could you have seen one like it, perhaps in Edinburgh?' I insisted and Craig's head jerked up at that.

'In Edinburgh?' Then: 'No. What makes you think that?' he added sharply.

'I don't know. Just an idea.'

He looked at me, frowning. 'There could be something in Edinburgh, but I'm not familiar with it.' And turning to Frank, 'What about you? Come across a mermaid stone in any of your activities?' he asked lightly.

Frank shook his head and continued to watch me, his gaze brooding and intent as if trying to interpret my thoughts. Then he shrugged. 'Not that I can think of. And there aren't many Pictish remains in Edinburgh.'

I thought of Arthur's Seat and all the evidence of runrig agriculture, but I wasn't going to argue with authority.

'What about your antiquarian societies?' I asked Craig.

'Can't say I've come across any mention of such a stone in their papers.' He paused. 'Why are you so interested?' he asked curiously.

'I know this sounds silly but as soon as Erland showed it to me I was certain that I have actually held something in my hand very like it. The crowned mermaid with her mirror.'

'And when would that be?' Craig asked

'Fairly recently – since I came back to Edinburgh.'

Craig stood silent, Frank at his side. Both tall men, they towered over me in what seemed a suddenly intimidating manner. Then Craig smiled, a polite and tolerant smile. 'Sorry we can't help you, Rose. But if we think of anything…'

He looked at Frank who nodded vaguely. The little group were staring over in our direction, impatient to discuss the possibilities of their latest find. 'Back to work, eh, Frank?'

'Perhaps this is your pot of gold,' I said encouragingly.

He grinned. 'Hope so.'

'Good luck,' I said rather lamely and made my way back along the drive and up to the house, disappointed and uneasy too, certain that there was some vital fact that I had overlooked. And angry at my inability to remember, for a reliable memory and an eye for detail are the essentials of my investigations.

So why had I lost the mermaid stone? Now it seemed that I must wait until I got back to Edinburgh to find out.

But I was to have my answer much sooner than that.

Emily was in the sitting room, her feet up, with her knitting. To my anxious question, she smiled reassuringly: 'I'm perfectly fine, really. Erland just insists on me taking a lot of rest. He makes such a fuss and I do it to keep him happy. Anything for a peaceful life. He tells me you liked our garden,' she added proudly. 'And that you were very knowledgeable about hedgehogs. Did he show you his pride and joy, the Ghost Orchid?'

When I said that it had reminded me of Hamlet's father, her eyes widened. 'Erland would love that. The story is that the Maid of Norway brought some of her most precious and delicate plants to remind her of home.'

He hadn't mentioned that. 'If that's true, Emmy, perhaps that's what gives rise to the legend that she was buried at Hopescarth.'

'I suppose so.' Emily's deep sigh told its own story, that she had heard the story of the Maid of Norway at least a hundred times and, as far as she was concerned, that was ninety-nine times too many. And laying aside her knitting rather reluctantly, she stood up: 'I promised Erland I would look out the botanical prints and that old watercolour – if I can find it.'

'If you're not too tired,' I said, although there was little sign of her pregnancy beyond a slight thickening of her waistline.

'I've told you, Rose. I'm very well – very well indeed,' she added a trifle impatiently. 'I do beg you, please don't join the chorus of those who want to watch over me as if I'm an invalid or a piece of Dresden china. And as if having a baby isn't the most normal event in a woman's life. Think of the poor tinker women who give birth by the roadside, or those who have to go back to work next day. I'm very lucky to be so cherished.'

Touching her stomach in a gesture I was to find very familiar, she said softly:

'I assure you the little fellow is doing fine and as I'm well past the danger time, you can expect to have a grand little nephew in the spring.'

As I let her lead the way across the hall and up the handsome oak staircase with its fine carved balustrade, I remembered that every night I prayed for what concerned me most.

Her safe delivery. Of either the son Erland longed for or a pretty little daughter.

In daylight, with the sun slanting through the stained glass window, I noticed lighter squares on the walls, where, presumably, picture frames had been removed. 'What happened to the paintings?'

Emily shook her head. 'They were so dreary, those old family portraits. Very plain indeed, the lot of them, but they did like to be immortalised. Their gloomy presence depressed Erland walking up and down stairs under the eagle eye of his ancestors. So they have been banished to the attic.'

Pausing half-way, she regarded the empty walls. 'We are about to celebrate by a long overdue decoration of the staircase and hall. Some nice fashionable wallpaper. I fancy roses, big, big flowers. So cheerful. What do you think?' she demanded excitedly. 'We had a quick look in Kirkwall this afternoon, but I don't trust Erland's judgement. I thought we might go together,' she added eagerly.

I said I'd love that. I was very willing to look at wallpapers although I wasn't any kind of judge. The modern taste for bucolic floral patterns I found rather threatening. Having to live with them would have reduced me to feeling rather like a small insect pursued across a garden full of predatory flowers.

Tapestries on Solomon's Tower – not for decor but to keep out some of the cold draughts – were as far as it went with me, I thought, following her along a corridor, which housed the main family bedrooms and a bathroom, that delightful addition to the modern age. We climbed another less imposing staircase. Linoleum-clad creaky wooden steps led to the attics on the third floor which Erland's grandfather had intended to house servants and nannies for his dream of a Yesnaby dynasty.

I looked round. Emily was toiling after me, a little breathlessly. I waited for her and we went up the last flight hand-in-hand. This part of the house, dusty and rather damp, smelt musty and disused My pushing open of the door, into a room with a sloping ceiling, was accompanied by what I recognised as the familiar scurrying sound of mice and the darting shapes of spiders.

Our entrance raised a cloud of dust from the floor. Emily sneezed. 'Sorry about the mess. This is the glory-hole for everything Erland doesn't want but won't throw away in case it turns out to be valuable. He wasn't the first Yesnaby to suffer from that disorder either,' she added wryly.

I believed her. Trunks covered in cobwebs bore faded labels from the far-flung outposts of Empire, no doubt carried by seagoing and soldier Yesnabys who had travelled beyond Orkney to more exotic lands. In one corner a rocking-horse, a broken Orkney chair and, partly hidden by a sheet, a beautifully carved cradle.

Emily seized upon it with a cry of triumph. 'So that's where it got to! Erland bought it in an antique shop in Edinburgh – it's supposed to be seventeenth-century.' Her touch sent it rocking gently. 'He brought it home the day I lost the baby – when I was expecting the first time. We had such hopes,' she added sadly. 'Poor Erland was quite distraught, worse than me really. Women are used to such things, I suppose, and I always believed that we'd have another soon. But Erland cried and cried, although he liked to pretend that I was the one so upset. Anyway, he couldn't bear to see the cradle in our bedroom. For him such a terrible reminder.'

I could see Erland, so sensitive to gardens with their flowers and plants, being heartbroken at Emily's miscarriage. 'I lost two more after that, you know,' she sighed, 'But I never gave up hope. And now…' As she pulled the cradle into the light, I rushed forward.

'You're not thinking of taking that anywhere?'

'Just downstairs,' she said.

'Not even across the landing.' I gave it an exploratory shove. 'Solid oak – it's far too heavy. Leave it to Erland.'

She smiled wanly. 'Perhaps you're right. Best leave it here until the baby arrives. I don't want to upset him.'

'You'll need a month or two to make blankets and have everything prepared. I could give you a hand while I'm here.'

She shrugged. 'I know and I appreciate the offer. But Erland is terribly superstitious this time. He doesn't even want to talk about it – without crossing his fingers. Poor darling – it would break his heart – I don't think I could bear it either if – it—'

She shook her head, her eyes suddenly tear-filled and I put an arm around her. 'You're not to have such thoughts, Emmy. Why, you've just told me that you're past the danger time. You feel well and you'll have a strong healthy baby. Believe it – have some faith.'

'You really think so, Rose?' she whispered.

'I know so. And I'm the one in the family who "sees" things too.'

We both laughed at that long-standing joke.

'Remember how the girls at school thought you had

magic powers to find their missing pens and lost hand-kerchiefs, Rose? And you generally were successful. It amazed them.'

'Nothing magic about applying some logic to a situation, Emmy.'

'Logic – something you inherited from Pappa, I expect.'

'I suppose so.' Important in my chosen career, logic had also landed me my very first case with my friend, Alice, who had recalled that I solved mysteries that baffled everyone else when we were at school together. 'All I ever made them do was to back-track, think where they had last seen or used the missing pen or whatever.'

'And it generally worked.' Emily paused. 'Sibella thinks the baby will be all right and she has the second sight,' she added but something in her voice scared me.

I didn't know why. Not then.

Chapter Fifteen

Emily looked around the dusty attic.

'Over there!' Triumphantly she pointed to a stack of frames. 'Now is your great moment – to be introduced to most of Erland's solemn ancestors. But first of all…'

And she pounced on a faded folder, blew off a great quantity of dust and said: 'Here are the botanical prints – but where is the watercolour of the garden? Yes, here it is. Oh, the glass has broken and the frame's cracked. What a shame!'

As for the painting, it was pretty enough and rather what I expected. A pleasant amateur effort and I could just imagine the lady of the house sitting in the warm sunshine, paying meticulous attention to every bush and flower, anxious to include each leaf and petal.

'Do you think the prints have any value?' Emily asked doubtfully, opening up the folder. 'They're mostly of Erland's precious orchids, but you know something about watercolours.'

The botanical drawings were brown-spotted, foxed with damp. Pointing it out to Emily, I added that they were, alas, beyond repair and of little value.

Laying them aside I considered the painting of the garden. For there was the mermaid stone, clearer, brighter, before it had been overgrown with ivy.

'You should find a place for this one. Definitely.' And as I said the words, again that irritating twitch of memory.

'Had you ever seen that stone—?' I pointed to it. 'Before you come to Yesnaby, I mean.'

Emily frowned. 'Of course not. How could I?' Her response was immediate and a bit impatient, reminding me of Gran's similar reaction a little earlier as she gave a little laugh. But I'm sensitive to atmosphere and I wondered what Emily had against the mermaid stone that she wasn't willing to talk about it either.

'The painting's not very good, is it?' There was that abrupt change of subject.

'Never mind that, Emmy. It is part of the house's history and that is what matters.'

She watched me thoughtfully. 'But you could do a much better painting while you're here. I'm sure of that.'

'Mine would be quite different. The Yesnaby lady did that with her whole heart, a painting of her own lovely garden. She didn't care whether it was good, or valuable or not, or even if no one in the family wanted it after she had gone. She did it to please herself and possibly even as a present for her husband.'

'Very well.' Emily smiled. 'I'm persuaded. I'll get Erland to have it repaired and perhaps a new frame. But I'd still like your version – the house perhaps or some other aspect of the garden. And Erland would love that too.'

As she moved it back against the wall, I was suddenly aware that the temperature in the room had dropped. It was so cold. I wanted to go downstairs again to that warm, comfortable – and safe – kitchen.

I'd had enough of the past. But not quite...

Emily saw me shiver and smiled. 'A quick look at the rogues' gallery then you'll have earned that cup of tea. Although I suspect they were all too dull and boring to be anything else but harmless.'

I had to agree. The original oil painting Erland had mentioned was black with age, depressing and, I suspected, worthless. As for the portraits, they all looked as if they had been the work of an unskilled artist better at painting doors and windows than the human face.

'Had enough?' Emily laughed.

I agreed. 'But wait a moment. Is that one we've missed, over there against the wall?'

Emily bit her lip. 'That's a portrait of Thora,' she whispered hurriedly as if she could be overheard. 'Erland was so upset by – by all that happened, he couldn't bear to look at it.'

Hardly surprising, I thought, but I was very curious to see what Erland's first wife had looked like as, somewhat reluctantly, Emily turned it to the light.

A woman with dark hair and hard eyes in the fashionable dress of the 1880s, standing by the mantelpiece of the drawing-room downstairs so that her reflection was in the mirror behind her. She looked over her shoulder towards the artist, her thin lips slightly parted, her hand raised, fingers to her bare neck.

'What do you think of it?' asked Emily. 'It might well be valuable. Painted by one of the Glasgow School.' And she mentioned a painter whose exhibitions I had seen in Edinburgh. 'He's quite famous now – if Erland ever wanted to sell it, that is.'

But I was hardly listening. My eyes were riveted to that long swanlike throat and the locket that adorned it.

A heavy gold, rather ugly locket.

In its centre a crowned mermaid, her tail studded with blue stones, possibly sapphires, the mirror she held, pearl-rimmed.

And this was an exact copy of the mermaid stone I had seen in the garden.

'What do you think?' Emily repeated.

'That locket!' I gasped.

'The Yesnaby family heirloom,' she said sadly. 'Supposed to be about two hundred years old, handed down to the wife of the eldest son and heir. Not that I'd care to wear it,' she added hastily. 'Rather ugly, don't you think?'

'Where is it now?'

Emily shrugged. 'At the bottom of the peat bog, I imagine. Thora adored it, her favourite piece of jewellery, and Erland said she was wearing it the night she disappeared.' She sighed. 'I'm afraid it's gone for ever now.'

'Gone for ever? No, Emmy, that can't be. You see, I know I've seen it somewhere—'

'Indeed. And where would that be?'

It was Erland. I hadn't heard him come upstairs and he stood by the door watching us.

Emily gave him a startled glance and hastily thrust Thora's portrait out of sight, back against the wall.

'I thought I'd find you both here,' he said.

'You're just in time to take the cradle downstairs,' Emily said firmly.

He frowned. 'If you're sure.'

She smiled. 'Absolutely sure, dear.'

Erland bowed and turned to me politely. 'I'm afraid I interrupted. You were saying, Rose?'

'Just that I don't think your Yesnaby jewel is lost for ever.' I waited but there was no delight or anticipation in Erland's expression as he said quietly:

'Indeed. And what makes you think that?'

'I'm certain I've seen it. And definitely much more recent than your late wife's disappearance.'

Erland studied me silently for a moment. 'Indeed, and where might that have been?' he asked carefully.

I shook my head, confused. 'That's the problem. I don't know. Somewhere in Edinburgh, I expect.'

'Indeed,' he repeated coldly.

I looked at him, bewildered. He had known about the missing locket when we were in the garden and I asked him about the mermaid stone. Surely he might have mentioned the coincidence of the Yesnaby jewel then, but he had not said one word.

Emily was telling him: 'Rose doesn't think it disappeared after all. Do you think someone might have found it?'

Erland made an impatient gesture. 'For goodness' sake, Emily, are you suggesting that Thora dropped it in her flight and that someone – someone from here, from Hopescarth – stole it?'

It was Emily's turn to look bewildered. She shook her head and Erland said sharply:

'You realise that anyone finding such a piece of jewellery would have made enquiries, returned it to the house? The only other explanation is that a thief carried it to Edinburgh where Rose believes she saw it.'

It sounded quite nonsensical. But my mind was racing ahead. The only thief or thieves could have been from the archaeology team. Now both Erland and Emily had turned to me awaiting some logical explanation.

'Do you think that is what happened, Rose?' Erland demanded.

Even as he spoke, I knew that the Yesnaby jewel had never been stolen by thieves and taken to Edinburgh. Nor had it disappeared into the peat bog with Thora.

In a sudden rush of enlightenment, memory flooded back complete in every detail.

I had seen it before. In an Edinburgh hotel room.

Last year. On one of my clients.

And the face in the portrait I had just seen triggered my memory.

For the woman who had sought my help and called herself Mrs Smith was beyond any shadow of doubt the same Thora Yesnaby who had disappeared from Hopescarth eleven years ago.

Chapter Sixteen

Edinburgh, October 1895

Having just completed the second of my discreet investigations into matters that ladies and gentlemen with reputations at stake preferred not to put into the hands of the Edinburgh City Police, I had received an invitation to the opening of a smart new hotel and restaurant on Princes Street, overlooking the Castle.

As it was unusual for respectable unmarried ladies to be invited without a husband or a male relative, I realised that this new establishment must be very modern indeed or else, ever hopeful, that there was a client in the offing.

The postman brought a note from Mr Brightwell that the hotel carriage would collect me and as I dressed with more thought than I usually devote to my daily toilette, I wondered if the invitation had been suggested by Mrs Alice Bolton, one-time school friend, now rich and influential. We had met again on my return from America and Alice was, I suspected, hell-bent on introducing Mrs Rose McQuinn, widow, into middle-class Edinburgh society.

I had just managed to tame my mop of yellow curls, with the frequent stabbing of many hairpins and unladylike curses, into a semblance of decorum, when the carriage arrived.

Adorned in my one tea gown (inherited from my tall, elegant sister-in-law, Olivia, and much shortened), I felt very vulnerable as I was whirled in solitary splendour towards the hotel.

Obviously I could have invited Jack Macmerry to escort me, but the presence of a detective sergeant of police partaking of polite afternoon tea at what I expected to be a predominantly female occasion, would have been sufficiently inappropriate to arouse one of Jack's famous scowls. Theatres and concerts were a different matter and he was not averse to having a widowed lady on his arm, but Brightwell's Hotel at four in the afternoon was a very different matter.

Climbing up the handsome staircase to the drawing room, I observed middle-class Edinburgh matrons were well to the fore and I was relieved to be greeted by Alice, who rushed over to introduce me to Mr Brightwell. He bowed over my hand, his sleek macassar-oiled head, the high forehead already beaded with sweat which extended to his hands, doubtless the effect of a rather too tight waistcoat.

Whatever his discomfort, he stayed by my side, his mission in life at that moment apparently to make me warmly welcome. I was impressed. His introductions included several titles and a lady whose name I gathered was Mrs Smith.

Urgently summoned by a harassed waiter, Mr Brightwell bowing profusely, left us and I was acutely aware of the elegant Mrs Smith's steady gaze. Although no longer young, she was still slim and her features striking under the veiled hat.

Her escort was a young man, considerably her junior, handsome, tall and sleek, black of beard and moustache. He bowed in my direction and side-stepping an introduction, quickly excused himself.

As though his departure left Mrs Smith vulnerable, she shot a nervous glance in his direction and said with a grimace: 'Business matters. You know. Gentlemen find these gatherings rather tedious.'

I could sympathise with that and I broke a silence that seemed likely to be prolonged by asking: 'Do you live in Edinburgh?'

'No.'

I had anticipated that reply as her accent was familiar. 'You are not from these parts, are you?'

'I am merely a guest in the hotel,' she said coldly, her manner indicating that further information regarding her background was not forthcoming. Her origins were her own affair, after all, so I changed course and asked if she was enjoying her visit.

She stared across the room. The young man hovered by the door. There was no doubt that she was relieved at his reappearance as she excused herself and neither of them were present at the afternoon tea with its dainty sandwiches and cakes.

I had been hungry too often in those pioneering years with Danny to be self-conscious regarding second helpings and as my solitary life in Solomon's Tower tends towards the spartan, I did full justice to each passing plate.

With little to contribute to conversations on topics dear to middle-class Edinburgh matrons, problems with servants and children's education, I was relieved when Alice drifted over.

'Sorry I have had so little chance of a chat with you.' An airy hand towards the little groups. 'So many old acquaintances, you know. However, the carriage is at the door. Can we set you down at Solomon's Tower?'

As we headed towards reception for our cloaks, weaving towards us was Mr Brightwell. Bowing, he asked if I could spare him a moment.

I indicated Alice and he said quickly: 'We will provide a carriage for Mrs McQuinn, madam.'

As Alice smiled assent he turned to me again. 'If you could oblige me – a matter of great concern.'

He looked flustered and rather put out, so, saying I would be with him directly, I took Alice aside. 'Of course I forgive you, Rose,' she whispered slyly. 'You were on my guest list, but perhaps your fame has appeared already. Judging by Mr Brightwell's demeanour, all is not well. Some thieving servants, perhaps. Another case for you to solve. Good luck.'

Mr Brightwell was pacing the floor, impatiently waiting, and led the way into his office where no expense had been spared in exotic plants, gilt-framed paintings, plush sofas and a large mahogany desk.

Inviting me to take a seat, with profuse apologies for having delayed my departure, he said: 'I trust I am not taking too great a liberty. I already know of your excellent reputation as an investigator and it was nothing short of providential when Mrs Bolton introduced us. I will come to the point, Mrs McQuinn. One of my guests has lost a valuable piece of jewellery. It happened this morning, while Madam was out of her room – in the bathroom.'

Mr Brightwell was inordinately proud of this modern

addition to his hotel, stressed so glowingly in his opening announcement in 'The Scotsman'.

'Madam returned to her bedroom to discover that the item left on her dressing table had disappeared.'

'Was her door locked during her absence?'

Mr Brightwell sucked in his lips and looked quite scandalised at such a suggestion. He leaned forward. 'Mrs McQuinn, this is a respectable establishment,' he said huffily. 'Considering the high reputation of our hotel, Madam did not even consider such a precaution was necessary. She had only to cross over the corridor, a few steps opposite, to the bathroom. Madam was absent for a few minutes only.'

His pause and delicate cough indicated that Madam had been availing herself of the water closet.

'Were there any other guests occupying rooms on the same floor?'

'None who were present at that time. There are four other bedrooms, two are unoccupied until Friday and the two couples occupying the adjoining rooms were out of the building. You have my assurance on that, since their keys were deposited at reception and I saw them leave myself.'

'Is it possible that any of your guests who were dining had seen the lady wearing this valuable piece of jewellery and had been tempted?'

As I spoke I was considering the possibilities that any of these absent guests might have re-entered the hotel, ran up the staircase and observed the open bedroom door. Mr Brightwell's eyes, however, rose heavenward. His furious exclamation indicated outrage at such a suggestion.

'Mrs McQuinn, I cannot imagine that any of our guests would behave in such a low fashion.'

'It does happen sometimes, even in the best hotels,' I reminded him dryly.

'Not in my hotel,' he declared hotly. 'Our guests are quite impeccable, persons of privilege, even of the nobility. You have my assurance on that. Besides, the lower classes could not afford to stay here,' he added with an air of satisfaction.

But having made his point he simmered down. 'As for Madam, newly arrived, she was in the dining room for luncheon but as there were few other diners we may safely dismiss the idea that Madam's necklace might have given cause for envy and temptation,' he added firmly.

It was my turn. 'If this is a valuable piece, Mr Brightwell, surely this is a matter for the police.'

'It is indeed. The piece in question, a locket I am told, is a family heirloom. But there is a complication and that is why I urgently require your services as an investigator.' Pausing for a moment, he said guardedly: 'Madam has personal reasons for discretion.'

'An assignation?' I asked delicately, remembering the young man I had seen with her who was so eager to avoid an introduction. 'A gentleman who is not her husband, perhaps?'

Mr Brightwell wheezed a sigh. And with a despairing gesture, 'You understand the situation, if this matter were made public...'

I did indeed understand. It formed the basis of most of my cases.

'Did the lady unpack her valise on her arrival?'

'Indeed not. When ladies are not accompanied by their own personal maid, this is the duty of the hotel chambermaid.'

A little light was beginning to dawn. I said: 'I think at

this stage, it would save time if I could see the lady's room and speak with her personally.'

He nodded eagerly, a relieved smile. 'I will be for ever indebted to you, Mrs McQuinn, for this incident could not have come at a worse time for my hotel's reputation.'

Following him upstairs, we halted outside Room 2 and he whispered: 'To have made this public, to have it spread over the newspapers would mean ruin. But I believe you have already met. I introduced you—'

Before he could say more, the door opened and the lady who stood there was Mrs Smith, with whom I had recently shared a somewhat vague exchange of social comments. The young man was not in evidence.

She invited me to be seated, her gesture to Mr Brightwell indicating that his presence was no longer required. Bowing, he withdrew and I produced my card.

Mrs Smith read it carefully. 'Thank you for seeing me, Mrs McQuinn. I will not beat about the bush, I find myself in a quite desperate situation. This missing piece – is a family heirloom and I am at my wit's end—'

She shook her head. 'This theft adds to the state of crisis in my life at present. I left my husband some years ago – the details need not concern you, but let us say that I took the locket as a matter of insurance, in case of financial need, its value is considerable.'

She paused, her lips tightened. 'I allowed my husband to believe that I was dead, that I had taken my own life. Alas, that was a grievous mistake. In fact,' she added bitterly, 'our whole life together had been a mistake, a marriage of convenience. We were not at all suited to one another and he was in love with a younger woman and wished to marry her.'

Regarding me intently, she hesitated and then went on: 'I now find that, although I need money desperately, I cannot sell the locket as I once thought. I have been warned that it might be recognised and as I removed a family heirloom without my husband's permission, I could be prosecuted for unlawful possession and theft.'

'A moment,' I said. 'As his wife, surely the locket belongs to you?'

She shook her head. 'Only as long as I remain so. In the event of my death it would have been passed down to his second wife, should he remarry. If there was no heir, it would continue to the next in line as it had through the preceding generations.'

Her eyes narrowed. 'So I decided on a plan, the reason why I am in Edinburgh at the moment. I am en route north to where my husband lives.'

Listening to her, I heard again that familiar accent. 'You are from Orkney, are you not?'

She froze. 'Where I am from need not concern you, Mrs McQuinn. Now may I continue? I intend reappearing, alive and well and demanding a divorce and the payment of certain debts I have acquired during my absence in order that he can make his own bigamous marriage legal, in return for the locket. A bargain don't you agree? Especially as it is not only priceless and of sentimental value to the family, but also of historic interest.'

Judging my reaction to this piece of information, she added: 'We can be certain that his new wife would not wish me to put in an embarrassing and very public reappearance after ten years, especially as this would make any heirs they might have had illegitimate.'

I asked the obvious question. 'There were no children by your own marriage?'

'None,' she said. 'I do not care for children, particularly dynastic ones – that it is a wife's duty to provide.'

At closer quarters without the veiled bonnet, her eyes were hard, her lips thin and it as at that moment I decided I did not like Mrs Smith. But then I do not have to like my clients, I thought as she added anxiously:

'Is there any way you can possibly recover the locket for me? It is only hours since it disappeared so it cannot have travelled very far.'

Perhaps I was not concealing my feelings of distaste for this assignment too well, for she leaned forward impulsively, touched my arm and said: 'Please, Mrs McQuinn – I will pay you a great deal of money for the locket's safe return. My whole future depends on it. You see, I have also met someone else...'

I told myself that my clients' morals are also none of my concern, otherwise I would certainly be out of business. And I was perfectly aware of the less agreeable facts I might have to face when I became a Lady Investigator, Discretion Guaranteed.

'It was a great stroke of fortune that you were a guest here this afternoon and I have Mr Brightwell's assurance that you are quite remarkable,' she added, hoping no doubt that flattery would work.

And it did, I am ashamed to say. That promised 'great deal of money' was also irresistible.

'Very well, Mrs Smith. I will do what I can. When do you leave Edinburgh?'

'Tomorrow – as soon as the locket is recovered. Otherwise my whole plan – my whole future must fall apart.'

'Then first of all, I need to know exactly the state of your room here when you left it briefly to go across to the bathroom.'

She frowned, thinking. 'The chambermaid had unpacked my valise and hung my garments in the wardrobe. The locket had caught in my hair as I was removing my gown and I asked for her assistance. I then took it off and placed it beside my jewel box on the dressing table.'

'Was the maid still in the room when you left it?'

'No. I asked her for extra towels and she said she would fetch them from the linen cupboard. I saw her there on my way to the bathroom.'

As I took out a pencil and notebook, Mrs Smith watched me intently. 'Is there anything else you wish to know? I have told you everything as I remember it.'

'Thank you, Mrs Smith. You have been very helpful. Now I wonder if you could do me a rough sketch of the locket?'

She sighed. 'I'm not very good at drawing but I'll do the best I can. It is gold, you know. On a chain.'

'I just need some idea of size, design, jewels and so forth.' I handed her a page from my notebook and as she drew I took a quick look around the room. But I had already solved the case. She had given me enough information to guess the thief's identity and it was unlikely that the locket was hidden anywhere in this room. Time was of the essence for I suspected it had already left the hotel.

Wishing all cases were this easy, I promised Mrs Smith that I would do my best to recover the locket with all possible speed. She was grateful and, taking out her purse, handed me ten guineas.

'There is another ten for you if you are successful.'

I accepted gratefully and hurried downstairs where Mr Brightwell was waiting in reception, delighted and relieved that I was willing to make a desperate bid to save his hotel's precious reputation.

'I would like to speak to the chambermaid who was on

duty when Mrs Smith arrived and who helped her unpack her valise.'

Mr Brightwell gave me a despairing look and shook his head. 'On that matter, I have made some progress while you were talking to Madam. I understand from the housekeeper that Maeve, one of the Irish maids I engaged – with excellent references, I assure you – attended to Room 2. The girl said that she must return to Ireland without delay and tried to borrow the fare from her future wages. It seemed that her mother was dying, or so she said.'

Pausing, he gave me a significant look. 'I understand that the girl hasn't been seen since and never returned to her other duties—'

'You are presuming that she is not likely to return?'

'I think that is rather obvious, especially as Mrs Rowe informs me that the maid's bedroom has been cleared of her belongings.'

I guessed those belongings would be few indeed and this was confirmed as I followed Mrs Rowe up to the dreary attic room where the less fortunate staff of the opulent modern hotel had their quarters.

I had already concluded that if the Irish maid needed money urgently, the most likely place for a knowledgeable Edinburgh domestic to turn stolen jewellery into cash was at a local pawnbroker.

The first that came to mind was one Jack Macmerry had pointed out in the High Street. A fence for stolen goods, no questions asked, he was under surveillance by the police – and Jack.

There was no time to lose. As I was leaving the hotel, I had another glimpse of Mrs Smith's young lover who had tactfully made himself scarce during my talk with his mistress. Bowing, he now held the door open for me.

For a moment it crossed my mind that he might be involved, but deciding this was highly unlikely I made my way to the old pawnbroker's shop.

His greeting was polite but guarded when I showed him Mrs Smith's sketch of the missing locket. Handing him my card, I knew before I asked: 'Have you seen such a piece?' that he had it in his possession.

The next move was on his part. If he knew this was stolen property, valuable and unique, then he would keep it well hidden until an opportunity arose to sell it to some foreign traveller who would take it far from Edinburgh.

'Have you money to pay for such a piece, an unredeemed pledge, madam?' he asked carefully.

I explained that the locket had been stolen and that the lady who owned it would give twice as much as he had paid the person who had pawned it.

Immediately defensive, he said: 'The young lady said it belonged in her family and that she needed the money for her fare to return home. She sounded genuine enough, very distressed and I had not the least idea that she had come by the piece by dishonest means. I do not want to get into trouble with the police—'

It was a standard reply and he went on: 'I gave her five guineas for it,' and opening the drawer he produced the locket.

Mrs Smith's drawing had not done it justice. A large oval, heavier and less attractive than I had imagined.

I would never have worn it. The gold casing embossed with a crowned mermaid and mirror, outlined in coloured stones and pearls, did little to enhance what I considered an ugly piece of jewellery.

'It is as well the young person brought it to an honest

dealer – I doubt she knew its real value,' he added ruefully, for he could not expect five guineas in return for stolen property and would be fortunate to once again escape prosecution.

Mr Brightwell was overcome with relief and gratitude but his emotions were nothing compared to those of Mrs Smith, who handed me a further ten guineas for my trouble.

I went back to Solomon's Tower very happy indeed and thrust my finer feelings aside, totally unrepentant at having been party to Mrs Smith's blackmailing intentions regarding the locket's future. I told myself that her husband was most probably a very unpleasant man and I was on the side of wives who often had very raw deals with brutal husbands, especially where property was concerned.

In addition I was glad that the young chambermaid would not be prosecuted and that she would soon be safely in Ireland with her family again.

Naturally I did not tell Jack any of this. I do not tell him everything and besides, to have betrayed Mrs Smith's confidences would have been outwith my role as a discreet investigator.

Next day, my conscience was cleared by a note from Mr Brightwell saying that the postman had brought a letter containing the pawn ticket. To be forwarded to Mrs Smith to recover her locket.

'As this is no longer required and Mrs Smith has left the hotel, I have destroyed it,' wrote Mr Brightwell.

The case was closed.

Chapter Seventeen

Emily had not noticed my confusion as we left the attics and was chattering happily. On the landing, excusing myself, I went into the bedroom, closed the door and leaned weakly against it. Staring out over the sea, I considered the nightmare situation I had found myself in.

Thora Yesnaby could not have lain in the peat-bog for ten years, to be conveniently discovered last year by the archaeology team. Last year, calling herself Mrs Smith, she had been very much alive with a young lover in an Edinburgh hotel. Then as Thora once more, she had made her way back to Orkney with the Yesnaby locket, which I had recovered from the Edinburgh pawnbroker.

I was aware that she was to use it to blackmail – Yes, that was the word – to blackmail her husband into divorcing her and paying dearly for the privilege, thus avoiding the scandal of bigamy and leaving him free to legally marry my sister Emily Faro.

This left only one terrible conclusion.

Her unexpected arrival in Hopescarth had upset someone so much that she had never left it again alive.

She had been murdered.

This had none of the marks of a crime of passion, of sudden anger and despair resulting in violence. This crime was one of premeditation and conspiracy, for I suspected that it could not have been carried out efficiently by one person acting alone.

The sickening thought led to the chief suspect, who even at this distance had to be the one with most to gain by her death.

Her husband Erland – my own brother-in-law.

Or – the dreaded whisper of logic – my sister Emily.

Why not, whispered the cold voice of reason? The truth could not be avoided. Thora could have been murdered by either of them. Or both.

I still could not see the gentle, rather vague Emmy assisting Erland to kill Thora and deposit her body in the peat-bog. But was I being completely honest without consulting her motives?

Emily had been pregnant again with the baby they both longed for. Was she to allow Thora to ruin their lives by coming back from the dead? To reclaim her rights of inheritance and break Erland's heart by declaring their marriage bigamous and the coming child illegitimate.

What if the shock of Thora's inconvenient arrival had caused Emily to miscarry and sent Erland into a murderous rage? In the annals of crime, there were many such tales of seemingly mild-mannered people who had been driven to such acts of violence.

And had Emily been present, a mute and horrified observer?

Before any condemnation, I had to put on their shoes, metaphorically speaking, walk around in them and share that time of nightmare.

A little honest soul-searching brought me directly to Danny McQuinn. I could make a comparison here, certain that Emily loved Erland as much as I loved Danny, and had I been called upon to do so, I might well have sacrificed my immortal soul and committed murder to save him.

So having set aside the moral issues, what did I do next?

The obvious most comfortable answer was to ignore, to forget the whole thing, pretend I had not recognised the mermaid locket in the painting. Forget the Edinburgh interlude and pretend that 'Mrs Smith' was merely Thora's double, any similar circumstances mere coincidence. Leave it at that, continue my holiday, blissfully happy and carefree.

And I knew that I could not do so.

Whatever the outcome of this case, the most devilish and personally distressing ever likely to come my way, I had to know the answer. I had to know the truth. Even, I told myself, for my own satisfaction, if it was one that must remain a secret between me and my conscience, never to be revealed without destroying those I loved most in all the world.

One thing I was well aware of. The bleak vague tones of Emily's letters that had so distressed me since I returned to Edinburgh. Now I could forgive her all. Compared with the load of anguish – and perhaps even guilt – she carried about Thora's body being newly discovered near the gates of Yesnaby House, the needs of her sister, safe in Edinburgh, must have paled in significance and could never have rated high on her list of priorities.

I looked out of the window, conscious that Orkney and its sentimental past had changed for ever. Nostalgia for this longed-for holiday had evaporated like morning mist over the sea. My horizon was now occupied by the grim purpose ahead of me. One I must conceal at all costs from Emily, especially in her present delicate condition.

But where to begin?

The grim discovery of Thora's body suggested an urgent interview with the doctor who had so cleverly diagnosed that death had actually taken place ten years earlier, her body amazingly preserved by the peat-bog.

I would be very interested to meet that gentleman. Could it have been mere incompetence relating to cause of death or devotion and excessive loyalty as a family doctor which had led him to keep silent about his suspicions?

As for the local policeman, even had he known anything about the science of preserved bodies in peat-bogs, which is doubtful, he would have hesitated to question the word of the higher echelons of Hopescarth society, namely the doctor and the local laird.

I went downstairs, my legs shaking. I had to get away, out of the house, to think. I was going for a walk, I said, the effort of producing a normal smile a considerable strain on my facial muscles.

They looked up at me, smiling. Emily and Gran, all as normal as I had pictured them in so many happy memories of childhood and girlhood days.

Now I feared I had lost them and those precious memories for ever. The grim reality of what I was about to investigate surely meant that I could never again regard my dear ones in this tranquil innocent light.

But my sense of horror was well disguised. They failed to notice what I feared was written all over my face.

Again they smiled. 'Be back before dark, lass,' said Gran. 'And if you're going on that thing,' (meaning the bicycle) 'be extra careful.'

'Just some fresh air this time.' I added a convincing deep breath, managed another smile.

Outside, I decided my first inquiry would be at the dig and as I hurried down the drive I watched anxiously in case Craig and his team had finished for the day.

I was just in time, he told me, the others had left and he was packing up his tools. He seemed surprised to see me and, I thought, pleased by this unexpected visit. Puzzled perhaps too, when without my usual care, or any preliminary of polite chatter, I launched into the subject of the peat-bog woman, hinting that it had been discussed at a teatime conversation I had just left.

'It is quite intriguing. Tell me, has it been written up anywhere?'

Craig turned the key on the last of the day's specimens in their wooden box and regarded me quizzically, so intently that I wondered if he could read my thoughts.

'The local newspapers made quite a thing about it. It even got a mention in *The Times* and I expect *The Scotsman* took it up as well.'

It was certainly unique enough to receive a mention in the Scottish newspapers, while the other nationals might follow suit with a paragraph or two. Why then had I missed it? I concluded that I hadn't noticed it because I relied on receiving copies from Jack and didn't always have time to read them.

Most likely I was on a case at the time or mention of Orkney would surely have stirred my interest. However, I doubted if I would have made the connection with Mrs Smith and the mermaid locket.

Craig went on: '*The Orcadian* will certainly have it in their files. Worth a visit to their offices anyway next time you're in Kirkwall, if you're still interested.'

I shrugged, hoping to indicate that it wasn't really all that important. 'You must have found it a rather gruesome experience. I mean, digging for old bones and finding something only ten years old.'

He nodded vaguely. 'The peat-bog is the very reason we suspect that the Maid's grave may have been hereabouts. That and the coins. The reason why we don't give up, why we keep on digging so persistently, year after year. We're certain, you see, that there is something here – and that with time and patience – we'll find it.'

'You think a body might have survived for six hundred years?'

'Possibly.'

There was a pause and I said: 'You must have been very disappointed at finding the late Mrs Yesnaby.'

Craig shrugged. 'I wasn't here, alas. Just my luck – or the reverse, I'm afraid,' he added ruefully. 'A moment-ous discovery and I was in Edinburgh at an antiquarian society giving a paper when Frank and the lads found it.'

I was disappointed. I had hoped for some valuable first hand information and I said: 'How did they react? It must have been something of a surprise.'

'Shock is the more appropriate word. As you can imagine, they all thought when a hand suddenly appeared from the ground—'

'A hand? Where exactly?'

He smiled, obviously indulging my morbid turn of mind. 'Over there, just below the bridge. Come and I'll show you if you like.'

I followed him along the well-worn path above what had once been the moat.

'The exact spot, as Frank told me. Down there, a

somewhat muddied but very well preserved hand appeared above the surface.'

He paused dramatically watching its effect on me. 'As you might imagine, panic all around. First thoughts were that they had discovered a murder victim. The local constable was summoned. The local doctor sent for.'

At last, that was all I needed to know for where to begin my inquiries.

Chapter Eighteen

'There was quite a stir in the village, I can tell you,' Craig went on. 'Nothing as dramatic as this had ever happened in living memory. In everyone's mind was the same thought: was there a murderer abroad in Hopescarth? Or was the victim from somewhere else and dumped here?

'Poor old Frank was shattered. It was worst of all for him. You see, he recognised the body. He knew Thora well. The lady of the manor had been very kind to him, especially after Lily stopped coming to the dig each year.'

'Lily?'

'Mrs Breck – his wife.'

I shook my head. I'd never have guessed that Frank was married. To me he seemed the personification of the crusty old bachelor, dedicated to a career.

'What happened?'

Craig shrugged. 'The usual story. Lily was a city girl.' He smiled. 'From Edinburgh, as a matter of fact. He'd met her when she came on holiday to Orkney. Anyway, she was swept off her feet. Thought archaeology digs were so romantic.' A grimace and he added: 'They got married and she used to spend every summer here at the dig.'

'Any children?'

Craig shook his head. 'Alas, no. I don't think Frank minded that at all. Well, the year Thora Yesnaby disappeared had been a particularly bad summer. No doubt Lily was keen to see the back of the dig which had been even less productive and ten times more boring than usual. She ran a small boarding house in Edinburgh to help make ends meet and when they packed up that year, Frank told the team that Lily wouldn't be coming back to Hopescarth in future.'

I looked at him quickly, but his expression gave nothing away.

'You think there was more to it – someone else, perhaps?'

He nodded. 'All this happened before I came to Hopescarth but from Frank's rare hints about his private life, I suspected that his wife had left him for someone else. No one could blame her, really. Frank was obsessed. The dig came first in his life. Even when Lily was here, I suspect he spent little time with her. His family were from Orkney and Meg – our landlady – who likes a gossip, once hinted that he fancied the lady of the manor.'

He sighed. 'No wonder he was so upset when they dug her out of the peat-bog. Not a very pleasant thing for the lord of the manor, either,' he added ruefully. 'His late wife turning up like that, a bit of a shock when he thought he'd buried her ten years earlier. As for your sister, it must have been dreadful, quite dreadful. Especially as she was—'

Suddenly realising you didn't say 'pregnant' to a lady, so I put the word in for him. 'I expect you know that she lost the baby.'

He nodded. 'My doctorate doesn't cover medicine but I

might hazard a guess that the shock maybe had something to do with that.'

So I had guessed right. I felt suddenly chilled as I asked: 'Did they get the Fiscal on to it?'

'I expect so.' Craig looked vague. 'By the time I came back from my lecture tour, it was old news. The sensational discovery of a corpse was over and Hopescarth could breathe again. They weren't looking for a killer in their midst after all.'

He looked at me. 'In our business, as I've told you, we know that peat can have extraordinary preserving qualities and the doctor confirmed that when he said it was most likely she had lain there since the night she disappeared. I gather Erland remembered that it had been a wild night, high gales, when she left the house. She must have stumbled and fallen, I suppose.'

He paused, biting his lip, hesitating as if he was unwilling to continue. 'I'm not sure how much you know about the lady—'

'Very little,' I put in eagerly.

He smiled. 'Again from Meg, I understand that she was – well, a little unbalanced to put it mildly. Overfond of the whisky too. Her behaviour could be completely irrational. Not an easy person to live with,' he added sadly.

'No one had the slightest notion about where she went after she ran out of the house that night. One theory was that she took Frank's fishing boat, which he kept in a shed down at the harbour, which also went missing. A few days later it was washed up in one of our roarsts – those terrible seas produced by the tide-races and the unevenness of the rock beneath them. It was reduced to matchwood, and the same thought was in everyone's mind. Thora must have sailed off that night with some insane notion of heading across to the mainland. And this seemed to be confirmed later when a woman's torso was washed ashore near the Troll's Cave.'

He grimaced and then brightened. 'I must take you there sometime, Rose. It's spectacular – and quite lethal if you're in the vicinity when the sea funnels up at high tide. Anyway, Erland identified the body but in the circumstances I suppose a bereaved husband can be forgiven for not looking too closely at what remained of a woman who had been in the roasts for a few weeks.'

I was thinking of that unknown woman. Who was she? Where had she come from to be so conveniently identified as Thora?

Doubtless the police wouldn't be too eager to keep the body around either. I wondered were there other cases of missing persons at that time. If not, then they would have been only too relieved to close the case on the missing Mrs Yesnaby.

'Didn't it seem rather odd though – Thora taking a boat out on a wild night in the first place? Did she intend to kill herself?'

'Suicide?' Craig shrugged. 'Who knows? Perhaps that was in her mind. I gather that no one who knew her was surprised. She was totally unpredictable. A creature of impulse and every time she had a row up at the house, which was often, Frank told Meg – she'd come down and sulk at the dig and demand that he row her over to the mainland.

'Born and bred here, Frank was a good sailor and so was Thora. She loved the sea, so sometimes Frank would take her out fishing in the early morning. Lily didn't like that much, especially as she was violently ill even crossing over on the steamer each year.'

'Have you any theories about what really happened?' I asked.

'If she didn't take Frank's boat, rumour had it that the boat had been cut adrift deliberately by one of the local lads whose family had a long-standing feud with the Brecks. They weren't popular and local fisherfolk thought Frank had got above himself, too big for his boots, as they say, having been at the university and getting friendly with the big house.

'The general idea was that in her highly emotional state – Thora had been drinking heavily, according to hints from the servants – she had taken the short cut down to the shore, missed her footing, fallen face downwards into the bog and smothered.' Silent for a moment, he went on: 'A dreadful way to go,' he added grimly.

Dreadful indeed, I thought, and highly unlikely. Not to say downright unbelievable, since the place Craig had pointed out was near the bridge. I'd have favoured Frank's missing boat rather than the story that Thora alias Mrs Smith, strong and healthy when last seen by me in Edinburgh, vengeful and determined to destroy Erland – and Emily – had come to Hopescarth and, fully aware of the perilous terrain surrounding Yesnaby House, had succumbed to such a convenient accident.

Unless she was very, very drunk and had been pursued – and pushed!

And another intriguing thought. What had become of her lover from Brightwell's Hotel in all this? That bothered me. Hadn't anyone at Hopescarth been aware of his existence? Had he come back with her to Orkney to await results of her blackmailing project? If so, why had he disappeared into thin air? More likely, I thought grimly, as a witness to Thora's murder, he had been killed and his corpse disposed of far from the peat-bog.

And if he had not accompanied her, but was aware of her destination, had he not read the newspapers and guessed from Mrs Smith's destination that she was in fact, Thora Yesnaby, 'dead these past ten years' according to the official reports? And that being so, would he not have panicked and confided his suspicions to the police, who would then have set an inquiry under way?

'You're very interested, Rose.' Craig jolted me back to the present. 'Is this just the detective in your blood?' he added with a laugh. 'I hear that your father is the famous Inspector Faro Orkney is so proud of.'

I hadn't told him that I was a professional investigator. I thought it would put him off me. It would have that effect on a lot of men, so I side-stepped and said: 'Mysteries have always intrigued me.'

'Even on holiday?' he laughed. 'You should give them a rest,' he advised gently.

I ignored that. 'Were any of the present team here when the discovery was made?'

Craig shook his head. 'No, only Frank, the others have gone their separate ways long since. Frank was in charge, the only senior while I was away. We mostly take on eager students in the summer. Often foreign ones.' He paused, thinking. 'I remember we had two lads from Germany that summer.'

I could hardly demand their addresses, or attempt to track them down at this late stage.

Craig was regarding me curiously. 'You could ask Frank tomorrow, see if he can tell you more about it, but I doubt he'll have anything new to add to what was in the papers.' Another pause. 'I think I should warn you, though, he doesn't like talking about Thora Yesnaby.'

The church clock struck through the silence, a pleasant peaceful sound that carried a fair distance on still evenings.

His manner suddenly urgent, Craig said: 'You must excuse me, I have to go – and clean up. I'm meeting someone at seven,' he added rather self-consciously. 'See you tomorrow.'

As he indicated his motor car, accommodated in a disused barn at Sibella's croft, I wondered whether he was meeting the innkeeper's wife who had shown such a proprietorial interest in him.

And I was left with a strange feeling that Craig Denmore was greatly relieved that he had been absent when Thora's body was discovered.

Chapter Nineteen

Somehow I got through that evening, so pleasantly domestic, Emily busy knitting the baby shawl while Gran turned the heel on yet another pair of socks for Erland.

We had a visit from Sibella, who sat very upright in the Orkney chair, her hands idle, saying little but absorbing all that was going on. Occasionally I would look up to meet her eyes watching me narrowly, increasing my strange feeling that she had an uncanny ability to read my thoughts.

Erland had supper with us. Most evenings he departed to his study but tonight we were to be honoured with his company – at least the suggestion was that I was the one to be honoured.

The four of us were to play cards. I looked at Sibella, who shrugged. 'I only read the cards. I don't play games.' And stretching out a mittened hand, 'If you wish, Rose, I may tell your fortune.'

I pretended to make light of her offer, although I would have welcomed some expert knowledge of what my future held. But not this night. This night I was afraid. I had too many family secrets weighing heavily upon my mind.

We had a few hands of whist, Emily and I playing against Erland and Gran. Erland won.

'As usual,' whispered Emily. 'He always wins.' And turning to me: 'But you were always so good, Rose. Thought you'd be a match for Erland.'

At this hint of a reproach from my partner for my lack of concentration, I apologised. 'I'm a little tired – and out of practice, I'm afraid.'

'Do you want to continue then?' Erland asked politely.

My mind was certainly not on the cards, but on a much deadlier game whose outcome I could not bear to contemplate. But realising Erland, such a busy man, had arranged this evening as a special treat for me, I did not want to disappoint him, or Gran and Emily, who both loved a hand at cards.

And so the game continued. As I watched the three players getting so excited and eagerly counting their tricks, I did my best but frequently forgot what was trumps, threw away my best cards, making more serious mistakes and provoking Emily's rather tight-lipped exasperation at my incompetence.

Nor were my powers of concentration helped by awareness of Sibella's steady gaze. What was she thinking? Was she aware of my misery? I avoided contact with those strange round eyes that I felt could look into my soul and drag out my secrets.

At that moment, my whole concern in all the world was to prove that my own sister had no knowledge of Thora's arrival in Hopescarth last year and that she had not been an accessory to her murder. Such was my desperation that I knew I would be perfectly willing to commit perjury. Especially when I remembered that the outcome of the grim discovery had brought about a miscarriage and destroyed the child that Emily and Erland longed for.

Erland had produced a bottle of wine to add a note of celebration to his sister-in-law's visit.

I had a feeling that Erland liked me. He was delighted to find that we had much in common and I had warmed to him in that tour of the garden.

Could that be only yesterday? So much had happened since. Now he was going out of his way to reward a welcome guest, who was, in fact, considering him as chief suspect in his first wife's murder.

At last the evening was over, the cards put away and Emily's reproaches laid aside. She continued to gaze across at me rather anxiously, and having forgiven me for making us lose so disastrously was now asking if I was sure I was feeling quite well.

Trust Emily, I thought grimly. And I said more sharply than was necessary: 'Of course, why do you ask? I told you I'm just a little tired, that's all.'

She smiled. 'You were so good at winning. Don't you remember, Gran always said: "Lucky at cards, unlucky in love."'

I laughed. That was in the days when I was desperately in love with Danny McQuinn, sure he'd marry someone else before I grew up. But time and fate proved me wrong.

As we spoke, Sibella left her chair unaided, though rising with the deliberate care and stiffness of age. Declining Erland's offer to see her home, she nodded in my direction, smiling:

'I should like Rose to come with me. There's still enough light and she hasn't seen where I live yet.'

Goodnight hugs and kisses followed and Sibella was solemnly presented with a large brown paper bag.

According to Gran's murmurings this held the day's left-overs and I wondered how Sibella could possibly tackle them with her birdlike appetite.

As we set off, she tucked her hand into my arm. 'There now, dear. We'll walk quicker like this. Don't let me lean too heavily on you,' she added, apologising for an arm that was thin, weightless. And cold too.

It was just a step across the stone bridge, near the spot where Thora's hand had emerged from the peat-bog. I knew I could never look at it again without shuddering.

A short distance past the dig lay Sibella's little croft, just visible from my bedroom window. When she opened the door, I was taken aback. Preparing myself for something strange and outlandish, it was all perfectly ordinary, neat and tidy. One large room with a bed, table, sideboard and two comfortable Orkney chairs before a peat fire.

At my side Sibella chuckled. 'Not quite what you expected, is it, Rose?'

Remembering Emily's hints, I was embarrassed. Wagging a finger, she said: 'What on earth have they told you about me? That no one ever knew what Sibella might conjure up or if the mysterious stranger passing by and seeking shelter might be reported as revealing cloven hoofs and a tail?'

Hands on hips she regarded me. 'You expected a house from Hansel and Gretel and instead you've found just a dull ordinary croft like you'd find anywhere on the island.'

Again she laughed. 'But there is one difference.' She pointed. 'Over there.' And pulling aside a curtain, she revealed a table and deep shelf full of bottles of assorted colours. In the central position a large black leather book. Very impressive, with its brass lock. Taking it down, she held it out for my inspection.

'What do you think this is, Rose?'

'A book of spells?'

She shook her head. 'Not quite.'

'The Book of the Black Arts?' I whispered and she nodded eagerly.

'That's what folk like to believe, and it ensures that I never need to lock my door at night. Actually the key, if there ever was one, was lost long ago,' she added ruefully. Then, touching the book fondly, she smiled.

'This contains nothing more sinister than some of my best herbal cures and recipes gathered over many years. I had it with me when your grandmother brought me up to Hopescarth, when I was feeling poorly. That was before Erland and Emily got married, when Emily came to Yesnaby House as companion to Thora.'

She turned those luminous eyes upon me as if expecting a reaction at the mention of Thora. There was none and she smiled.

'Your gran did well out of that. Erland persuaded Emily that they needed a housekeeper as well. And Mary Scarth was not loath to leave Kirkwall. She liked the idea of living in the grand big house. And when I first came to live with them, I'd swear he gave me this croft because he never knew a moment's peace while I had what he thought was the Book of the Black Arts under his roof. Here you are.'

I took it from her carefully. It felt very heavy, old and very cold.

'No, my dear. This is not the real manual of magic printed in white characters on black pages which gave its owner unlimited power. However, as with all the devil's gifts, there was a snag, a price to be paid. The owner of the book, dying, could be carried straight to hell. Only for a smaller coin than was paid for the book could it be resold and anyone young and gullible could be forgiven for thinking the peedie black man at Kirkwall Fair was giving them a great bargain.

'Rumour had it that once, wicked greedy Earl Robert eagerly accepted it as a gift, ignoring its opening page: "Cursed is he that peruseth me." I often wonder if he realised the load of destruction he had in his possession, since a witch of that time had placed him under St Ringan's curse, used only by those who had suffered intolerable wrongs without other means of punishing their oppressors. A curse richly deserved by the earl and his sons.'

As she paused for breath, I said: 'I seem to remember being told at school that it could curse an entire family by making their men sterile and their womenfolk barren.'

I didn't add my own fears for the Scarths and Faros, their bad luck with child-bearing, miscarriages and infant deaths. And the fact that neither female Scarths nor Faros seemed capable of producing vast broods of children.

Sibella took back the book and placed it on the table. 'There are some very interesting cures here, for every mortal illness. The ones for curing bleeding noses with pig dung are not in great demand but you'll find farmers still using cow dung for bruised limbs.'

Smiling, she turned the page, to more ancient writing, brown with age. 'Here's one: sweetened urine for jaundice, and milk in which sheep droppings have been boiled for smallpox.' She sighed. 'I've tried some of those myself although I draw the line at this one: Mice roasted for whooping cough and snails dissolved in vinegar for rickets.'

Closing the book, she shook her head. 'Many are just plain common sense, or what I've often thought would be better defined as "uncommon sense".' She smiled reassuringly. 'But there are other cures I prefer not to dwell upon.'

I regarded her thoughtfully. 'How good are your spells? Are you still in business?'

'I'm getting rather old for the staying power needed these days. A lot of concentration, you know, and I soon weary. But in my time, I've done my share of exorcising toothaches. I used to be very good at that. And I could cure a child's ringworm and get rid of warts by placing special stones in a bag and throwing them into the sea. There isn't much scrofula these days, but the trick was to place white money – silver, that is – upon the sore and for a bad eye, a piece of gold,' and she smiled wistfully, as if living again those lost days of the seal woman's power.

'Doonfa'-sickness, as they call epilepsy, is still with us. Parents believed that if I pared the poor bairn's nails and cut off a lock of hair during one of the fits, buried both on the spot where he or she had fallen, the epilepsy would vanish.'

She sighed. 'Miracles they said I could work, but miracles are the work of the good Lord. A lot of my success was making folk have faith in themselves and faith that their prayers would be answered too.'

Pausing to look out of the window, she said: 'You'd better be going back to the house, Rose. I promised you'd get home safe in daylight, but there's one thing more I'd like to show you,' and seizing Gran's brown paper bag she led the way into the garden to a large wooden shed next to the barn where Craig kept his motor car.

There wasn't a sound coming from inside but as soon as she opened the door, all hell broke loose. And I discovered that Sibella's compassion for the island's population extended to birds and animals, none of whom feared her approach for she talked to them constantly.

Ignoring my presence, those who were able fluttered or jumped down from straw-lined ledges and came right up to her feet. There they sat, staring up at her trustingly, waiting patiently for titbits. Now I understood the reason for the leftovers from Gran's table.

Every inch of space in the hut's dim interior was occupied by cage or pen, row upon row, shelf upon shelf, where sick birds and an assortment of wild creatures were enjoying a health-giving but raucous convalescence. Packed full of herbs, medicines and ointments as their condition demanded, here many that would otherwise have found their way into the local cooking pots remained alive, nurtured and cherished by Sibella until the day they either expired naturally or made noisy pleas to resume their lives back in the wild.

Closing the door, she led me to the edge of the tiny garden overlooking the shore where rocks gleamed black in the gathering twilight.

'Down there,' she pointed. 'That's where I came from, Rose. See, by that big rock yonder. That's where Hakon carried me ashore from the sea and that's where he'll be waiting for me – when the time comes, and I'm ready to go.'

Turning, she smiled at me. 'Some days, you know, I feel his presence – that he is very near... Especially now on evenings like this, I feel his love like a cloud around me.'

She didn't have far to stretch to put her arms around me and gently kiss my cheek. Her lips were cold, papery, but her heart was warm as she said: 'I'm glad I had the chance to meet you before I leave Hopescarth.'

'I'm glad too, Sibella,' I said, thinking if only I could

confide my fears in you, you might provide all the answers.

But such terrible knowledge was not for Sibella, and my eyes suddenly brimmed over as, waving goodnight, I made my way back to the house and the family who waited for me.

And the terrors that swirled like demons, inescapable in the growing dusk.

Chapter Twenty

I wasn't sorry to find the kitchen deserted. Erland, Emily and Gran had retired. That was the general rule in Hopescarth: 'down with the sun and up with the larks.'

Thankfully I went upstairs to my room, lit the lamp and, preparing for bed, I tried to reorganise my thoughts and formulate some sort of plan.

Even as I did, something deep inside whispered again: 'Why not forget all this, forget that you met Thora, alias Mrs Smith, in Edinburgh? Pretend it was just someone who resembled her portrait and that mermaid lockets are everywhere, a popular form of Scottish jewellery, like the luckenbooth and thistle.'

I knew that would have been the sensible thing to do, but as Jack Macmerry never tired of commenting, taking the easy way had never been one of my characteristics. If there was a mystery to solve, I had to dive into it headlong, regardless of the consequences or the destructive forces that might lie ahead.

Of course, Jack was right.

I began my list. The first person to see was Frank, who

had been in charge of the site when the body was found.

The second was obviously the doctor, who had so incorrectly stated the date of Thora's death.

Third, the local policeman. I would have to handle that with skill, a tone of casual curiosity, along the lines of: 'an interesting thing to happen, it must have been an exciting time for you,' etc. etc. I did not want him to suspect that I had any ulterior motive for my inquiries.

At ten o'clock there was a tap on my bedroom door and guiltily I thrust my notes out of sight.

The door opened and there was Emily.

'I was going to the bathroom and I saw your lamp still on. Thought I'd just look in and say goodnight.'

She sounded anxious and this was an excuse. I knew my strange behaviour had been worrying her as she added: 'You aren't even in bed yet. You were so tired downstairs. I thought you'd be asleep before your head hit the pillow.'

'That was a long time ago, Emmy.'

She sat down on the bed. 'Well, and what did you think of Sibella's peedie croft?' she giggled.

'Smaller than I imagined.'

'And less tidy. Gran is forbidden to step over the threshold. On her one and only foray with mop and bucket she moved some of Sibella's precious bottles. There were spiders' webs, she said. But Sibella was furious, said keeping her croft clean was her business and no one else's.'

Emily sighed. 'Poor Gran. They are often at loggerheads and I seem destined to be piggy-in-the-middle. Gran was right put out by Sibella's animal sanctuary too, said it smelt, which is true. However, we got around that as it appeals to her sense of waste not, want not, where the leftovers and vegetable peelings can be suitably disposed of.'

I said I was very impressed by the little hut and its

occupants and Emily smiled. 'I thought you would be. Sibella never kills a living creature and that drives Gran mad too, when the doors and windows have to be thrown open for wasps and bees – and spiders – to depart peacefully. I have to say I don't feel quite so kindly towards spiders.'

She leaned back against the pillows. 'Do you know, until a year or two ago when she was a lot stronger than she is now, Sibella wasn't past wading out on to the rocks to bring back a seabird with a broken wing, or clambering down cliffs to rescue an injured sheep. Or some old ewe bleating in distress and likely to die in the lambing. She has an amazing affinity with animals. None of the rest of us have inherited that.'

Pausing, she looked at me. 'I remember you were absolutely terrified of big dogs. There was one round the corner from the school that used to bark at us.'

For a moment, I wanted to say that was no longer the case and tell her all about Thane. Then I realised that without proof of his existence such a confidence was inadvisable. And I had enough complications at the moment without a deerhound who might or might not exist.

She patted my hand. 'You are quite comfortable here, aren't you?'

'Of course. It's a lovely room. Thank you, Emmy.'

When I stifled a yawn, she said anxiously: 'I'll go down and fetch you some warm milk.' I declined the offer firmly and again taking my hands, she looked into my face intently. 'Rose, is everything all right? Are you sure?'

I hadn't fooled my sister. She suspected something was amiss and sounded so concerned that seeking some plausible excuse, I pointed to the table. 'I must write to Jack right away. He'll be worried about me.'

That wasn't true either but Emily nodded as if she understood and I went on: 'I have postcards to write. One to Mrs Brook. And my friend Alice Bolton – and Nancy. Nancy is a relative of our Mrs Brook,' I explained. 'She's nanny to the children of the explorer Gerald Carthew.'

Emily was very interested in Mrs Brook and we talked about the old days in Sheridan Place and her marvellous cooking. After a while, Emily went back to bed, satisfied that I was not falling victim to some malaise or fever.

I slept fitfully, full of strange dreams of Sibella and her animals and the portraits of long-gone Yesnabys.

Morning came with its chorus of seabirds and, after another of Gran's hearty breakfasts, I set off to the post office with the inevitable list of groceries and in fervent hope that I might waylay Frank on his way to the dig.

I was in luck. I had almost reached the village and there he was, trudging up the road, looking as grey and dour as ever. Wondering if he ever smiled or if his face was set permanently in that state of melancholy, I felt sudden sympathy for the wife who had left him. Frank could not have been much joy to live with at the best of times but after long hours digging in mud and cold and fierce winds, I could not imagine him being a lovable or engaging companion, much less a passionate lover at the end of the day.

As for Lily, after several years of enduring miserable summer digs, I wasn't in the least surprised that she had at last elected to remain in Edinburgh.

As Frank approached I greeted him cheerfully. 'Craig was telling me that you discovered the peat-bog burial. How very exciting.'

He gave me a scornful look. 'All in a day's work, Mrs McQuinn.'

I laughed. 'Surely that doesn't happen every day!'

He merely shrugged in reply.

I was genuinely surprised. 'I imagine you would be more used to dealing with Pictish burials. How did you spot it?'

He looked even more unhappy, if that were possible, at this question and I felt guilty that I was being relentless, especially recalling Craig's statement that Frank had been sweet on Thora.

He sighed deeply. 'Local bobby thought we had a murder on our hands at first. He was a bit disappointed, I can tell you. Didn't get much excitement beyond the local salmon poachers.'

'Were you in charge of the dig at the time?' I asked knowing the answer.

'Denmore should have been but he'd gone gallivanting away to a conference as usual.' He sounded bitter.

Encouraged, I asked: 'Have you been with this group long?'

He shrugged. 'Umpteen years, if you call that long. On and off, every summer and for all the finds we've made it's been time wasted. Especially as the professor here—' he stressed the words heavily— 'always claims any as his own.'

So there was no love lost there. 'Then why do you stay?' I asked gently and received a baleful glare in return.

'Because this is where I belong. I've always lived here apart from a few months every year in Scotland.'

He made it sound like a foreign land, I thought, as he looked towards the sea. 'My wife still lives there, but I hate cities. And that includes Edinburgh,' he added with a malevolent look. 'All I want is to know what happened to the Maid all those hundreds of years ago. Just as my father did before me. But we were just plain crofters, scratching a living from the soil and it was me, when I was a lad, that made the first find. A bronze ring,' he added proudly.

'However, we weren't educated enough, the authorities didn't trust an ignorant crofter's son who had never been to the university so they called in their own folk to take over,' he ended glumly.

I ended an uncomfortable silence by asking innocently: 'Do you go back to Edinburgh for the winter then?' knowing from Craig that he didn't any longer.

He looked sad, shook his head. 'I'm happy to stay here. This is my life.'

'Your wife must miss you.'

He grunted at that and I realised I was treading on forbidden ground. 'Where does she live in Edinburgh?'

'Newington. Minto Street. I don't suppose you know it.'

'Oh yes, I do. I live in Solomon's Tower – at the foot of Arthur's Seat. It's just a step away.'

And with a sudden desire to be friendly and helpful I produced one of my cards. 'If you'd like to write her address on the back – I have a friend who lives close by,' I said, thinking of Alice Bolton.

Frank stared at the card. I thought he was going to hand it back, but he thrust it into his pocket without a word and I said: 'If you give me Mrs Breck's number in Minto Street, I'll call on her when I get back. Letters can take a while—' I blundered on— 'I could take a message, something you'd like to send her. Flowers perhaps?'

He stared at me as if I'd suggested something quite outrageous. 'What do you mean, letters can take a while? My letters get there all right.'

'Good! It was only a suggestion – you know, a package, a present or something.' I was floundering badly now, wishing I had never raised the subject with such a difficult man, especially when without another word, he turned on his heel abruptly and walked quickly away in the direction of the dig.

Poor Frank, problems with the wife, so that was why he didn't want to go back to Edinburgh. I felt contrite, remembering Craig's hint that Lily had found someone else.

No doubt they had settled for an amicable separation and that was why he sounded so bitter, and of course, I had hit on the sore point of his existence. A chip on his shoulder about the dig as well as the wife who had deserted him for the bright lights of Edinburgh. And a lover.

I could sympathise although I was doubtful after this interview whether Frank could provide any information that would lead me to Thora's murderer. Our conversation hadn't been in the least enlightening. I had merely succeeded in antagonising and embarrassing him and I suspected that he would give me a wide berth in future.

A pity, but what had I been hoping for? Some flash of inspirational deduction on his part? I realised how unlikely that was as I walked towards the post office to ingratiate myself with Meg Flitt.

Chapter Twenty-One

Meg was standing by the window as I entered the shop. Suspecting that Frank and I had been under observation, this seemed an opportune moment to quiz his landlady for any other information.

'Frank has been telling me about the peat-bog woman. How exciting to have something like that on the doorstep,' I gushed, hoping to sound ingenuous, but from her dour expression, failing miserably.

'Horrible, I'd say. Especially if it was someone we knew like Mrs Yesnaby. All those years believing she had been drowned. Dreadful, it was.'

'Dreadful, indeed,' I echoed sympathetically and studied a shelf containing a few Orkney postcards. I chose a couple and said casually: 'I see in the window that you also advertise board and lodgings. Do you get many guests?'

'We're full. In the summer we take the lads from the dig and that's all,' she added firmly as if I might be making a request for a room.

'That must be interesting – I mean, quite different from the usual travellers who are just passing through.'

She gave me a cold look. 'You wouldn't say that if you had the archaeology team upstairs, tramping up and down through the house with their muddy boots, having damp clothes drying all over the kitchen.'

So much for respecting progress and the acquisition of knowledge about the ancient inhabitants of Hopescarth, I thought as she went on: 'Dr Denmore is all right. Pays his rent on time and he's very polite and considerate. My Wilma thinks he's wonderful, can hardly keep her away from the dig and he encourages her to have big notions about her future, when she grows up,' she added with a hint of disapproval.

I smiled. 'Doesn't that please you?'

'It does not,' she said sharply. 'It's never too soon for Wilma to know her place, and that's not gadding off to college over there on the mainland somewhere.' She managed to make the coast of Scotland sound like the dangerous unexplored regions of darkest Africa.

Then thumping the counter: 'Her place is here, on the island, with her family. Helping me in the shop and when the right time comes getting married and settling down with a decent local lad. Like her mother and her grandmother before her,' she said piously. 'That's what I want to see for her, not these grand ideas above her station that will just let her down and break her heart.'

And handing me my change: 'While we're on the subject, Mrs McQuinn, I don't approve of my Wilma being encouraged to ride a bicycle either.'

So much for female emancipation, I thought. As another customer who had followed me into the shop was listening agog to this conversation, I took my leave somewhat disconcerted at the way my first day of inquiry had begun, with two highly unfruitful encounters from which I had learned nothing of the slightest use.

Unfortunately, I had also probably succeeded in antagonising both Frank Breck and Meg Flitt who would be writing me off as a nosy foreigner.

The next person on my list was the local constable who, by a stroke of good fortune, was at that moment walking towards the church.

About to pursue him, I changed my mind. What if he did not believe this was merely morbid curiosity? What if his training, unlikely as it seemed, should prompt him to ask why I wanted all these details?

No, the local constable must wait, his time might come later, as I noticed two women walking into one of the handsome houses near the church and set back from the village street by a high wall.

'Dr Stern' proclaimed the brass plate on the gate and the fact that an old man with a limp was also heading his way up the path indicated that this must be the surgery hour.

That limp was inspirational. Bicycling, I had pulled an imaginary tendon on my ankle. That would serve splendidly as an introduction as I trailed behind the limping man, slowly and rather painfully as befitted that injury, while compiling a mental list of some searching questions regarding the late Thora Yesnaby.

Shown into the waiting room, dominated by a clock with an extremely loud and aggressive tick and offering scant comfort to the ragged nerves of the few patients nursing their aches and pains, I took a seat near the door, where the entrance of a stranger to the area was greeted with some curiosity.

Unwilling to satisfy this beyond a polite 'Good morning,' I sat in silence awaiting my turn. Some ten minutes later I followed the limping man who emerged from the surgery.

Dr Stern was seated behind his desk. He was not quite as I had imagined the Yesnaby's family doctor. For one thing, he was considerably younger than I had expected, a good looking man – at least I believed his features to be handsome under the facial hair of beard and moustache so fashionable for gentlemen, a trend set by our Royal Family and one I found distinctly unattractive.

He wrote down my name and regarding me across the table: 'You are not from these parts Mrs McQuinn?'

I told him Edinburgh and he smiled. 'A delightful place, I know it well. So what brings you to Hopescarth?'

'A short holiday at Yesnaby House.'

Satisfied, he nodded absently, and asked what was the trouble.

As I explained the pulled tendon, he came round, knelt down and, with hands that were firm but gentle, rotated my ankle. 'Does that hurt?'

'Ouch,' I winced convincingly and watched while he produced a roll of bandage and proceeded to wrap it rather too tightly around what he presumed to be my injured limb.

'I don't think there is much damage, but try to keep off it as much as possible for a day or two. If you have any further problems, come back and see me again. Where did you say you were staying – Mrs McQuinn—' he asked consulting his notes.

'With my sister, Mrs Emily Yesnaby – one of your patients, I believe.' After a hopeful pause, I added that I found Hopescarth quite charming.

'Do you not find it a little dull after Edinburgh?'

'Not at all.'

He smiled. 'I did my degree at Edinburgh University. I still miss it.'

I realised the advantage of being the last patient. Dr Stern might have a little time to spare for gossip and, in particular, for enlightenment regarding the body of Thora Yesnaby.

'What brought you back to Hopescarth?' I asked.

'My father was in poor health and I came to help him in the practice.'

'When was that?'

'Six months ago.'

'So you weren't on the scene when the great discovery was made.'

He looked puzzled. 'What discovery would that be?'

'The peat-bog woman, of course. I have heard so much about her.' I added enticingly: 'As a matter of fact, she was my brother-in-law's first wife, so I am rather curious.'

The doctor shook his head. 'I read the account in the newspapers, of course. My father dealt with it and was, well, rather reticent about the incident but I gather he found it very upsetting, especially as he had been the Yesnaby's family doctor for many years.' Another shake of the head. 'It is never a pleasant experience, you know, for a doctor to have to examine the corpse of someone who has been a personal friend.'

'Do you think that had something to do with your father giving up the practice?'

'Perhaps so.'

As he said the words, Dr Stern's manner changed abruptly. Reluctant to discuss an unpleasant topic he managed to imply that he found a stranger's curiosity a little vulgar. The conversation threatened to come to an abrupt end as he rustled some papers on his desk but I wasn't ready to leave just yet.

'Now that your father is no longer active in the practice,

I trust he is happy in his retirement.'

'I believe so,' was the rather cold reply.

'Does he find plenty to keep him occupied in Hopescarth? I presume he still lives here.'

A curious glance from the doctor. 'He decided to retire to Kirkwall. The house here is small – we are rather cramped – three children, you know, and the surgery,' he added with an apologetic gesture.

I told him my stepbrother was a doctor in Edinburgh. At the mention of his name, Dr Stern beamed. 'Well, I never! Vince Laurie, I knew him well – we were students together. Belonged to the same golf club after we graduated. A small world indeed.'

The next part was easy. Gran and my early days in Orkney.

'Father is very near there. Up beside the Bishop's Palace in Johnston House. You must know it well. We see him as often as we can.'

'He is in good health?'

The doctor frowned. 'As well as can be expected.' And perhaps because I was Vince Laurie's stepsister, seeing me to the door, he was suddenly confidential.

'I fear he was never quite the same man after the discovery of the first Mrs Yesnaby. It upset him dreadfully and I noticed a remarkable change in him when I returned to Hopescarth.' He shook his head. 'Quite remarkable – even considering the tragic circumstances.'

Had that change something to do with signing a death certificate he knew to be false? Had that preyed on his mind?

And I left resolving that my next visit would be to Kirkwall.

Chapter Twenty-Two

On my way back through the village, I remembered that Gran had said something about salt, unimportant enough to slip my mind during my interrogation of Frank Breck.

Back to Meg's shop once more and this time I was in luck. Leaning against the counter chatting to her was Andy Green, the local policeman.

Meg was in a better mood than at our earlier encounter and seemed eager to introduce me: 'Mrs McQuinn is Mrs Yesnaby's sister.'

The young policeman grinned. 'On holiday, I hear.'

I smiled. 'Word gets around.'

He laughed. 'Certainly does. Nothing goes past us here in Hopescarth,' he added rather proudly.

The shop bell indicated another customer and, picking up the salt, I handed over the money and followed PC Green outside.

'Walking today?' When I said yes, he shook his head. 'That bicycle of yours has created quite a sensation, Mrs McQuinn. I expect they're quite commonplace in Edinburgh these days.' He sighed. 'I wouldn't mind having one myself, it would make my daily rounds a lot easier. Can't expect anything as grand as Dr Denmore's motor car for a while.'

'Splendid, isn't it? I gather it is needed to transport precious artefacts from the dig.' And regarding this as a suitable prelude to the information I wanted, 'I suppose there is nothing as exciting now as the peat-bog woman though.'

'So you heard about that in Edinburgh, too?'

'I believe it was in all the newspapers.' And avoiding a downright lie, 'It must have given your local residents quite a shock.'

'Aye, it did that. Thought they had a murder on their hands,' he added and I detected just a tinge of regret.

'What did you think?' I asked eagerly.

He shook his head. 'Just what I read in the newspapers like everyone else. Just my luck to miss all the excitement.'

Just my luck, too, I thought despairingly as he went on, 'I'm a newcomer – from St Margaret's Hope.'

'I expect the constable here told you all about it. Such a sensation.'

He shrugged. 'Only read what was written in his notes. And that wasn't very much. Jock was a bit inarticulate, specially about writing, even when he was sober.'

'I would like to see his notes, if they are still around.'

'I dare say they are...somewhere, but...' As he shook his head, regarding me suddenly with a curious, even suspicious, expression, I hastily explained the reason – my brother-in-law's first wife. I felt very uncomfortable as a look of distaste very similar to Dr Stern's greeted my morbid interest.

'I expect Jock's notes are still in the files at the station,' he said firmly but didn't add what I already knew from experience. That they would not be available for public scrutiny.

I was reluctant to confide in him and set aside his bad opinion of this nosy woman by revealing that my interest was official. That I was a professional investigator. But I bit back the words that might arouse his own suspicions, the very last thing I wanted.

'Has the constable – Jock, you mentioned – retired now? Perhaps I could have a word with him.'

He gave me a sour look. 'Jock is dead.'

'Recently?' This was another blow I had not anticipated. The doctor who had issued the death certificate retired to Kirkwall in poor health, and the other important witness, the local constable, also dead.

Andy was saying: 'Jock died just two weeks after Mrs Yesnaby's body was found. He had a bad heart. Perhaps the shock of it all killed him, the exertion and so forth,' he added vaguely.

Another bad heart. Another shock severe enough to disable the local doctor and kill a policeman.

Too many coincidences, I thought grimly as I asked, 'What happened exactly?'

He regarded me silently, frowned and said: 'Ye ken, Jock wasna' convinced. He questioned the doctor's verdict, I dinna' mind telling you. Even though folk would take more notice of the doctor than the constable.' A moment's hesitation. 'Jock believed it was murder. He couldna' take in this preservation business and that a body could lie in the peat for ten years and look as if she had died yesterday.'

He sighed. 'Poor auld Jock. Always arguing about it, they told me. Then he had an accident, chasing some poachers, they guessed. Reckoned he'd had a drop too much to drink, fell down the cliff on the Hopescarth road.'

'Did they call in the Fiscal.'

He looked at me as if I had taken leave of my senses and suggested the Angel Gabriel. 'Whatever for? What good could the Fiscal do? This was natural causes.'

He was smiling rather pityingly, but his eyes were hard. 'We're used to looking after ourselves in Hopescarth. Making our own justice, if you like. After all, if we called in the Fiscal every time anyone died of a heart attack, or had an accident through drinking too much, he'd never be away from the island. Fishing boats are always being lost, ye ken, the men drowned, their bodies washed ashore and that sort of thing.'

Pausing to let that information sink in, he added, 'Is the Fiscal mannie the way they do it in Edinburgh?'

'Yes, usually when a dead body turns up in—' for 'suspicious' I hastily substituted— 'unusual circumstances, calling him in is a matter of course.'

He regarded me solemnly. 'You seem to know a lot about it, Mrs McQuinn.' And rubbing his chin thoughtfully, 'Wait a minute – are ye no' a Faro?'

When I said yes, he laughed. 'Ye're the daughter of our policeman who went to the mainland and made a name for himself. Inspector Faro.' And regarding me triumphantly, 'Now I get it – that's why you're so interested in our little mystery. Well, well, stands to reason, runs in the family, doesn't it!'

'As a matter of fact it does. I'm a private investigator.'

His eyes widened. 'A lady – investigating – crimes?'

He sounded quite shocked and I asked defensively: 'And why not?'

'Dead bodies and all that. Doesna' sound quite – decent. At least not for a nice lady like yourself,' he added hastily.

I laughed. 'Mostly it's quite mundane matters, frauds

and thefts, and domestic incidents, runaway wives and so forth.'

A sigh of relief. 'I'm right glad of that,' and I thought I had better add a homely touch:

'My fiancé is a detective sergeant in the Edinburgh Police.'

'Is that so?' he smiled. 'I took you to be a widow.'

'I am. But aren't widows allowed second marriages?'

Laughing, he saluted me mockingly. 'Point taken, madam.' And with a bow:

'Out of order, that remark. Beg pardon.'

'Tell me about Jock,' I said.

Regarding me thoughtfully, he said, 'The night it happened, ye mean? Well, I dare say Jock made a routine report but a dead body turning up in a peat-bog after being missing for ten years might not have justified a visit to Hopescarth by the Fiscal to survey the remains.'

He shrugged. 'Fiscals dinna' bother much about long-dead corpses, like I said. There werena' any suspicious circumstances. This was what we would call an open-and-shut case.'

There seemed nothing to add to that. But the lack of information on Thora Yesnaby's resurrection from the peat-bog was adding up to a very sinister picture. I had not bargained for the strange coincidence of my meeting with 'Mrs Smith' in Edinburgh.

'What about the unknown woman who had been buried earlier as Mrs Yesnaby?'

He frowned and shook his head. 'I never heard. Maybe it was before his time. And a bit difficult to open an accident inquiry after ten years.'

I thought, why had I ever imagined it would be simple to interview the main participants involved in the legal aspects of the case? The old family doctor, first on the scene, was now feeble in health and, I suspected, mind. And probably, even on his better days, fiercely loyal to the Yesnabys.

In addition, the local police constable, sole representative of law and order, was dead. If he had urged an official inquiry, suspecting 'murder' and threatening to make trouble, that left a very nasty conclusion. By repute, Jock was a heavy drinker who may, or may not, have notified the Procurator Fiscal regarding an inquest before he conveniently fell to his death off a cliff, when returning home one dark night.

Jock's demise had been skimmed over as an accident when, in fact, there was a strong possibility that there had been not one but two murders in Hopescarth.

'Incidentally, did ye ken that Jock was Meg's husband?' was Andy's parting shot. 'She took it very badly.'

Any plan of going to Kirkwall alone, without Emily insisting on accompanying me, I realised, would require skilful negotiation. The carriage would be put at our disposal, the suggestion eagerly seized upon as a splendid opportunity to select suitable wallpaper for refurbishing the hall.

It didn't take much stretch of imagination to guess that Emily's idea of a pleasant day's shopping, interrupted by frequent intervals for pots of tea and cake in several different cafés, would completely frustrate my own urgent reasons for that Kirkwall visit.

The only alternative was to arrange other means of transport as I did not greatly relish bicycling a round trip of thirty miles in the present spell of notoriously unsettled summer weather. Regardless of the time of year, Orkney was subject to sudden – very sudden – unpredictable downpours, which I would be quite unable to deal with. There is no possibility of carrying an umbrella while riding a bicycle and a rain cape would be hopelessly inadequate.

So once again I returned to Meg's post office, as the seat of local gossip exchange and a seemingly inexhaustible mine of information. My situation, however, was tricky in the extreme and I approached wondering how on earth I could angle the conversation around to Meg's late husband, PC Jock Flitt. A very delicate touch would be required, bearing in mind that Meg was by nature a somewhat prickly lady and I was further frustrated to find when I entered the shop that the counter was busier than usual.

As for my inquiry, regarding transport to Kirkwall, my timing had been perfect. Friday was market day and there would be plenty of carts heading in that direction and passing through Hopescarth.

Meg said that one of the farmers would give me a lift if I didn't mind a rough ride and was prepared to leave by six in the morning.

So leaving a message with her to warn them to expect a passenger, I returned to Hopescarth, thoughtfully considering the many gaps in my knowledge about Thora. Vital things about a woman whose life differed from Emily's portrayal of an invalid wife, who, I had also been allowed to assume, had died of natural causes, leaving the way open for my sister to marry the bereaved husband.

I wasn't alone in my assumptions. The Faro family, Pappa and Vince, had also believed in this romantic fable. And it seemed that our dear Emily had deliberately, if not actually lied to us, then gently led us away from the truth concerning the woman she was companion to.

The visit to Hopescarth had been enlightening in that respect. What had emerged was a very difficult, unbalanced, hysterical and often violent woman, overfond of whisky, who had stormed out of the house one night eleven years ago and had led Hopescarth to believe that she had either taken her own life or had been drowned in a tragic accident.

I thought of Thora roaming about the huge house, devious, making secret plans. The Thora I had never known, built of other people's word pictures. To this image I now added another version: that of her alter ego, my client 'Mrs Smith', met briefly in Edinburgh. A greedy, vengeful blackmailer to whom I had taken an instant dislike.

My thoughts continually drifted to that mysterious young lover, met so fleetingly at Brightwell's Hotel. What fate had overtaken him in the drama of the real Thora Yesnaby? I heard again Mrs Smith saying that she had met 'someone else'. Had I been in error to presume this was the same young man who was with her in the Edinburgh hotel and who, I presumed, was sharing her bed?

Had they parted before she left Edinburgh? What had transpired when she sailed to Orkney? Had they some plan that she was to travel alone and, after confronting her husband, they would meet again?

If so, most important, where was that meeting to take place? And when she did not arrive to keep that appointment, was her lover not deeply concerned? Did he make any inquiries?

And if he was the new man in her life, the one she hoped to marry, then surely he would have been frantic in his efforts to come in search of her?

The thought persisted that, had he accompanied her to Orkney, then it was most unlikely that she would have been murdered. His presence would have saved her life.

Unless he had also been murdered and his body disposed of elsewhere.

A tricky proposition for an amateur killer – or killers, since bodies are not all that easy to get rid of.

So what had become of him? Presuming that he was still alive and well, where was he now? The mysterious lover, who refused to be dismissed from my calculations, had to fit somewhere in Mrs Smith's violent end here in Hopescarth. He hovered on the edge of my mind, a fleeting ghost, an enigmatic shadowy figure, who alone could provide answers, the vital clue to the disastrous arrival of Mrs Smith at Yesnaby House.

There was another missing link in this puzzle. The Yesnaby locket, or Hopescarth jewel, which I had tracked down for my client Mrs Smith in the Edinburgh pawnshop and which Thora allegedly was last seen wearing.

One could sensibly accept a grimmer conclusion to its disappearance without a trace: that it lay somewhere in the depths of the peat-bog, a valuable historic treasure for some future generation of archaeologists.

Yet the more I sought to find answers, the more confused I became. And the possibility stared me in the face that I was on the wrong track completely.

Chapter Twenty-Three

I found Emily alone that evening. Gran was at a Women's Guild meeting at the church and Erland at work on his monthly accounts, closeted in his study and not to be disturbed.

This was our first evening alone together since my arrival and our conversation began casually enough with the usual family gossip to be expected between sisters who had been long apart.

An opportunity not to be missed to say how shocked I was to see Thora's memorial in the kirkyard and learn how she had died. Especially as I had presumed – a little reproachfully, I must admit – that she was a frail invalid.

Emily looked surprised. 'Did I give you that idea?'

'As a matter of fact, you did.' And when she frowned: 'I thought you were employed by Erland originally as Thora's companion.'

She nodded. 'That was true. What Erland had in mind when we first met in Kirkwall.' She sighed happily. 'That meeting was one of those accidents which change a whole life.'

And smiling at the memory, 'It was market day and the harbour cafe was crowded. I was alone at a table for two and he asked if he might be permitted to join me. I said yes and thought he had the most beautiful voice I had ever heard. He didn't look like a farmer either, too well-dressed, you know.'

Another sigh. 'As we talked, we got along famously. He was waiting for someone from Bergen – one of his shipping acquaintances. As I was leaving, he said how he had enjoyed my company and asked if he might see me again. I never hesitated. I said yes, of course, and gave him Gran's address. I never doubted that he would call. And he did. Gran was a bit shocked at the idea, a perfect stranger and all that sort of thing, he might be anyone! Of course, he charmed her instantly.'

She smiled. 'You know the rest. I was rather taken aback when he told me that he was married. I presumed when he wanted to see me again that he was a bachelor. Then in the next breath he told me about Thora and explained that she was an invalid and needed a companion. Especially as he was often away and had to leave her in that big house alone. And even before he asked me if I would consider such a situation, I knew I would say yes. He was delighted. He confessed that he had been thinking about me ever since we met in the harbour cafe and knew I was the right person.'

She paused, stretched and patted her stomach in that now familiar protective gesture. 'And so I came to live at Hopescarth. I admired and respected Erland and, although I soon felt that I had always known him and, secretly, that he was exactly the kind of man I had been waiting for, it was beyond my wildest dreams that I would ever be his wife. In those early days, I honestly never gave it a second thought.'

She shook her head. 'I didn't care that he could never be mine, just to be near him, to see him every day, I thought that would be enough.' A sigh at the memory. 'I felt a little like Jane Eyre with Mr Rochester.'

I laughed. 'Yes, I do see the resemblance.' I didn't add: 'Mad wife and all.'

Emily looked at me sadly and sighed. 'I was never like you, Rose. You always knew that you loved Danny right from being a little girl. Remember when he rescued us both from those criminals Pappa was tracking down in Edinburgh – when they kidnapped us?'

I nodded and she went on. 'How I envied you because I never met anyone like Danny and I didn't expect to – until I met Erland.'

She paused and frowned at me. 'I sometimes think we're an odd family, born to love only once. Perhaps it's in our blood, Sibella and Hakon, Gran and Magnus, Pappa and Mamma, you and Danny, me and Erland…'

Feeling suddenly disloyal, I banished a quick vision of Jack Macmerry as Emily said, 'I soon found that I had been misinformed about Thora. She wasn't physically frail, far from it. Her problems related to the whisky bottle. She was completely unbalanced and could turn quite violent. Not with me. With Erland. On several occasions I saw her physically attack him, he had scratches on his face, once a bloody nose.'

She shuddered. 'Any less caring husband would have had her put away.'

In the slight pause, I said. 'As bad as that?'

She shook her head. 'Worse. Fortunately these bouts were mostly directed at material things, ornaments and plates. Erland, who was so often away in Norway, had the idea that a companion to look after her and care for her would help. He said I was so gentle and sweet, I would be quite perfect and that I'd be around if she tried to do herself a mischief.'

Did he never think that Thora might do Emily a mischief, was my instant reaction to this as Emily continued:

'The thought seemed to haunt him that she might try to destroy herself in one of her mad rages.'

Was that why Erland had so readily accepted that Thora had committed suicide, had walked into the sea?

Emily sighed. 'As I wasn't qualified for anything, like you, from the practical viewpoint, I thought this was an excellent chance to earn some money. I was paid a good salary every month; I was very lucky.'

As she spoke, I thought that in common with so many other women, Emily regarded marriage as the only possible career open to a respectable, well-brought-up young woman.

'Gran is a very demanding person, as you know, Rose. I had always seen myself tied to her, an ageing grand-daughter at her beck and call for the rest of her life. But Erland provided a place for her too. He seemed to understand and,' she smiled, 'Gran was transformed when she came to Hopescarth with me. He gave her a new lease of life, too. Quite remarkable, she seemed to immediately shed twenty years.'

Not quite what you implied in your letters, sister mine, I thought, remembering her description of Gran as 'frail and needing care'.

'Gran even decided to heal the breach with Sibella. I didn't know then that we even had a great-grandmother.'

'Nor did I. A very well kept secret.'

Emily nodded. 'But dear Erland was ready once more. He offered to take Sibella under his roof.'

She paused and I asked, 'You were on good terms with Thora?'

Emily frowned. 'Yes, at first. She seemed to like me. In a way she regarded me as a novelty, a new toy to play with,' she added uncomfortably. 'Yes, I was fairly sure she liked me. Better than Erland anyway.'

'Really?'

'Yes, really. Erland was her husband, he loved her and was kind to her but she despised him. Never made any secret of that. She used to tell me that he had just married her for her wealth – because Hopescarth needed her money in order to survive.'

There was another pause before she continued, reluctant to remember: 'Thora liked to torment Erland by flirting with other men whenever she got the chance – any male visitors who came to the house.'

Another vision, this time of Mrs Smith and her lover. That fitted Thora Yesnaby too.

'She liked the archaeologists, they were always in the house, although Erland disapproved of the dig on Hopescarth land. But Thora was always inviting Frank Breck. She really led him on.'

'Didn't Erland object?'

She shook her head. 'He didn't seem to care. He had lost Thora long ago – if ever he had her, in all truth – and whatever marriage they once had was over. I suppose it might have been different if there had been children. Erland always wanted a family.'

Again that gesture now so familiar, smoothing her stomach where the outline of Erland's baby was not yet visible. 'Even if I hadn't – cared – I would have been sorry for any husband, especially such a wonderful man as Erland, being treated so badly.'

She paused, looking towards the window. 'Then there was one day I realised it was more than being sorry. I was in love with him. And I knew he loved me too. Terrible, wasn't that, Rose?'

'I don't think it was terrible. You both deserved some happiness. Sounds perfectly natural to me.'

But Emily shook her head obstinately, said firmly: 'Not as long as Thora was his wife. Erland would never have suggested anything – like that. It wouldn't have been proper for either of us.'

I let that pass. 'How about a divorce? Did he never consider that?'

'Thora would never divorce him. Once she knew that he loved me, she would never let him go. She told him so. That he didn't deserve the right to be happy.'

As she spoke, I wondered about those ten years away from Hopescarth. What circumstances had caused her to change her mind, make her willing to exchange the Yesnaby locket for a substantial divorce settlement and that 'someone else', her lover in Edinburgh?

I patted Emily's hand. 'It must have been awful for you both.'

'It was. I had decided I couldn't bear it any longer and told Erland that I was going to leave Hopescarth and go back to Kirkwall. By one of those odd coincidences, I had just told him, had it all planned the very day they had that last dreadful row. I only know that it was more violent than usual and it served to strengthen my purpose. I knew I had to leave him. I was doing the right thing, my presence was just making matters worse. By staying, I was giving Thora a stick to beat Erland with emotionally.

'And that—' Her eyes widened as she repeated. 'That was the very day she disappeared. Don't you think that was very strange? Fate stepping in like that.'

I thought it was very strange all right, but not for Emily's innocent reasons or the intervention of a benign fate either. And knowing what I did, I had not much faith in 'odd coincidences' either, as Emily continued:

'At first, Erland said he thought she had just gone down to the dig. To see Frank, was what he implied. She liked to cry on his shoulder, especially when Lily – Frank's wife – returned to Edinburgh. Next day when Thora's bed hadn't been slept in, Frank was the first person Erland asked, but he denied that she had been with him. He didn't know where she was.

'Erland then went to Sibella. Thora liked Sibella. Another shoulder to cry on. And Sibella was always ready with soothing new cures and remedies for Thora's imagined ills. But she hadn't seen her either.'

'Did Sibella like her?' I interrupted.

'Yes, and I think she was sorry for her. Since the reconciliation with Gran, Erland had given her the croft and would have been very happy to have her living in the house with us. There are enough rooms, but good sense prevailed. Sibella and Gran under one roof...'

Her heavenward glance said it all. 'And Sibella was another new toy as far as Thora was concerned. Certainly some of her cures seemed to help, or maybe it was simply because Thora believed in them.'

'How did Erland react to Thora's disappearance?' I put in.

Emily shrugged. 'I think he was just, well, relieved that she had gone. A few days afterwards I noticed a change in him. He no longer regarded the door being flung open with dread. He was like a man who had just had a great burden lifted from him. One day he said to me: "I don't think Thora's coming back, I think she's gone for good this time."'

'And that made a difference to your relationship.'

Emily coloured slightly. 'Yes, we became lovers – at last,' she whispered.

'Good for you, Emmy. And about time, too.'

'She looked amazed. You're not shocked?'

'Of course I'm not shocked. Tell me – had Thora ever left home before?'

'Oh, often. Full of threats that she was never coming back, Erland told me. But she was always home before nightfall,' Emily said bitterly. 'Somehow I knew that it was different this time too. I could feel it all over the house. That we were rid of Thora's evil presence and now Erland and I were together – we could get married – some day, quite soon.'

She paused again, regarding me thoughtfully. 'Do you know, he never shed a tear – not one – when she was – I mean, when that poor woman's body, who he thought was Thora, was washed ashore.'

She shuddered at the memory. 'Thora, his wife, and him so tender and gentle, but not one single tear,' she repeated.

I had no comment to offer, thinking that if he had his own reasons for knowing that this was not Thora, and was eager to accept a replacement body, then a certain lack of any emotion but thanksgiving was quite in order.

Again Emily seemed to read my thoughts. 'Of course, I questioned him when he came back after identifying the body, but I don't think he had looked too closely and I was told that after long periods in the water, bodies are fairly unrecognisable.'

Another shudder, as she whispered: 'This poor woman – arms and legs gone. Poor Erland, what an ordeal. Later, once we were married, he said it was a good thing that Thora was dead. That if she hadn't vanished when she did, if we had both had to suffer much longer, then he would not have been responsible for his actions.'

She closed her eyes briefly. 'Wasn't that a terrible thing for someone like Erland to admit?'

Though Emily didn't understand the significance of her words they were making plenty of sense to me. And setting Erland up as prime suspect for Thora's murder.

'I never was sure we were rid of her, really, Rose. It seemed too good to be true and I always felt the bliss I had with Erland would have to be paid for.'

I hoped that I was wrong but I now had the same ominous feeling.

Chapter Twenty-Four

At the mention of Kirkwall there was, as I had anticipated, some opposition to my plan.

After a shocked silence, Emily asked if I hadn't realised that we could go together in the carriage, that Erland would be most willing to take us both. Had I any idea how uncomfortable a farmer's cart would be for such a journey?

I side-stepped the issue by saying I really wanted to make an early start – at the crack of dawn – and I wouldn't impose that upon them.

Emily, a late riser, did look a little downcast at the mention of six o'clock but an argument seemed inescapable until Gran reminded Emily that she couldn't go with me. Had she forgotten that they were having afternoon tea with the doctor's wife?

I decided I had best mention that I had already met Dr Stern in case my visit to the surgery was mentioned. This immediately threw them both into the state of panic, which I had been hoping to avoid. Why had I gone there? Was I feeling ill? And so forth. I explained about the tendon in my ankle, blaming the bicycle for that imaginary injury.

'I might have known it. There's no place for a dangerous thing like that on these roads,' said Gran in the gloomy manner of one hourly expecting a fatality.

'No need for a doctor, Rose,' Emily cut in sharply. 'Sibella's great at treating sprains and suchlike, isn't that so, Gran?' To which Gran had to admit rather grudgingly that Sibella had fixed her sprained wrist in no time at all.

I listened patiently and said weakly: 'I happened to be near the surgery when it happened, so I thought I'd get advice. Dr Stern told me he had taken over from his father.'

'We miss the old doctor. Such a nice man, too,' said Gran. 'As for that young lad...' She shook her head dubiously. 'His father was Erland's family doctor. And very good to Emily when she had all her troubles.' 'Troubles' obviously referring to the miscarriages.

'I gather he's retired to Kirkwall,' I said.

'Yes, he's in Johnston House – remember, Rose? Up the hill from where we lived,' said Emily.

And I had a stroke of unexpected luck as she added: 'If you're quite set on going to Kirkwall, I'm sure he'd love to meet you. He'll be very interested in you having lived in America. It was his ambition to go there as a young man.'

Pausing, she smiled at Gran. 'I've just thought – it's his eightieth birthday next week. I always remember because it's the day after Erland's. If you have time, Rose, you could maybe take him a plant for his room, from the garden here. He isn't very mobile any more and he would love that.'

I awoke at dawn next morning and crept downstairs. On the kitchen table, as well as Gran's provisions for my journey – adequate for several farmers, I thought – there was also a basket containing a plant, a card and some of her biscuits for the doctor.

I let myself out and set off briskly down the drive. How sharp and clear the air, before it had been 'breathed by everybody,' as Gran used to say.

The farmers' carts were already on the road past the post office and as I waited for a lift, Wilma looked out of the upstairs window.

'Hello, Missus Rose. Where's your bicycle?'

When I explained that it was too far to ride into Kirkwall, she beamed down at me. 'Can I go to the house and practice then – if I tell Mrs Yesnaby you said so?'

I wasn't too keen on that idea, however, I weakened and said: 'If you think you'll manage alone – I don't want you falling and hurting yourself.'

'I won't – I won't. I promise!'

'Very well. There are plenty of straight paths round the house. If you promise to stay there.'

'I will. I will! I'll be careful and I won't fall off.'

At that she gave me a warning glance as her mother appeared behind her, asking what was she doing out of bed with the window wide open.

The cavalcade of carts were now assembled and what followed was not the most comfortable ride to Kirkwall, as Emily had predicted. Alec Burray, elderly and enigmatic, had invited me to share the cart seat on his harvest load of vegetables.

Prepared to expect the worst, I was relieved when the day promised to be kind, blossoming into a warm sunny morning, almost windless, and I began to look forward to the cart ride as an interesting experience. Especially when a halt was called halfway at Skailholm where it was traditional that the farmers halted for a pot of ale.

They trooped into the inn where I had observed Craig Denmore on such excellent terms with the blacksmith's wife. I followed, curious to see Maud again, whose hair was already immaculately arranged, not a curl out of place, leaving some doubt as to whether she achieved this miracle by sleeping sitting bolt upright in bed.

I was recognised again. 'What's yours, then?'

My request for a glass of milk raised her well-defined eyebrows. 'You're brave to travel with that lot,' but I detected none of the hostility in her manner so evident when I had been accompanied by Craig and his motor car as she asked: 'Enjoying your holiday, are you?'

I said very much and she continued to look at me in that rather intense way, as if I was something of a curiosity myself.

'Doesn't it seem a bit dull after Edinburgh?' So she knew that too.

'Makes a pleasant change. I used to live in Kirkwall before I was married.'

She nodded. 'Your family comes from here.' A statement, not a question, so Craig must have told her and her next remark left me in no doubt of that.

'Aye, your grandfather was a policeman—'

'Maud!' It was Lenny, red-faced and busy. 'Cut short yer gossip, lass,' he said, indicating the farmers noisily clamouring at the bar.

Sipping my glass of milk, I noticed one customer who wasn't with the cavalcade. Breakfasting alone, he was staring out of the window, as if anxious to dissociate himself from the rowdy arrivals.

Although he was seated, I got the impression of a tall man, heavily built, middle-aged. His bearing, his stern expression, combined with a shock of straight sandy hair and a moustache hinted at a military man.

What happened afterwards was rather odd. On her way

to the bar Maud touched his shoulder, whispered in his ear. Nodding in agreement, he turned his head sharply in my direction. Immediately leaving his table, he came over to me, holding out his hand.

'Mrs McQuinn, I believe.'

I was certain that we had never met before as he explained: 'Mrs Lenny told me who you were. And that you have Hopescarth connections.' He smiled. 'As a matter of fact, I am heading in that direction myself.'

That voice – the accent! 'You're from America?' And as I said the words my heart leapt with sudden hope. Was this stranger a contact, at last? Someone come to bring me news of Danny?

He shook his head. 'Folks over here often make that mistake. I'm Canadian – from Toronto. I have kin hereabouts. Jim Mainwell's the name.'

The prospects of a possibly interesting conversation were challenged by the loud clanging of a bell. The farmers immediately banged down their empty ale pots and surged towards the door.

I stood up. 'That's for me, too. I'm off to Kirkwall with them.'

I wanted to know more about Mr Mainwell, but Alec Burray, his complexion heightened even more with the effects of the ale, shouted:

'Come away, lass. Or we'll be leaving without you!'

As I ran to the door, the military man who was standing still, watching me, raised a hand in salute.

Farmer Burray noticed the gesture and allowed his face to fold into a grin as he helped me up on to the seat beside him.

'Nice fellow, eh? Sorry we had to tak' ye awa', lass,' he added with a knowing wink.

I tried not to bristle at the implications and coldly replied: 'He has connections in Hopescarth.'

'Oh aye. That'll be nice for you,' he remarked, his glance arch and disbelieving.

I knew there was no point in arguing or being outraged at any lewd suggestion. This was normal male behaviour, in Edinburgh as well as Orkney, so I prepared to enjoy the scenery, especially as the day was growing warmer, the sky cloudless.

Up hills and down hills we travelled, horizons often shrouded behind tall hedgerows, deep in summer's wild flowers. Our progress was marked by an escort of raucous seabirds, lured by prospects of scavenging, adding to the noise of sheep and hens carried on the carts, and the lowing cattle being driven alongside.

And for me, the calendar tipped backwards and I was deposited once more into childhood memories, long before the tall rose-red cathedral spire of St Magnus appeared on the skyline. Emily and I had gone to Sunday school there long ago.

Eventually a huddle of rooftops heralded the street and the cottage where Emily and I had lived with Gran.

I laughed out loud. 'This is just perfect. I've come home again.'

Farmer Burray seemed pleased and suddenly keen to impress me with his knowledge of past days. He and his fathers before him had travelled these roads on market day for generations past. But he found it difficult to believe that I was of Orcadian descent and had spent my growing-up years here.

There was more to come and I realised that I was in for yet another lesson on local lore when he said:

'Bet ye didna' ken the word "orc" was Celtic for pig and

that "ey" was Norse for island. Put them together, lass, and ye'll get the Islands and the People of the Wild Boar,' he said triumphantly.

In reply I told him that my family, Faros and Scarths, had lived here for generations and they would know.

Faro, aye, he kenned the name well, but what had lured them awa' to a place the likes o' Edinburgh? From which I guessed that the name of Chief Inspector Jeremy Faro had not reached Alec Burray.

Chapter Twenty-Five

Outside the cattle market I left the cart in a noisy throng with their bleating, mooing, clucking charges and made my way up the hill past the cottage where Emily and I had spent so many years.

As I stood by the fence, a woman with a baby in her arms came out and asked me if I wanted something. I said that I used to live here.

I suppose I was hoping that she would ask me in, as I had been warned to expect by Gran, with traditional Orkney hospitality and the offer of tea and bere bannocks. I was really looking forward to accepting her invitation so that I could sit in a once familiar kitchen and relive those nostalgic moments of childhood.

Alas, the present occupant of Gran's cottage did none of these things. I suspected this was a new breed of neighbour who had not heard of the island's famed old ways, as, hushing the awakened baby, she smiled politely and closed the door.

Somewhat deflated, I walked past the cathedral up the hill to the Earl's Palace. Pausing by the railings, I regarded it through those peaceful sheltering trees, trying to equate this imposing ruin with Erland's story. Was this what Hopescarth had looked like in Huw Scarth's days of glory when he had followed his rainbow and found his pot of gold?

On up the hill to Johnston House. A sign on the gate: 'Residential Home for Retired Gentlemen', I decided might cover a number of possibilities as I walked down the drive.

Once inside, I found that the desk in the dark-panelled reception area – that smelt of polish and something less pleasant I associated with hospitals – was occupied by a brisk nurse wearing a white starched apron, and with a white starched face to match.

In answer to my question she pointed to a door. 'Through there. Dr Stern is in the garden at present.'

I hesitated. 'This is my first visit. I come on a friend's behalf. I haven't met the doctor before.'

Pursing her lips, she regarded me suspiciously, managing to make my request to have him identified sound rather fast and improper. Under her steadily watchful gaze, I made my way out along a path where a nurse was pushing a wheelchair. A tap on the window behind me revealed the brisk nurse again and indicated the shawled occupant as Dr Stern.

I mouthed a thank you and hurried across the grass where a young nurse, aged about sixteen, I guessed, turned to greet me and at my request I was duly introduced to the unmoving figure hunched in the chair: 'Sir, this is Mrs Erland Yesnaby's sister, Mrs McQuinn.'

She said the words very slowly and loudly, with a glance in my direction, hinting that the old doctor was hard of hearing.

'I am very pleased to meet you, Dr Stern,' I smiled.

His hostile glance as I took hold of that skeletal hand did not augur well. 'My sister, Mrs Yesnaby, sends you her warmest greetings. She has asked me to give you this—' I indicated the plant in its basket— 'and to wish you many happy returns on your birthday.'

Even as I heard myself saying the words I realised how foolish and incongruous such a greeting must have sounded.

The doctor glared at the flower in its pot. I could have sworn that its petals shivered under his icy gaze and as he made no attempt to take it, I relinquished it to the young nurse's tender keeping – I hoped!

With a smile, I held out the biscuits. Snatching from my hand, he examined them contemptuously and without a word of thanks, thrust them down the side of the wheelchair.

Staring at me suspiciously, he said: 'Mrs Yesnaby is dead. And I don't know who you are.' His tone suggested that he didn't care much either as he continued:

'Erland would be sending me something stronger. Like a good malt whisky.' Another glare, a hint that I had been admitted to his presence on false pretences. 'And Mrs Yesnaby had a fine taste in whisky.'

I stammered out that the present was from my sister, Mrs Emily Yesnaby, but shaking his head, he grunted and deliberately turned his head away muttering: 'Whisky – that's what I want. Not all this rubbish. Tell her that from me.'

An apologetic glance and a despairing sigh from the young nurse indicated that the lack of whisky was a constant source of aggravation and arguments from her charge.

Did everyone drink to excess in Hopescarth, I thought helplessly, remembering Thora and PC Jock Flitt's unfortunate demise, as a result no doubt of over-indulgence.

Dr Stern made an impatient gesture, banging his fist against the arm of his wheelchair. 'Let's get on with it, shall we? I'm cold. No point in standing around here.'

Wondering what to do next, how to ingratiate myself with the doctor, I fell in step alongside. Then I had an idea and said to the nurse: 'I could take over from you, look after him for a while.'

Sadly she shook her head, whispered: 'You would need Matron's approval, madam. Unauthorised visitors are not allowed to take out – residents out in wheelchairs.'

At that pronouncement I surveyed the situation with deepening gloom. It looked as if my journey, from which I had entertained such hopes of obtaining valuable information about Thora Yesnaby, was fast proving to have been a complete waste of time. Evidence was clear that this was going to be exceedingly difficult, if not impossible, to bring up the subject.

Dr Stern, after his outburst about the whisky, had lapsed into a huffy silence. Or bored, his eyes closed, he now seemed to be asleep. This lasted for a few rounds of the path through the shrubbery and around the rather dismal lawn. He had obviously dismissed my presence, if he was still aware of it, while I was considering what should be my next move.

As we approached the house, the nurse gave me a sympathetic look: 'Are you on holiday, madam?'

I told her I was staying at Hopescarth and that my sister was the second Mrs Yesnaby.

'It was her suggestion that I should visit Dr Stern. He

was greatly liked by the family, a close friend as well as the family doctor.'

The nurse frowned. 'His memory is quite acute – about some things – that he wants to remember, that is. And he does hold some very forceful opinions.' Her tone implied that he was a very difficult patient.

Politely I bade him goodbye. Either he didn't hear me or was fast asleep and I walked out of the gate and down the drive, aware that I was tired too with that early morning start and far from comfortable journey in Alex Burray's farm cart.

A church clock struck mid-day. Here I was in Kirkwall with time on my hands, at least four hours before the return journey to Hopescarth.

If only the visit to Dr Stern had been more rewarding. All I had found was a complete waste of time with a confused, ill-tempered old man. My own temper wasn't much improved either as I made my way down to the local hotel, still relatively quiet before the farmers and cattle dealers arrived for their mid-day meal.

As the waitress hovered, I realised that opening Gran's contribution would be severely frowned on, and tackling soup followed by steak pie reminded me that I had never before set foot in this hotel or eaten meals anywhere except at home with Emily and Gran, who would have been shocked at such extravagance.

In considerably better humour at this novel and very pleasant experience I sat at the window table overlooking the harbour. Some of the diners were staying and as they collected their keys at reception I watched them climb the carpeted stair to their bedrooms and had a sudden impulse to do likewise. Book a room, go upstairs and close the door. Spend the rest of my holiday here, very pleasantly drifting about Kirkwall and maybe taking a ferry to some of the islands.

I sighed. Oh, the joy to leave the horrors awaiting me back at Yesnaby House. Just pretend they had never happened. Dismiss them from my mind. If only I could do so with an easy conscience. If only I could have been someone else at that moment instead of Rose McQuinn. Someone who could thrust aside the murder of her brother-in-law's first wife.

But paying the bill I abandoned that fantasy and decided there remained one somewhat forlorn possibility to justify my visit to Kirkwall.

PC Green had suggested that I might look in at the offices of *The Orcadian*. I vaguely remembered the location and at the counter requested back numbers relating to archaeological digs in the Hopescarth area.

And at last I had a piece of good fortune. A journalist seated at a nearby desk overheard my inquiry. He came over, asked: 'Are you planning to visit Hopescarth, miss?'

When I said yes, he smiled. 'Maybe I can help you? What exactly were you interested in seeing?'

I explained that I was visiting my sister in Yesnaby House and was curious about the peat-bog burial. Deciding to avoid exhibiting a morbid interest in Emily's predecessor, I took refuge in one of my assumed roles: I was gathering information for a travel piece on Orkney for an Edinburgh magazine, which had particularly stressed archaeological finds.

The man smiled. 'You've come to the right person.' And holding out his hand: 'Eric Mawson. And I was on the spot when it all happened.'

'You actually saw the body exhumed?'

He shook his head. 'Alas, no. It was removed very

speedily on the doctor's orders. Apparently deterioration sets in very fast on exposure to the open air. Writing it up was my assignment and I think I can lay hands on the very articles you want.'

A few minutes later I was seated at a table before a large file of the newspaper's back numbers.

Chapter Twenty-Six

'Peat-bog burial', said Mr Mawson triumphantly, skimming through the pages. 'Here it is. I'll leave you to it.'

Dated 28 October 1895, the article began:

Mrs Thora Yesnaby of Yesnaby House, Hopescarth disappeared from her home ten years ago in September 1885.

A woman's badly decomposed body, washed ashore in a storm near Marwick Head on 30 November, was identified by the distraught Erland Yesnaby as that of his missing wife and laid to rest in the family grave at Hopescarth….

The November date was of particular significance since Erland and Emily were married on Christmas Eve 1885.

The account continued:

The body discovered in the peat-bog a few days ago has been identified as the real Mrs Thora Yesnaby. The family physician, Dr Joseph Stern, claimed that, the victim of a tragic accident, she had lain there since the night of her disappearance when she had stumbled into the peat-bog on leaving home…

I scanned the rest. The preservative qualities of peat and so forth were discussed but there was one surprising omission.

No one had queried the identity of the woman buried in Thora's grave.

As I copied the details into my logbook, I turned back to my entry dated 2 October 1895, relating to my recovery of a locket for a client Mrs Smith, a resident at Brightwell's Hotel, Princes Street, Edinburgh.

Since Mrs Smith was the alias of Thora Yesnaby, this confirmed that her visit to Hopescarth and the discovery of her body took place within three weeks of her departure from Edinburgh.

I laid aside the file wearily. Although I now had some actual dates for reference, I knew that recent crimes are difficult enough to solve but dealing with those of a year past suggested all the possibilities of a nightmare.

However, I should be grateful. All I needed to know was the location of the prime suspects during the three weeks covering her probable departure from Edinburgh to the grim discovery of her body. I thought cynically, no wonder her corpse looked so fresh. And I would have hazarded a fairly accurate guess that Thora's arrival at Yesnaby and her departure via the peat-bog happened almost simultaneously.

That was a logical conclusion. Otherwise too many other people would have been involved and as it was, the murderer was taking a great chance. Some acquaintance from Hopescarth might have encountered her on the journey from Stromness and realised that she had not been dead for ten years after all, and was returning home very much alive.

In small communities like Hopescarth, such fascinating revelations, such sensational news, would have moved faster than a forest fire, and that was one risk her murderer could not afford to take.

I had to find out from Emily, by subtle means, if Erland was at home during last October. And if he was in Bergen, had he an alibi? I hoped so and, in that case, the prime suspect must be her young lover.

Did he have a motive? Truth and the motive were inescapable and alas, firmly pointed to Erland who I knew from my Edinburgh interview with 'Mrs Smith' was the reason for her visit.

The only person who knew the exact date of Thora's return, who had met her and learned her grim purpose, had also been her killer. This was a fact. I could not ignore it whatever my reluctance to do so.

The indelible picture in my mind was of Mrs Smith arriving off the Leith steamer soon after I had restored the locket to her. Alone or accompanied by her young lover? It was very frustrating that I had merely caught a glimpse of him. Mrs Smith had avoided an introduction so I had no name for him, not even a false once, since he had probably registered as Mr Smith at Brightwell's Hotel.

There was so much valuable information readily available, the kind I was used to tracking down had I been investigating this case in Edinburgh. Of course I could write to Jack to check the relevant details but my stay would be almost over before I might expect a response. To say nothing of lengthy explanations regarding the purpose behind my inquiries and the necessity of telling him about my interview with 'Mrs Smith' and why hadn't I mentioned the twenty guineas, my fee for recovering the locket?

Alas, there was no easy way. I had to solve this murder here in Hopescarth – alone – before my holiday ended or return home and leave the mystery for ever unsolved.

To be tormented for the rest of my life by the suspicion that my sister Emily was married to a murderer. Or, reason whispered, that my sister Emily might be accessory to such a crime.

My thoughts returned again to Thora. How did she reach Hopescarth from Stromness? Had she hired a carriage? And I toyed with the possibility of searching out firms of hirers in Stromness. But the hope of finding the same cab and the same driver – and of his remembering the fare he had taken to Hopescarth a year ago, whether or not she had travelled alone – was remote indeed.

Even with such information, could I risk stirring up muddy waters which might involve Emily? Her welfare was my main concern, in need of greater protection than Erland, especially as anxiety might bring about disaster to her early pregnancy.

As for Thora, if she hoped for anonymity, I did not doubt that she had taken refuge in the easiest of all disguises for any woman. Most convenient and readily at hand were widow's weeds, features hidden behind heavy veils, vague and impenetrable as her sorrow. To be revered, respected and unapproachable. And also considerably to her murderer's advantage.

Again I considered that hired carriage, the driver showing little interest in his heavily veiled passenger beyond taking her fare. There was a possibility of course that he might have heard a few weeks later about the archaeologist's grim discovery. But unless he was of an exceedingly inquiring turn of mind, what was there to connect the corpse who had lain undiscovered in the peat-bog for ten years with the widowed lady, the fare he had carried to Hopescarth?

Returning the past issues of the newspapers to Mr Mawson with expressions of gratitude, I wandered back into the streets of Kirkwall – a pleasurable experience, at least. In order to make my visit plausible since Emily and Gran would expect a detailed account of how every minute was spent, I bought some chocolates for them and a special cheese for Erland.

As I walked past our old school, the bell rang and children came hurrying out of the gates, talking shrilly. I stood aside, guessing that many would be children of my own schoolmates who had settled down in Kirkwall and married farmers, local lads.

The realisation made me wish for a moment that I had kept in touch with those long-lost companions.

At last it was time to join Alec Burray and the farmers on their return journey to Hopescarth and beyond. This proved to be a much quieter affair, with considerably fewer animals and Gran's much appreciated picnic. Some of the farmers were in a merry mood and quite inebriated. Obviously profits from sales had been skimmed off for whisky and ale.

Once again, as we broke our journey at the Skailholm Inn, I wondered if the military gentleman would still be there. Maud drifted over and as if she knew what I had in mind, said: 'That man who stayed here last night got a lift to Hopescarth this morning, soon after you left.'

'I don't suppose you get many Canadians.'

She shook her head. 'First since I've been here, usually looking for their ancestors.'

'Did he say who he was visiting?'

'Frank Breck, I expect. He works with Craig. Lily Breck, his wife, once said she had a brother in Toronto. I've known her for years. We were very friendly when she came for the summer each year. She's a city lass like me, wanted to get away from all that mud at the dig once in a while and didn't care too much for Frank's lodgings. Used to come over with the farmers' carts for a change of scene.'

And suddenly confidential, 'Mr Mainwell is worried about Lily. Never did keep in touch over the years but when he was in Edinburgh he thought he'd call but she wasn't at the address he had been given any more.'

'Frank told me she lived in Minto Street.'

Maud shrugged. 'Maybe he went to the wrong house. Funny thing is, though, I haven't heard from her for ages either. Used to keep in touch, a card at Christmas, that sort of thing. But after she stopped coming to the dig, I wrote and it came back "gone away". I gave the letter to Craig for Frank, asking him to forward it to her new address and ask her to get in touch. But she never did.'

As she spoke, I remembered Craig saying he thought she'd found someone else. That was the general opinion. Perhaps Frank's manly pride was shattered, but surely she might have confided in Maud.

'Do you think maybe she had decided to leave Frank?'

Maud gave me a hard look. 'You mean, had she got another man?' she laughed. 'Anyone who knew Frank wouldn't have blamed her. But I think she would have told me. On the other hand, maybe she didn't want him to find out.'

She shrugged. 'Well, I was sorry we lost touch, because I liked her and I thought we were good chums.' And with a sigh, 'But there it is. Life's like that, isn't it?'

She sounded disappointed and my mind drifted back to Kirkwall and girls at school swearing eternal friendship. Where were they all now? Even their faces were forgotten. The classroom their solitary bond, the grown-up world the great divider.

Friendships, firmly made, that grew apart, unable to cope with the march of time and changing circumstances, I thought sadly as the cavalcade moved homewards.

Chapter Twenty-Seven

I was set down once more outside the post office by a weary Alec Burray, who had been somewhat inarticulate on the latter part of the journey. That suited me as I had a great deal to mull over concerning the information acquired from the newspaper files, as well as Maud's revelations regarding Lily Breck and her brother.

Leaving the farm cart and heading down the road towards Yesnaby House, the sound of a noisy engine from Stromness direction announced the imminent appearance of Craig Denmore's motor car.

He drew to a halt more or less alongside. 'Where's the bicycle?'

The information that I had been in Kirkwall with the farm carts raised his eyebrows in shocked surprise. 'At least I can offer you more comfortable transport back to the house.'

Accepting gratefully I told him of my meeting with Mrs Breck's brother at the Skailholm Inn.

Craig nodded. 'He was here earlier and Frank took him off to show him the more spectacular sights of Hopescarth, like the Troll's Cave.'

'I haven't been there yet.'

Perhaps he thought I was angling for an invitation as he said very quickly: 'I'll take you – it's just round the corner, in a manner of speaking, from Sibella's croft.'

'In that case, I'll have no difficulty finding it on my own.'

He put a hand on my arm. 'Steer clear, Rose. There are warning notices – strictly out of bounds to strangers in the area.'

I laughed and he gave me a stern look. 'The Troll's Cave is a very dangerous place for the unwary. There's a funnel through the rocks that goes right down to the shore. A sort of chimney.'

'A chimney?'

'Yes. The roarsts funnel up at high tide. Make a sound like dragons roaring, according to young Wilma, who is heavy on imagination but strictly barred from going anywhere near.' He smiled. 'I presume an Orcadian lass knows all about the roaring roarsts?'

'Of course,' I said without confessing that I had only heard about them since I arrived in Hopescarth as Craig continued:

'Frank has good reason to remember them. That's how his boat was washed ashore, smashed into matchwood.'

No need to complete the picture of the boat believed to have carried Thora Yesnaby to her death. The thought crossed my mind to wonder why the place had such a fascination for Lily's Canadian brother as Craig went on enthusiastically:

'I'll take you there at low tide. The spout rising from the sea is quite dramatic from the cliff top, well worth seeing. We can take a picnic, if you have time.'

I certainly had time for a picnic with Craig Denmore,

even moonlight on a stormy night would have been acceptable, as I thanked him calmly.

He grinned. 'I have a tide-table somewhere. I'll consult it for the low tides.'

We had reached the bridge leading across to the drive when Frank and Mainwell appeared from the direction of the dig.

As Frank prepared to make some reluctant introductions, I said we had met before. I thought Jim Mainwell looked flushed and angry. Whatever we had interrupted, he was clearly upset and Frank had no desire to linger.

He said brusquely, 'I'm taking him to stay at our lodgings overnight.'

Mainwell seemed less that delighted at the prospect. 'I was hoping to stay for a few days.'

'I explained that there may not be room at Mrs Flitt's.' Frank's sharp response managed to indicate that he certainly hoped there wouldn't be.

'Oh, I dare say Meg will find something for you.' Craig smiled soothingly at the newcomer, earning a bitter glance from Frank. 'Incidentally, if you'd like a look at Kirkwall or Stromness, I can take you on my next visit.'

'Thank you, sir. I would be delighted. I have only a short time here.'

'An excellent idea, Craig,' Frank put in gratefully, sounding relieved to have someone take his brother-in-law off his hands.

As I prepared to step down from the car, Craig took my arm. 'Wait. I'll deliver you to your front door. It's a tedious walk up that drive.'

Looking back and watching the two men head towards the village, I had a weird sensation of everything being out of focus, a sense of brooding disquiet as I asked:

'What do you think of him?'

Craig knew exactly who I was talking about. 'A pity he had to come all this way to see his sister. Someone should have warned him in Edinburgh.'

'Frank told me she lived in Minto Street. That's very near my home. And when we were at Skailholm Inn on the way home, Mrs Lenny mentioned that she and Lily had been good friends when she spent the summers here, but that they had lost touch.'

'I think the answer is rather obvious, don't you?' Craig sighed. 'Lily has another man and poor old Frank can't bear to have us know. Still keeps up this elaborate pretence that all is well as usual in Edinburgh.'

As we drew up in front of the house, I said: 'If Lily has found someone else, why doesn't she get a divorce, free herself from Frank?'

Craig shrugged. 'I haven't the slightest idea, Rose. Divorces and marriage breakdowns are very personal things and Frank is a very sensitive and secretive person. Doesn't talk much about himself if he can avoid it. Even though I've worked with him for years, I honestly know him no better than I did in those first days.'

Silent for a moment, he added reluctantly: 'Maybe Lily preferred to leave him quietly – just take the opportunity to walk out when she returned to Edinburgh. Frank does have a very violent temper on the rare occasions when he gets angry. Perhaps Lily wants to avoid a confrontation.'

'Surely she kept in touch with someone,' I said desperately. 'What about her family, apart from her brother in Canada?'

'I have no idea. You'll need to ask Frank about that.'

His tone was not encouraging and I couldn't imagine asking Frank such a question.

But there was something wrong here. I could feel it.

'If they had lost touch, why this sudden decision to come all the way to Orkney? Hardly the easiest journey in the world.'

Craig shrugged. 'Who knows? An attack of conscience, a desire to see his long-lost sister. Happens sometimes when families get older.'

He regarded my worried expression critically. 'Don't concern yourself about Frank and Lily. Married couples split up regularly and discreetly. They don't advertise the fact, possibly feel a little ashamed, especially when a man has to admit that his wife left him for someone else. I expect the simple truth was that Lily was bored to death and that's why she abandoned the summer dig – and Frank.'

This confirmed what Maud had told me.

'You're a sweet person, Rose. You worry too much.' His hand on my arm was a surge of warmth that set my blood racing. My knees went suddenly quite weak at the thought of what it would be like if Craig Denmore ever crossed the boundary and kissed me.

Oblivious of his effect upon me, he was smiling, changing the subject, saying: 'You haven't said what prompted the visit to Kirkwall, all alone.'

I said defensively: 'I'm used to being on my own rather a lot.'

A look of compassion as he said gently: 'Poor Rose. I forgot.'

The last thing I wanted from him was sympathy for the poor young widow. And because I desperately needed to tell someone, to share my fears and perhaps even seek reassurance, I decided to confide in Craig.

I began at the beginning. The garden at Yesnaby and

seeing the mermaid stone. The feeling that I had seen it somewhere before.

'Yes. I remember,' Craig interrupted. 'You asked me about it. Did I know where there was a similar stone?'

'I didn't know then that Thora was wearing a locket with the same design. Have you seen it – in her portrait?'

He shook his head. "Fraid not. The portrait was never on display on the rare occasions when I've been invited to cross the threshold. So?'

'So I remembered where I had seen that same locket.' I paused dramatically. 'In Edinburgh – just last year.'

It had to come out then. I handed him one of my cards.

He read it and whistled. 'A detective – like your father.' He grinned. 'Who would have guessed it? How on earth—?'

And I told him about Mrs Smith, my client, who had the locket stolen from her hotel room. Craig didn't seem all that impressed. He listened silently and I was disappointed when he merely shrugged.

'Could have been a copy, of course.'

'Not this time, Craig. Not when Mrs Smith was also Thora Yesnaby.'

That bombshell went down like a damp firework.

He gave me a puzzled glance. 'I don't get it, Rose. How could she be the same woman? Thora had been dead for years—'

'So we all thought, but when Emily showed me the portrait of Thora – which had been stored away in the attics – that was why you never saw it – I recognised her as the woman I had known as Mrs Smith.'

Craig was silent, thoughtful in the pause that followed. 'Are you absolutely sure about all this, Rose? I mean, could you have made a mistake? After all, I mean, it isn't impossible for people to have doubles. And portraits aren't always accurate images.'

'I agree. I realise it could have been merely a very strong resemblance, but I wasn't wrong about the locket. Of that I am certain. You see, I had held it in my hand.'

Again he whistled, said slowly: 'You realise what you're telling me, Rose? That Thora, after pretending to be dead for years, came back to Hopescarth and got herself murdered? That someone pushed her into the peat-bog? Who on earth would want to do that – and why, for heaven's sake?' He laughed shakily. 'Really, Rose, this is too fantastic, beyond belief.'

I said nothing and he gave me a sharp look. The obvious and only answer to the identity of Thora's killer had also occurred to him.

He said slowly: 'Bit inconvenient for Erland, wasn't it, though? Especially when he thought he had buried her remains in Hopescarth kirkyard ten years ago.' He paused, frowning. 'Wait a minute. What about that other woman – in the family grave? The one who drowned – who was she?'

Even as his words sank in, the answer was there, staring me in the face.

But I still couldn't see it.

Chapter Twenty-Eight

At breakfast next morning, Emily handed me a note: 'For you, Rose.'

She looked curious as I read it. 'Who is it from?'

'Craig Denmore. He's taking me to the Troll's Cave.'

Erland looked up from his newspaper, his face anxious. 'Do be careful, Rose.' And then the oft-repeated warning: 'It can be very dangerous.'

'I promise to take care,' I assured him. And with a certain pride: 'I'm sure Craig will look after me.'

Erland shrugged. 'You know how to get there?'

When I said I had been told it was close to Sibella's croft, he shook his head. 'It is indeed, but you can easily miss it. The best way to approach is by the shore.'

'You will take care,' Emily said anxiously and I couldn't resist saying again:

'Don't worry, I'll be in very good hands.'

When I went upstairs, I looked again at the note. 'Meet this afternoon at 3 at the Troll's Cave. Craig.' A brief scribble on a piece of paper torn from a notebook, the time altered from 5 to 3, as if he had written it in a great hurry.

I was delighted at the prospect of seeing him again so soon. A calm sunny day too, especially as access to the cave was dependent on the weather and tides.

I walked down to the shore, the cliffs rising sheer above me. The sea looked warm and friendly too, very blue, with gentle waves lazily lapping the shore and a few seals basking in the sunshine, looking for all the world like human bathers after a strenuous swim.

I found it hard to believe that this tranquil scene could be transformed within minutes to a place of death and destruction, that the sea's lace-edged calm could change suddenly from smooth sapphire into fierce white foam, ready to suck the unwary down into the needle-sharp rocks below the surface

The entrance to the cave was a natural crevice set back against the cliff about four feet above the sand, an access to be skilfully negotiated over rocks, treacherous with wet seaweed.

I made my way carefully, leaping from one smooth rock to the next, thankful that since Craig's terse note hadn't mentioned a picnic, I had both hands free. I was early with half an hour to spare. The dark interior of the cave held globules of reflected light but I decided against penetrating too far into that gloomy cavern. Especially as imagination had no problem at all in conjuring up the resident trolls with leering faces hiding in every crevice.

Suddenly I felt scared, my scalp tingling as I nervously glanced over my shoulder, trying to see beyond the cave's shadowy depths.

Once I thought I heard breathing, fancied a nearby movement where there should have been none and told myself it was merely glancing sunlight.

Perhaps Craig had got here first after all.

Nervously I called: 'Craig, is that you?'

Then out of the darkness, a shadow exploded, swooped down on me. A trapped bird, I thought and ducked to avoid a glancing blow.

I cried out as something struck out at my head.

But it was a human hand that struck me. Hard.

The darkness shifted and absorbed me into its depths.

I was in the land of no-time. The centuries had turned back. In earth time, the flight of a single arrow, the shiver of a solitary leaf falling upon the ground.

I was wading through the shallows, a tall ship lying at anchor in the dying moonlight of a cold autumn dawn. Men came ashore in boats, in furs and rich raiments, huddled against the piercing wind, the seabirds screaming above their heads.

In their midst, women wept into hooded cloaks. Ahead of them, a man solemnly bore the body of a child aloft, high above the sea.

A small exquisite girl child, her face waxed pale by death. Only her hair moved, a cloud of straight yellow hair, braided and entwined with pearls.

One of the younger women ran forward weeping, returning with sea-thrift and blue flowers, a mourning wreath to set about her mistress's brow as they made their way towards the sole habitation, a crude stone building like a hermit's cell on the skyline, dwarfed by the bleak landscape.

The child's death had been sudden, unexpected, and had taken all by surprise. The sound of a carpenter's hammer on the shore mixed with the boom of the sea, a funeral knell, numbing the dirge of weeping women.

At last, as all shivered, waiting, their work completed, the mourners watched with folded hands, trembling against cold and sorrow as the small body, wrapped in cloth of gold, was reverently carried to its bier, swathed in a black velvet cloak.

I followed at a respectful distance, conscious even then that I was an observer only and that they would shrink in horror from this ghost of a time still to come.

Climbing the steep hill with no path I walked in the footsteps of the mourners. In my dream this was a familiar place although against that dawn horizon there was nothing to break the cold barren landscape but the outline of the hermit's cell.

We stumbled over boulder and rocks towards it, as a voice called: 'Where shall we lay our young majesty to rest?'

The man who came forward, staff in hand, with the important air of a priest, replied: 'Here she shall lie, facing across the sea. Towards her own beloved land.'

At his words, a keening wail from the women.

'Let it be so, as I command,' the priest went on. 'For one day, we shall return and give her proper burial with a solemn mass and all honours due to a beloved queen.'

I watched them move forward, a watcher beyond time, when suddenly I was no longer alone.

At my side. A huge animal. A deerhound.

Past and present became one.

'Thane,' I whispered.

But this deerhound was different. This deerhound had a human voice.

'Leave us. Go – hurry – or the sea will take you. Wake from your dream, Rose. Wake…'

But as he circled me, frantically barking, I was already in the sea, its cold spread was gripping my feet, crawling up my legs.

One last glimpse of the cortege of the dead. The deerhound

*wavering, dissolving into the air, his barking growing fainter,
as I called weakly:*

'Stay with me, Thane! Don't leave me!'

*I was aware of danger, of quicksand. Unable to move, the
thick wetness growing higher, higher. Past my waist…*

*My eyelids were too heavy to open but I knew, although I
dreamed, that I was in deadly peril. That I must escape from
this nightmare, awaken to find myself safe again in my warm
bed at Yesnaby House.*

*I blinked furiously, a trick I had learned from Pappa long
ago, to rouse myself from childhood's grisly nightmares. But
the effort of opening my eyes, squeezing my eyelids together
was like moving lead weights.*

I kept on…

It worked. Suddenly I was awake.

Suddenly I was awake. But far from safe. Or my warm bed.

Confused, I thought at first that I had fallen asleep in
the bath. Dark, the lamp had gone out, the water grown
cold. So cold.

Then, horror-stricken, my eyes fully open, I had
stepped from one nightmare into another.

I was lying in water, the sea was rushing through what
had been the mouth of the Troll's Cave.

I was trapped…

As I tried to stand up, the weight of the sea hurled me
on to my back again. I coughed up salt water, tried again to
rise, realising that I had been carried unconscious by the
water and drifted into the depths of the cave… Or I had
been carried by human hands. And left to drown.

I tried get on to my feet. But there was no light to see
by. At that moment I lost all reason and panicked for there
was no way I could get through that solid flood of water.

No way I could reach the entrance of the cave, which had vanished under the tide.

I began screaming although there were none to hear my cries. And I became aware that my head, too, screamed with pain, with the force of the blow I had been dealt by that unknown assailant.

It was only the brutal force of the sea that had brought me back to consciousness. Obviously I was not meant to recover my senses. The intention was plainly that I should be trapped in the cave.

And left to drown. And this was no troll or trolls at work, no supernatural agency here.

Someone was trying to kill me.

And I knew in that instant not to give in to panic. My life depended on logical thought against this inferno of sound, these fierce waves tearing at me. I had to use my reason – my poor ever-diminishing reason that told me I must die, that I must drown in the next few moments, if I could not think clearly.

Think clearly. And battling to keep my head above the rising waves, I put out my hands like a blind woman, edged forward.

And was rewarded. By firm rock beneath my hands. Running them downwards, I touched a ledge. About a foot wide and a yard above the floor of the cave. As I struggled to scramble on to it, the sea tore angrily at me, dragging me under.

At last I was on my feet, above the water. For a moment it seemed that I was safe. Soaked, cold. Alive, but for how long?

The water too, that raging sea, continued to rise and I remembered that this was the tide that flooded the cave. The dreaded 'roarin' roarst'. There was a funnel Craig had told me about. A chimney-like funnel. Somewhere far above my head on the cliff top where one could watch the waters spouting out.

A spectacular show, he had called it.

And with just a glimmer of hope, I realised that the presence of a chimney meant more than one exit from the cave. If I could find it and if it was wide enough to take a human being.

At least I was small, and slim too. Perhaps that would save me if I could escape by squeezing through.

I began to struggle along the rocky ledge, searching for the gleam of sky that would show me where the funnel exited. And even then my heart failed me, as sense whispered: What if it is night out there too, how will you see it?

How long I had been unconscious, I could only guess. But I remembered I had left the house shortly after two o'clock, so was it still a warm summer afternoon outside? And even as I thought of promises, I thrust out of my mind the horror of the evil intent that had lured me to my death.

Inch by inch, I crawled along the ledge, clinging desperately to any protruding rock, for if I missed my footing and fell back into the foaming water, then there was no hope for me. I would drown.

Then at last I saw it. A few feet above my head, an unmoving area of light. A gleam of sky.

Here was my chance of survival, a very small chance and only if I could reach it. Struggling forwards, I tried to be patient, aware of my pounding heart and moving slowly and with care not to make any mistake and slip. Taking my time, remembering that it was not yet full tide when the trapped seas would be roaring out of that tiny space.

After what seemed like hours of careful negotiation, the spout came nearer, glowing like an angel's halo above my head. And I guessed that although the space was too small for a full grown man or even an average-sized woman, I was small enough to squeeze through.

Had I been taller I could have stood up and scrambled through, but I was too short and now had to desperately seek out footholds on stone worn slippery smooth. Sometimes I got a foot on to a protruding rock and then found it too weak to support my weight as a sliver crumbled, broke off and fell back into the water, almost taking me with it.

Sometimes I screamed as I regained my balance and sobbing with exhaustion, summoned up enough breath to call for help in the forlorn hope that someone walking on the clifftop would hear my cries.

'Help… Help…' I shouted at intervals but how could a human voice compete against the roar of the waves echoing in the cave?

Then at last when all hope seemed to fade, my shouts were heard, my prayers answered…

A face appeared, filling the round aperture above my head, blocking out the sky.

The face of my rescuer!

'Thank God – thank God,' I sobbed and reached my arms up as far as I could for that saviour to seize.

The face moved forward. A man's face.

For a moment it was in focus.

'Grab hold of my arms. Quickly – heave me out,' I cried, sobbing with gratitude at my deliverance.

Chapter Twenty-Nine

'Help me out!' I called again.

But Frank Breck stared down at me, unseeing, bewildered.

'Help me! I am going to drown....'

He did not move. Then his face, my last hope of surviving, disappeared.

Perhaps he was going for help – for a rope.

I could not wait for that. Again I tried to climb but my foot slipped and I plunged back, screaming. A second later and I would have submerged under that boiling, thrusting water. I only just regained my balance on the narrow ledge, no longer able to distinguish between the sound of the waves dashing against the funnel sides and my own heartbeat.

I could not believe that Frank would abandon me to drown. But there was no time to reason out his odd behaviour as the water was higher now, growing more ferocious.

The ledge had saved me, otherwise I would have been drowned on the floor of the cave or in the fury of the rising tide. As I struggled to climb those last few feet, I tried to think calmly. If Frank, as I hoped and believed, had panicked and gone for help, it was almost too late now. I had only minutes, perhaps seconds, before the waves gained full strength and funnelled up out of the spout.

Clinging with one hand, I used the other to feel for any possible footholds on the slippery rock face worn smooth by centuries of the roarst. I knew, even as I made one last effort, that no one was coming to save me, although Frank could have done so quite easily. Kneeling down, I still believed his arms could have reached out and dragged me to safety.

There was a projecting lip in the rock wall near the funnel, just above my head. My last hope. I eased my way carefully along praying that it would take my full weight when I tried to stand upright—

And then the dreaded waters were my saviour. With a great roar, an extra strong wave propelled me forwards and upwards. A moment later I was lying, half out of the chimney, clawing at the rocks, the sea rushing behind me, rising in a great spout of water.

My progress was watched by a screaming cloud of gulls, swooping down over my head. Doubtless used to the wave washing fish and other delectables on to the rocks, their bright eyes and cruel beaks as they hovered indicated that this was an interesting new morsel.

Waving my arms to keep them at bay, I struggled to my feet on firm land, dripping water, shivering but safe.

Safe, but terrified – as the dreadful realisation dawned.

Someone had tried to kill me.

Someone – and logic whispered Craig Denmore – had sent a note, telling me to met him at the Troll's Cave.

At high tide!

And he had come to make sure that I was in the cave. Had hit me on the head and left me there to drown.

As for Frank Breck. Where did he fit in? Was he Craig's accomplice? Was this some plot concerning the Maid of Norway's dowry or was I too close to the truth of Thora's murder for comfort?

Squelching water at every step, my clothes weighed down with water, I staggered along the cliff path.

On the horizon the dig appeared to be deserted, the nearest hint of habitation, Siella's croft. Too weak and exhausted to face the walk to Hopescarth, I pushed open the gate, feebly pushed open the door.

Sibella was sitting by the fire and at first glance I hardly recognised her. I shivered, not with cold this time, for on each occasion we met her appearance was a shock and I realised that she was starting to look – well, not quite human.

She heard me come in, turned those strange round eyes slowly towards me. I stretched out my arms and collapsed on to the floor, the water pouring from my hair and clothes.

'Rose! Rose, what has happened to you?'

She helped raise me to my feet. Choking, I sobbed that I had been in the Troll's Cave, as she seized towels and stripped off my wet clothes. At last, huddled over the fire, shivering and inarticulate, I gasped out the story which was already sounding more like a nightmare than reality.

I could see by Sibella's expression that she thought so too.

'Who sent you that note?' she asked calmly.

When I said Craig, she repeated almost in a whisper: 'Craig.'

A moment later she added: 'But he would never send

anyone there at high tide, Rose. No one who knows anything about this area would ever do such a terrible thing. They know the consequences, there have been many drownings there…'

I could think of nothing to add to that.

'Are you absolutely sure it was Craig?' she said.

I thought for a moment she looked worried, even scared as I said bitterly: 'Who else?'

Shaking her head, she nodded grimly, repeated: 'Craig.' And thrusting a bowl of soup into my hands: 'Drink this. There are herbs in it which will stop you taking a chill,' she added, turning her attention to towelling my hair, a thick sodden entanglement. I winced when she touched the lump raised on the back of my head.

'It's a miracle you managed to escape the roarst. Most folk drown. However did you get out of that funnel?' And regarding me in wonder: 'I expect you have to thank the fact that you are so small. Most grown-up folk could never have got through, they'd stick halfway,' she added with a shudder. 'Even children have been caught like that and drowned.'

Regaining strength and some of my composure, I told her about the ledge and how I had worked my way towards daylight.

'Frank Breck was there, outside on the clifftop. He heard me shouting for help.'

'So that was it. You were lucky, lass.'

'No, Sibella, I wasn't. Frank looked down, saw me and just walked away. All he had to do was lean over and grab my arms. I thought at first he had gone for help, but there was no sign of him anywhere when I managed to get out.'

Bewildered by all this, Sibella shook her head as I continued: 'And there's more. Someone was already in the cave, waiting for me.' I touched the bump on my head. 'Feel that! It's fortunate that my hair is so thick, otherwise the blow might have split my skull.'

Touching my head gingerly, she looked even more perturbed when I told her how I had been attacked, a little disbelieving, as if I had imagined the whole thing.

Taking the empty bowl from me and when I said it was delicious, she offered a refill. 'Drink this. Then you must get back to the house quickly and into dry clothes. We'll sort out what happened to Frank later. Don't worry, Rose. There must be some simple explanation.'

Whatever the soup contained, I had stopped shivering and began to feel a little better. Anger was fast replacing my feelings of terror.

Sibella bundled up my wet clothes and wrapped me in a blanket. 'I'll walk with you, lass. See you safe home.'

I put out a delaying hand. 'Before we go, Sibella, there is something I want to tell you about. I'm not sure that anyone else but you might understand. They might dismiss what happened as hallucination, the result of being hit on the head. When I was unconscious and the sea was coming in, slowly then, I had a dream. At least, I think that's what it was.'

And I told her about seeing the Maid of Norway carried ashore by the mourners, every detail as I could remember it.

'I'm sure the place was Hopescarth – here somewhere nearby. Although it was quite different then. No house of course, no garden, but there was an ancient building no larger than a tool shed where the garden is now. One of those tiny early Christian chapels you see on deserted islands, their history lost long ago.'

'Like Eynhallow, you mean.'

'Yes, but smaller than that. The kind a hermit might have built.'

She smiled. 'Or a saint, Rose. Or a saint.' And with a sigh, 'If the Maid is buried here, if your vision was true, I think perhaps you should keep it to yourself, for the present anyway.'

And I guessed she was warning me about Craig when she said: 'I think your vision was a blessed one, Rose. I always knew somehow right from our first meeting that you were different – one of Us,' she added in a whisper, leaving me no doubts about who 'Us' referred to.

Again she smiled. 'Someone watches over you, Rose.'

There was only one thing I had omitted from my dream. And there seemed enough fantasy without adding a deerhound with a human voice.

But she accepted that part of the vision too.

She nodded eagerly. 'Sometimes in moments of peril, animals can talk, warn us. There are many examples of their extra sense of danger, a sense that humans had once, in the early days of civilisation, but have now lost.' She regarded me gravely. 'However, some of us, a very few, retain a few shreds. That's all.'

I looked at her. 'And is that what magic is all about?'

She nodded. 'Part of the secret. Having this extra awareness is what makes witches and warlocks – and animals that can talk...'

'I know an animal like that, Sibella – the one in my dream!'

I had never told anyone at Hopescarth, certainly not Emily or Gran, about Thane, my deerhound, who had his own baffling and mysterious existence on Arthur's Seat and I watched Sibella's expression carefully as I spoke.

But she didn't look cynical or question me, as I expected

and walking towards the drive to Yesnaby House, I saw she was entranced by the story of Thane. Wanting to know more about him. So I told her how he had saved me from the tinkers and from a murderer.

'And who else has seen him?'

'He keeps out of sight and only chooses to make friends with those he trusts. Like Jack – my policeman friend.'

She laughed. 'Ah, Jack. The one you can't make up your mind to marry.' And wagging a finger at me: 'I think you'd do well not to let this Jack go, if your deerhound approved of him.'

And there at the most interesting part, where I wanted to know more, our conversation was terminated.

We never reached the drive. As we crossed the bridge, the sound of a motor car indicated that Craig Denmore was on the road behind.

Despite reawakened terror at this confrontation, there were many questions for which I must have answers. And none which could await a more opportune moment.

Chapter Thirty

Glad of Sibella's presence at my side, I nevertheless had a sudden desire to take to my heels, to run from the helmeted and goggled driver bearing swiftly down upon us.

No longer the fascinating, handsome Craig Denmore, with whom I was allowing myself to fall just a little in love, this new image was sinister, terrifying, as the motor car snorted to a halt alongside.

'What on earth has happened to you, Rose?' Craig demanded. Doubtless we made a curious spectacle, the old woman and the girl wrapped in a blanket, bare-legged and carrying her boots.

It was Sibella who spoke up. 'Rose had an accident at the Troll's Cave,' she said stiffly, 'and I'll be obliged if you will take her up to the house as quickly as you can.' Then with a warm protecting arm around me: 'I'll see you later, lass.'

'Wait, Sibella, please.' I wanted her to stay with me. I felt safe in her presence, but she was already walking away, that odd walk, dragging her feet, more evident than ever.

Again the startling image that Sibella was – reverting? I

wondered if Erland and Emily noticed or just dismissed it as the normal pattern of old age.

'What on earth were you doing in the Troll's Cave?' demanded Craig who looked puzzled enough to deserve a 'not guilty' verdict as he leaped down to help me into the passenger seat. 'I warned you that it was dangerous and I told you to wait until I looked up the tide-times,' he added sternly, staring down into my face as he started the engine.

As it roared into life, he shouted: 'You could have drowned!'

'And I almost did. No thanks to you!' I yelled back.

'Can't hear a word. Tell me when we get you home.'

It was a short drive but a cold one sitting wrapped in Sibella's blanket. The front door was closed and I trudged round to the kitchen entrance which was never locked.

Craig followed. The kitchen was empty and I guessed that Emily would be having her afternoon nap. Gran wasn't in evidence either, leaving me with some anxious moments wondering if I'd be safe enough with Craig.

After what had happened, alone with him in an empty house. I had only myself to blame for trusting him, confiding my fears about Thora Yesnaby and the story of that stolen locket in Edinburgh.

Suddenly a thought unbidden clicked into place.

'Get dressed,' he said, handing me the bundle of wet clothes. 'I'll wait.'

I shivered. 'I feel like a drowned rat.'

He grinned and said softly. 'A very pretty drowned rat.'

At any other time how my heart would have raced at that tender look, I thought as I ran upstairs safe in the knowledge of Emily's presence just yards away behind her closed bedroom door.

The note Craig had sent was still where I had left it on

the dressing-table. I read it again and now angry and confused, with no time to look out dry clothes, I put on a robe, bound my wet hair with a ribbon.

Downstairs, Craig was still there standing by the stove. He had made a pot of tea. Pouring out two cups, adding milk and sugar, he smiled as I sat opposite him at the table.

Looking me over, he shook his head. 'You silly girl, Rose. You know you could have drowned.'

I repeated: 'I almost did.' And as the whole terrifying scene returned, throwing down the note I sobbed out: 'How do you explain this – telling me to meet you there?'

Slowly he picked it up, read it and frowning, read it again.

'It is your writing, isn't it?'

He looked up. 'Yes, but I don't understand.' And shaking his head. 'I didn't send this to you, Rose.' Stretching across the table he took my cold hands, rubbed then, as if restoring life into them. 'Rose, how could I have asked you to go to the Troll's Cave – to meet me? I had to take some artefacts to the steamer, to catch the tide. As well as people to see in Stromness. I left here at eleven this morning.'

'How do you explain your note, then? Someone was expecting me. They were waiting in the cave.' And fighting back hysteria, I thumped my fists on the table. 'I was hit over the head. I have a huge bump to prove that.'

Craig still stared at me, bewildered and I thought angrily, quite unbelieving. 'Someone tried to kill me in your Troll's Cave.'

He shook his head. 'Surely not, Rose.'

'As sure as we are sitting here.'

He listened patiently without interruption or denial as I told him what happened. At the end, he said: 'You believe you were attacked, knocked unconscious. And this person – whoever it was – left you in the cave to drown.'

Pausing, he stared at me wide-eyed. 'That is just incredible, Rose. I can scarcely believe such a dreadful thing—'

I knew it sounded like that, but I went on: 'The incoming tide, the shock of the cold water brought me back to my senses and then I realised that the cave was being flooded. I fought my way to the funnel you had told me about. As I tried to climb out, Frank came—'

'Frank?' His head jerked up.

'Yes, I saw Frank. He was there outside on the clifftop. I shouted for help and he looked down at me.'

'You were lucky that he was there to save you.'

'To save me!' I screamed at him. 'You don't understand, do you! He just stared at me and walked away.'

'Maybe he didn't see you—'

'Oh yes, he did. I was only an arm's length below him, struggling in the mouth of the funnel—'

As I spoke Craig seized the note, looked at it again, said triumphantly: 'That's it! This note, I knew I'd written it. It's one I sent addressed to him – with his name cut off.'

Biting his lip, regarding me narrowly, he said slowly: 'Someone else used my note to Frank.'

'You don't believe it was him, do you? Or that I saw him.'

He looked at the note again, apparently reluctant to believe ill of Frank Breck. 'Weren't you suspicious when you got this? I mean, did it sound like me? A bit brusque and businesslike, not particularly friendly. Didn't you think so?'

'Yes,' I admitted.

He smiled, looking relieved. 'Weren't you surprised?'

'Not really. This was the first communication I'd ever received from you – perhaps you always write curt notes, how on earth was I to know?'

I spoke sharply but he wasn't listening any more. 'If it really was Frank who sent this,' he said grimly, 'then he has some explaining to do.'

'Attempted murder, assault, among other things,' I said.

'Let's not be rash. Anyone on the dig or in our lodging could have picked up the note and altered it.'

'All right. Give me one good reason why.'

He shook his head. 'Why should Frank want to do this – try to kill you? You've hardly met – you've certainly never harmed him.'

'I don't know the answer to that, but I intend to find out. I do know however, that I wasn't the first of his victims.'

Craig stared at me. 'What do you mean – first of his victims?' he demanded. 'What on earth are you saying?'

'I wasn't the first he left to drown,' I said triumphantly.

And one of the missing pieces of the puzzle that had been bothering me suddenly veered into focus as Craig sighed wearily.

'That bash on the head, Rose? Frank Breck never drowned anyone.'

'Oh yes, he did. He killed Lily.'

'Rose, you're crazy. Lily's alive and well in Edinburgh.'

I shook my head. 'No, she isn't. She's dead. Of that I'm certain.' At his dismissive gesture, I went on: 'Here's my proof. Your friend Mrs Lenny was telling me she and Lily were great friends.'

He nodded. 'I know that. Lily used to go across to Skailholm any chance she got. I don't blame her for that—'

'Then please listen, will you? According to Mrs Lenny, Lily's letters ceased abruptly at the end of that dig eleven years ago when she returned to Edinburgh. When according to Frank she made the decision not to come back.'

Craig sighed. 'Eleven years – that's a long time. These things happen. Even to the best of friends—'

'Please hear me out. The time that Lily disappeared for good, mark that well. It was just before Thora Yesnaby also disappeared. In fact, one could safely say they both – left – Hopescarth around the same time.'

'So? I don't see the significance of that.'

And it was at that moment I decided that Craig Denmore might be a great archaeologist but he would never make a detective.

'Lily lodged with Meg,' I said.

Craig nodded. 'They both did.'

'Presumably any letters from Lily would have been forwarded on to Frank.'

He thought about that. 'Perhaps they didn't write to each other. Married couples often fall short on correspondence. Feel they've already said everything there is to say,' he added cynically.

'Jim Mainwell told Mrs Lenny that Lily also stopped writing to him and that he had completely lost touch with her—'

'Hardly surprising. It does happen in even the best of families, you know.'

And somewhat guiltily I remembered Emily, and in particular Pappa on his travels with Imogen, as he went on: 'Besides, brother and sister with a big age gap – not a lot in common. And I suspect that Lily had met someone else and left Edinburgh as well as poor old Frank.'

This was the second time I had been given that piece of speculation. It wouldn't do this time. I said: 'You make it sound very simple, all part of good old human nature and the vagaries of time. But I think there is a more permanent and less endearing explanation,' I added triumphantly.

'So you really believe Lily is dead.' He laughed at my solemn face. 'Come along, Rose. What on earth gives you that idea? Just because she's abandoned her husband and chosen to discreetly disappear so he can't track her down.'

'She didn't abandon her husband willingly, Craig.' After a pause to let this sink in, I said, 'He murdered her. He drowned her off Marwick Head.'

'Rose! Of all the mad ideas!'

'Mad, is it? Then listen carefully. I am certain Lily didn't find someone else and leave Edinburgh. Simply because she has been dead and buried for eleven years. I think Frank killed her, put her in the sea and let his boat drift ashore to be conveniently wrecked by the roarsts. As you once said, reduced to matchwood. It was very fortunate indeed for him that Thora Yesnaby happened to disappear around the same time.'

Craig stared at me. 'What are you saying?' He sounded shocked.

'What I am saying is that the woman's torso Erland conveniently identified as Thora, was in fact all that remained of Lily Breck.'

'Lily Breck!' Craig shook his head violently, said vehemently, 'Rose, this is nonsense. You have too much imagination and what you are suggesting just isn't feasible. Believe me—'

'Believe me, it is quite feasible. He killed her, just as he left me to drown. He knew that I was a private investigator, a female detective. And that worried him. He was scared as hell that I might find out the truth.'

'The truth! I don't see your reasoning – why should he be scared of you?'

'Because when I asked where Lily lived in Edinburgh, he said Newington. And by a coincidence, that's just half a mile away from where I live and I showed him one of my cards. Just to be friendly I suggested calling on her – taking a message from him, or some flowers – when I returned home. I was quite ignorant then of the intricacies of Frank's domestic life – I imagined my offer would be doing him a favour.'

I thought for a moment, recalling his expression, his look of horror.

'He was very sharp with me. Cautious I now realise, aware of the danger if I went to her address in Minto Street and found out that she hadn't been seen there for eleven years. And that he had told everyone a pack of lies.'

I paused for breath. Craig hadn't said a word.

'Tell me, what did Lily look like?'

'I've only seen a photograph of her taken with Maud – Mrs Lenny. She was tallish, slim, dark hair.'

With Mrs Smith in mind I said: 'From the portrait I've seen, that would describe Thora too.'

Enough resemblance for a well decomposed torso of an unknown woman I thought grimly and resolved to see Maud's photograph of her old friend.

Craig was staring at me in amazement.

'You don't believe me, do you?' I asked

'I don't – want – to believe you,' he admitted reluctantly. 'You see, I can't equate my image of Frank as a valued and trusted colleague with that of a wife-murderer who tried to kill you too.'

And shaking his head as if to banish the unpleasant thought. 'In my profession, all the murders we encounter have taken place centuries ago and the killers, where applicable, have turned into history and respectable dust. Murders don't normally happen to people we know,' he added with a sigh.

We were interrupted by footsteps on the stairs. Voices.

Craig whispered: 'I'll go now, if you'll excuse me. I'm not a welcome sight at this particular kitchen table.' And rising to his feet, 'You've given me plenty to think about, Rose McQuinn,' he added grimly.

Time will tell, I thought, relieved that I had been wrong about Craig and that I could still keep some of my romantic illusions intact.

He passed Emily and Gran in the doorway, leaving me to explain as best I could what I was doing in the kitchen with him. At five in the afternoon – in my nightrobe.

Cheerfully ignoring their shocked expressions, I cleared two teacups off the table and said: 'Decided to have a bath. Not a good time, I'm afraid.'

It was also a very transparent lie because the sound of a bath running was audible all over the house.

Emily gave me a hard look. 'Was the water not too cold?' she demanded sternly.

I shrugged. 'It was all right,' I said and thought that any water would pass that test compared to the roarst in the Troll's Cave.

Gran was looking out of the window: 'Craig Denmore's motor car is just going down the drive.'

'Oh, is it?' I said. And by way of a rapid but feeble explanation for his presence in their kitchen: 'He was leaving me a note.'

Gran nodded vaguely and wandered over to the sink,

frowning sternly at the two teacups as if they might be ready with some more plausible explanation of their own.

I withdrew hurriedly and left them both to work out my odd behaviour and reach their own conclusions.

For the moment I had more important things on my mind.

Such as having a word with Frank Breck next morning.

But I was already too late.

Chapter Thirty-One

When I came down to breakfast, Craig was talking to Erland.

He had brought bad news. Frank Breck was dead.

'An accident with a rifle,' he explained. 'Early this morning. He was going out shooting, the gun misfired. I drove him in to the hospital but it was too late.'

Emily and Gran were seated bolt upright at the table. Erland stood with a hand on Emily's shoulder, anxiety in his face as he watched her as if the shock of this bad news might affect their unborn child.

I had to see Craig alone. I knew that was why he was at Hopescarth and a look, a silent message passed between us.

'What rotten luck,' was my somewhat inadequate comment. And seizing my cape from the peg, I said: 'I need to catch the post,'

'Wait. I'll take you,' Craig put in quickly.

A moment later we were outside. Sudden death was an outrage against this bright shining morning, with seabirds, a radiant sky and scene of blissful peace.

As Craig handed me into the passenger seat, I asked:

'How did it happen? Was it really an accident?'

Craig started the engine but a little way out of sight of the house, he braked to a standstill again.

'I didn't see Frank when I got back late last night and I gathered he was going to take Jim Mainwell out shooting. He needed a second rifle, one he didn't often use. It had belonged to his father and he kept it in Meg's shed. He was cleaning it apparently—'

Craig stopped, drew a deep breath. 'It misfired. Fortunate that I had the old girl here—' he patted the wheel— 'parked outside as I had some artefacts for loading on to the early steamer in Stromness. I drove him straight to the hospital.'

Pausing, he shook his head. 'They couldn't do anything for him. But I think you should know that – that he talked to me before the end. About Lily.'

Turning to face me, he sighed grimly. 'It seems you were right in your calculations, clever girl. He killed Lily. There was more to it than her being fed up with the weather and the dullness of summer at the dig. As some of us suspected, she told him she had a new fellow in Edinburgh and was leaving him – for good.

'They were walking on the shore, late that night and had a terrible row. Frank went wild, hit her with a piece of driftwood. Realised she was dead, panicked and pushed her out to sea in his fishing boat. The roarsts completed the job for him – beyond his wildest expectations,' he added grimly.

'Luck was on his side, of course, since Thora had run away and everyone believed that what was washed up at Marwick Head was what was left of her.'

Again he paused. 'Poor old Frank. Apart from the occasional letter forwarded to Lily from Edinburgh which he destroyed, Frank felt he was safe.'

'What about the new man in her life?'

Craig shrugged. 'We will never know. Maybe he was just an invention to get rid of Frank, or if he existed, decided she had changed her mind. Whichever way, it seems highly unlikely – and Frank must have prayed daily – that he would never come to Orkney in search of her. Anyway, as the years passed, Frank must have felt that he was safe.'

He looked at me and smiled grimly. 'Until a young woman came to visit her sister in Yesnaby House. And by the hand of coincidence that young woman lived just half a mile away from Lily in Edinburgh. You know the rest. A female detective! Of all the wretched luck – he had to get rid of you. And his guilt about Lily told him that you were also a kindly lady who might feel it was your duty to be sociable and get in touch with Lily when you got back.

'In a way it was my fault too. I told him you wanted to see the Troll's Cave and did he know where we'd put the tide-tables? The rest was easy. He took one of my notes to him about an artefact consignment, cut off "Dear Frank" – waited for you in the cave and felled you with a blow. He was certain the roarst would do the rest, but to make certain, he watched the funnel from the clifftop,' he added grimly.

'But luck wasn't with him. You hadn't drowned and were struggling to get out. Worst of all you had seen him. He knew that was the end of the line. Better to end it now than on the gallows. The past had caught up with him. Not only a sharp young woman, who was moreover a self-made detective, but also Lily's brother, a policeman from Canada, who was asking a lot of questions—'

'What about Thora?' I interrupted. 'Did he confess to killing her too?'

Craig shrugged. 'I didn't ask. Jim was waiting outside. They only let me stay because Frank insisted. I tried to avoid the gory details but Jim had guessed that Lily was dead – and left it as brief as possible, a row, a fight, not meaning to kill her. Jim has friends in Edinburgh, so he'll visit them for a while before going back home.'

'Was he very upset?'

'Hard to tell. Said the truth might as well go to the grave with Frank. How could anyone prove it now – after all this time? And a scandal like that, the newspapers and so forth. I think he wisely decided that they should both be left to rest in peace.'

Smiling wryly, he turned to me. 'Well done, Rose. That's your mystery solved.'

'One down and one to go. Did he kill Thora?'

Craig shrugged. 'That we'll never know now, I'm afraid. However, I doubt it,' he said. 'Now you can go ahead and enjoy the rest of your holiday. We'll maybe manage some of those picnics yet.'

The engine's roar put an end to any possibility of answers to the many questions regarding that second murder and, as we had reached the bridge, our ways parted.

Thanking him, I said: 'I'll walk down to the post office. I expect you have loads to do.'

He grimaced. 'None of it very pleasant, I'm afraid. I'm more used to dealing with long-dead bodies, not those of friends and colleagues. Andy Green will notify the Fiscal but I imagine it'll be an open and shut case. As far as the law is concerned, accidents with rifles aren't all that unusual. Frank had no surviving family,' he went on, 'so after the inquest, I'll have to arrange the funeral. I doubt in the circumstances, that Jim will want to stay for that. Then I'll have to advertise for another archaeologist for next year's dig. Someone who is enthusiastic enough to take on an Orkney dig, weather regardless.'

He sighed deeply. 'Won't be easy to find, I'm afraid. Poor old Frank. He'll be hard to replace, he was good at his job, I'll say that for him. Quite dedicated.' And looking down at me, 'Let me know when you want to go into Stromness or Kirkwall. We can make a day of it. You came a long way to be with your sister, so try to put all this behind you and enjoy your holiday,' he added solemnly.

I watched him drive away, considering his advice. So I was to go back to Hopescarth and enjoy the rest of my holiday. With everything neatly filed away, a killer found who had murdered his wife, had tried to kill me and, tormented by a guilty conscience, had very obligingly committed suicide, surviving long enough however to confess all to Craig.

Simple, wasn't it?

Unfortunately, I didn't believe that. Oh yes, I did believe the part about Frank having murdered Lily and his reasons for feeling he had to dispose of me. The arrival of Jim Mainwell must have seemed like the last cruel twist of fate.

But the burning question still remained – had Frank also killed Thora? He had not confessed to that for the simple reason that he had loved her and he certainly didn't do it.

Someone else killed her.

There was still the enigma of that unknown young man, Mrs Smith's lover at Brightwell's Hotel unaccounted for.

And I still had at least one more murder to solve.

At the post office I found Meg in a state of shock, surrounded by a crowd of locals to whom she was breaking the terrible news. The men shaking their heads, full of deadly warnings about old rifles, the women sighing like a

Greek chorus, recalling every other violent death on the island.

It was all quite dreadful. I managed to squeeze past and put my postcards on the counter.

Meg saw me and said: 'Mr Mainwell wanted a word with you – asked where you lived. You might save him the journey. He's upstairs in poor Frank's room, sorting things out.'

Followed by her curious look I went upstairs, unsure what condolences to offer, spared the embarrassment when Jim put aside a sheaf of papers, stood up and solemnly shook hands.

'Please take a seat, Mrs McQuinn.'

'I'm so sorry about Frank,' I began. He nodded absently and picked up the address card I had given Frank when I asked where Lily lived.

'Mrs Rose McQuinn. Lady Investigator, Discretion Guaranteed.' Regarding me gravely, he said: 'Was Frank, by any chance, wanting you to look into Lily's disappearance?'

'No. I discovered quite by accident that Mrs Breck lived near me in Edinburgh.'

'Not any longer, Mrs McQuinn. And not for a very long time, I guess,' he added. Holding up a packet of letters addressed to Mrs Lily Breck: 'These were returned to me. But Lily had indeed "gone away". And that is what I came over to investigate.' Pausing, he smiled. 'Yes, ma'am, I'm in the Canadian Mounted Police – a Mountie, maybe you've heard of us – the ones who always get their man – or woman, as the case may be.'

Leaning back he regarded me critically. 'So we are in the same line of business. I'm older than Lily and we lost touch after she married Frank. I remembered she always adored children and, I gather, never had any of her own. I wrote to tell her about the birth of my twin daughters and asked her to be godmother but she ignored the letter completely.'

He sighed. 'I made allowances, perhaps she couldn't bear the thought of her brother having children when she had none, but early last year, when my dear wife died, I wrote to Lily again. I expected some response, some sympathy – perhaps the possibility that she might want to see her little nieces, but again there was nothing. Not a word. I was hurt but there was more to it than that. I was alone, my little girls were being taken care of by friends so I decided I must see Lily again, put a bridge over those lost years.'

This was so much my own story about Emily and losing touch, except that I had found my sister alive and well – and, reason whispered, perhaps married to a murderer, as Jim went on:

'Then something occurred that made it imperative that she be found, her whereabouts traced, alive or dead,' he added grimly. 'An old man on our mother's side who struck it rich gold-mining in '49, died childless in California. We were the only family – remote cousins, it is true, but his money was to be shared between us. A few thousand dollars, not a vast fortune but enough to keep us comfortably off with a few careful investments.

'I thought of my little girls' futures and what it would mean to them and to Lily. I guessed that an archaeologist's wife might be glad of some extra dollars. Hence this trip to Scotland, but the only information I could get from her last Edinburgh address was from the lady who had helped her run the lodging-house and, although they had been close friends, she hadn't had a word from Lily since she left eleven years ago, to spend the summer with her husband in

Orkney. When neither of them returned that autumn, it seemed odd because all Lily's possessions still remained in the house.'

Pausing, he added grimly: 'By now I was beginning to be alarmed and decided to talk it over with a detective in Edinburgh, a contact from the old days. His advice was to come up here. Well, as soon as Frank set eyes on me, he made up a stack of lies that Lily had gone off with some other man years ago. And there it was. If Lily had lived, Frank would have been a rich man too.'

He sighed. 'I'll be straight with you, Mrs McQuinn. I believe that Frank killed Lily and got away with it, since I gather from Dr Denmore that another woman's body was conveniently washed up by the sea. Lucky for Frank that there wasn't an active police force on the island, or much crime in this remote area.'

And confirming what Craig had told me, he added: 'There's no way to prove any of this. Frank has killed himself and they're both gone now. So I will willingly let the matter rest there.'

I'd already decided not to mention that Frank had tried to kill me in the Troll's Cave when footsteps on the stairs and a tap at the door announced Meg who was not very good at concealing her feelings or her curiosity. She was obviously dying to know what Mr Mainwell had wanted to discuss with me so urgently.

'There's food downstairs, if you want it,' she said to him, squinting at the papers and books he'd spread on Frank's desk. 'How's the sorting out going? I'll be obliged if you'll take anything away that you want.'

Jim shook his head. 'There isn't anything really.'

'Then what am I to do with all his possessions?'

'From the contents of his wardrobe, ma'am, you won't

have much trouble there. Just a few well-worn clothes and boots. And his old books. What I was really hoping for was some picture of my sister to take back home.'

As he spoke, he opened a desk drawer. 'Ah, this is more like it!' But the photographs were mostly of artefacts taken before they went across to the mainland and the museums. Skimming through them, he sighed. 'But nothing of Lily, I guess that was too much to hope for.'

'I'll see if I have anything downstairs,' said Meg.

We followed her down and she took from the sideboard cupboard a large cardboard box and, searching through the contents, she shook her head. 'Nothing of your sister, I'm afraid.'

And handing him a group photograph, she said: 'This was taken a couple of years ago. Frank thought I might like a copy. It's the only one I have of him,' she said sadly, laying it on the table. 'But you can have it, if you like.'

I looked at it. A good photograph with the shadow of Yesnaby House in the background. A group of students. In the centre, Frank scowling as usual. A young bearded man smiling at his side.

A man I recognised…

Chapter Thirty-Two

A face I recognised. Knew – and loved!

My heart was pounding. I could hardly breathe.

'The man with Frank – who is that?'

'Which one?' Meg asked.

'With a beard, standing next to him,' I pointed.

And before she said the words, I already knew the answer.

'Why, that's Dr Denmore, of course. Before he shaved off his beard.' Meg laughed. 'Mind you, I have to say it is a great improvement. He said he never liked it much but it saved the bother of shaving every day—'

I was no longer listening.

The photograph trembling in my hands was of Mrs Smith's young lover!

I set it down on the desk, murmured that I had to go now, my sister was expecting me for lunch. Leaving them staring at me, curious about my abrupt departure, once outside my legs began to tremble.

The puzzle was complete. The photograph had given me the answer to the second murder.

The very last answer I wanted to the question of whether or not Mrs Smith had abandoned her lover in Edinburgh. How he had apparently disappeared from the scene when she had come back to Orkney on the steamer, travelling unobserved to Hopescarth as Thora Yesnaby.

Craig Denmore was her escort, the anonymous young man from the hotel, keen to remain in the background. He was no stranger to Hopescarth, they knew him well. His appearance would draw no comment, in their midst, a familiar sight every day, Dr Craig Denmore, the archaeologist.

If I needed further proof, he had lied to me about the beard. Even if I hadn't recognised him, he had known right from when we first met who I was.

And dear God, I had confided in him, all my suspicions about the double murder.

I couldn't face Emily and Gran yet. So I went into the kirkyard and sat among the tombs of the dead, trying to work out what exactly had happened when Thora arrived so unexpectedly at Yesnaby House.

I did not doubt that she had confronted Erland alone. I fervently hoped that she had met him without Emily's knowledge.

Meanwhile Craig would have stayed discreetly out of sight in his lodgings. The more I considered that, another grim possibility sprang to mind.

That Thora had never met Erland at all. Craig had decided to get rid of her and steal the Yesnaby locket.

Was I secretly hoping that was the answer, that her death had nothing to do with Erland and Emily?

It was no great comfort to suspect that Craig knew the archaeological world intimately and how unscrupulous collectors of antiques did not question too closely the origins of the pieces they coveted. If that was the reason, then the locket had indeed disappeared for ever.

Another grim thought. The disposal of Thora in the peat-bog would not have been difficult for a strong man like Craig.

I saw Craig then going off on that lecture tour, taking the locket with a ready buyer from abroad, praying that in his absence one of the team would make the discovery of Thora's body.

But bearing in mind Craig's aristocratic background, was I certain that he would risk killing her solely for the price of the locket? Surely not. There was that rich father, Sir Miles, with the whisky distillery – Craig's inheritance. As for the locket itself, it was certainly too modern for his personal taste.

The cold-blooded murder of Thora did not fit the pattern. I could not visualise him as the passionate jealous lover, who would kill his mistress for taking another lover. I had already marked Craig down as a man who would have his choice of women and, from what I had learned about Thora, finding a new lover had never been one of her problems.

Craig might have been disappointed but there is a long way between disappointment and murder, especially for a clever young man with good looks and a family fortune. Brief memory of Brightwell's Hotel suggested an ill-assorted pair, the older Thora and Craig, the discarded lover, who would bow out calmly saying: 'Thank you and goodbye.'

And another chilling doubt: Had he lied about Frank too? Had Frank really made that death-bed confession?

My dismal theories had a new accompaniment. Rain. Huge drops as large as coins spattered down, robing the dismal gravestones in appropriate mourning black. With no wish for a second soaking, I hurried back along the road leading to the drive.

Absorbed by the complexity of my tortured reasoning, Craig's motor car was almost upon me before I heard it.

Dear God, was he trying to run me down? I leaped aside and landed in the wet hedgerow.

The machine wheezed to an angry halt a few feet down the hill. Craig jumped out, shouting:

'Rose, you idiot! Didn't you hear my horn blasting away?'

'You nearly killed me!' I sobbed.

'I didn't see you until I was at the top of the hill. You know I can't stop quickly on a steep slope.' Close to me now, he said: 'What's wrong, Rose? You look dreadful – that white face doesn't become you.' And taking my arm, 'What's happened? Are you ill?'

I looked up at him. 'I have just had a terrible shock.'

He nodded sadly. 'I know. Poor old Frank. It was awful.'

'Not Frank this time, Craig. This time I've just solved Thora's murder.'

His grip on my arm tightened. 'Get in – I'll drive you home.'

'No!' I struggled to free myself from his grasp.

'Get aboard, for heaven's sake. We're both getting soaked standing here arguing.'

'I can walk, thank you—'

'No, you can't. And I want to talk to you. There are things we have to discuss – now that Frank has gone.'

Weakly I followed him. I wanted to talk to him, too, but as he handed me into the passenger seat, it did occur to me that maybe he intended to kill me. And I had no defence.

Conversation was impossible above the engine's roar

but, as we reached the bridge, I said: 'Put me down here.' He ignored that, so I added: 'I'll walk up the drive.'

'I'm taking the old girl home,' he said. 'She doesn't like getting wet. It isn't good for her.'

The motor car's 'home' as I knew, was the old barn beside Sibella's croft, convenient for the dig. And I thought of the cliff path, how easy to drive past the croft then push me out – down – down – and into the sea.

But Craig merely drove very neatly through the open barn doors and, switching off the engine, turned to me and said: 'Well now, we always seem to be meeting in the rain.'

'And parting too,' I said

He gave me a sharp look. I took a deep breath and said: 'We have met before, you and I. In Edinburgh. You must remember the occasion surely? At Brightwell's Hotel.' I managed a mocking smile. 'And yet when we talked yesterday and I confided my fears in you, you never said a word about that.'

He turned his head away. 'I don't know what you're talking about.'

'Oh, I think you do. We met briefly at an afternoon tea there last October. You had a beard then.'

In a guilty gesture, his hand flew to his chin as I continued: 'You were there with Thora Yesnaby. She was using another name – Mrs Smith – and I gathered you were lovers—'

'Don't be ridiculous, Rose.' He laughed harshly. 'I never met Thora. I remember Mrs Smith though. I was staying at the hotel testing it out as a possible new venue for one of our conferences. Mr Brightwell said he had a guest staying who was also going to Orkney.

'We were introduced and had lunch together. She told me she was returning home after having lived in France for several years and would be grateful for a travelling companion. She didn't care for the idea of making the journey alone, without even a maid. Naturally I agreed to escort her.'

Pausing, he looked at me. 'Whatever made you think we were lovers?' Without giving me a chance to reply to that, he went on: 'She had a French count who wanted to marry her and she was hoping for a divorce. It never occurred to me that there was any connection with Erland Yesnaby, whose wife had drowned years ago.'

I wanted to believe him. His story was plausible enough. Having seen him in Mrs Smith's company, and her remark about having a lover, I had presumed the rest.

He was staring at my grim expression. 'Marry her! For heaven's sake, Rose. Your imagination let you down there. Didn't you think she was a bit old for me? My father would have had a fit. Besides, I have a young lady back in Inverness: right age, good family, excellent breeding prospects. Necessary for dynastic purposes. The future of the distillery and that sort of thing.'

I must confess to being just a little disappointed by that information.

'We've known each other all our lives. However—' Pausing, he sighed and his look was both tender and searching as he put an arm around my shoulders.

'A pretty young widow would give Father a heart attack. Apart from the fact that you are a high-ranking policeman's daughter, your chosen profession might not meet with the family's blessing. And I doubt whether the bicycle would find a warm welcome—'

'Don't try to get round me by changing the subject, please,' I said sternly, reluctantly shaking free from his embrace. 'I want to know why you killed Thora.'

'The answer is easy. I didn't. I never even knew then that she was Thora. I believed like everyone else that she had been dead and buried in the Yesnaby grave years before I set foot in Hopescarth. I'm telling you, Rose, I only knew her as Mrs Smith, a woman I met casually in Edinburgh. And I'd never seen that portrait of Thora you told me about.'

He sounded exasperated. 'As I was saying – if you'd only listen. We reached Stromness, a boring voyage and she stayed in her cabin most of the time, nursing the whisky bottle, I'm afraid. We hired a carriage to Hopescarth and stopped at Meg's. When Mrs Smith said her destination was Yesnaby House, I told her she should have kept the carriage as it was a long way up the drive in the dark. She said she knew that but wanted to surprise them.

'I felt obliged to see her as far as the bridge.' He stopped suddenly. 'That's all I can tell you, Rose. I'm sorry. I have nothing more to say.'

I stared at him in amazement. 'I don't believe it. You're making this up!'

'No, Rose. He isn't.'

A voice behind us.

Someone had been listening to our conversation.

Chapter Thirty Three

A figure moved out of the shadows by the door.

It was Sibella.

'He's telling the truth, Rose. Now, both of you, enough of this nonsense. You'll catch your death sitting out here. Come indoors, where it's warm. Now!'

We followed her across the yard, meek as two naughty children and sat down by the fire.

She smiled at Craig. 'If there are any important pieces I miss out, you'll need to remind me. My memory's not as good as it once was.'

And turning to me, 'Before she went up to the house, she told Craig she wanted to see me first. When she walked in, I thought I had seen a ghost, a very unwelcome ghost. For me, she had been dead for the past ten years. I had grieved for the poor demented lass who we all believed had drowned in the sea down yonder.'

She sighed. 'I saw immediately that this Thora was different. I asked her where she had been all these years. "Living abroad", she said. And then I asked her why she had come back.'

Pausing she looked across at Craig. 'You were going to leave politely at that point, but she said he was to stay, that she'd maybe need a witness for her business up at the house. I asked her what that was and she laughed, said: "To return the locket and in return for it get a large divorce settlement. My lover is a penniless French count, we can only marry if I can provide him with a dowry. In return I won't make it public that Erland's marriage is bigamous and any children are illegitimate."'

Sibella sighed. 'She turned to me and said: "I presume that he married his precious Emily and that there are children?" And I could have bitten my tongue for I spoke too soon, told her that Emily was going to have a baby after all these years. If I had hoped for her compassion, I soon found out how wrong I was.

'She screamed with mirth, clapped her hands. "That's even better for my purpose, then," and I knew that she had no pity or goodness in her heart and that she meant to destroy Emily and Erland.'

Pausing, she shook her head, said slowly: 'And I couldn't allow her to harm a hair of my precious Emily's head.' Turning to Craig, she went on: 'You remember how agitated she was that night? She behaved like someone demented.'

Craig nodded in silent agreement and Sibella said: 'She kept shouting that she needed a drink. She'd already had more than enough I was thinking. I hadn't any whisky and that infuriated her. She dived among my jars scattering them, shouting: "You're lying. You're lying. Everyone has whisky."'

She sat back in her chair, her face stricken and Craig took her hand, said: 'We tried to calm her down, so she demanded some of Sibella's herbs, the ones she used to get in the old days—'

Sibella took over again. 'Said there was a special one. I knew which she meant. She held a jar up, screamed: "This is it!" It was a drug and not to be taken lightly. "Just a few drops then," I said but she snatched it from me. And at that moment, I knew exactly what I had to do. It was like a revelation, like a voice whispering in my ear. A plan. And I thought, whatever happens this night, Emily and Erland need never know. They will be safe. For them Thora has been dead for years. So unless their lives were to be ruined for ever and my Emily lose her precious baby, then Thora – must – must remain dead.

'So I took the bottle and gave her enough, I hoped, for a fatal dose.'

She stopped, regarding me with those strange luminous eyes. 'I killed her, Rose. Poisoned her. The only thing I did not know was how long it would take to work on top of all the whisky in her system she'd had before she came. And would it work quickly enough to stop her going up to the house.

'I watched her gulp it down. Demand more. Amazingly she said: "I feel wonderful now, ready to go and shatter that happy family." She swayed a bit and Craig took her arm.'

Sibella looked at him. 'He had no idea what I had done, poor lad.'

There was a long pause before Craig spoke. 'I was still shocked, I suppose, at finding my travelling companion was the resurrected Thora Yesnaby. I hadn't any idea what Sibella had given her, but as she screamed that she wanted more, Sibella held the jar away from her and she grabbed a knife off the table and screamed: "Give me that or I'll kill you both!" She lunged at us, I grabbed her as she dragged Sibella on to the floor.'

He stopped, shaking his head and I visualised the dreadful scene as Sibella said: 'The drug had given her tremendous strength and we could hardly hold her. The next thing I knew, I had her head and banged it on the floor. She lay quite still.'

'Everything was so quiet, I think we both knew that she was dead. Between us we had killed her,' he added softly.

'No, lad. My fault – my drug and striking her head like that. We didn't know what to do next. We had a dead body on our hands. "The sea?" I asked him.'

'"Not again", I said. "We can't hope for another roarst and a second burial",' Craig said. 'I had a better idea. The peat-bog. It was just a short distance to carry her. You know the rest.'

He paused and they looked at each other. Silently, reliving the horror of those last hours.

'I went off next day and it was our secret,' he said.

'Always has been, lad. No one ever knew of Thora's second arrival at Yesnaby.'

Or of Erland and Emily's lucky escape, I thought as I asked: 'What happened to the locket?'

In answer Sibella unlocked a drawer, took it out. 'That's where it's been for the past year.'

And for the second time I held it in my hand.

'Time it was resurrected from the peat-bog, Craig,' she said. 'And returned to Erland. He'll be delighted.'

There isn't much more to tell. I went back up to the house and slept soundly. I still had more than a week to enjoy my holiday with Emily and nothing more nerve-wracking to anticipate than Wilma's promised bicycling lessons.

Jim Mainwell returned to Edinburgh. I didn't expect to see much of Craig and I wasn't expected to go to Frank's funeral. Ladies stay at home and make the sandwiches, is the general rule.

Early that week, however, one of Craig's students made an interesting discovery. A piece of jewellery shining in the thick green moss of the peat-bog, identified as the Yesnaby locket. Craig had been good to his word and the young lad received a handsome reward from a grateful and surprised Erland.

But there was still one more discovery in store for me. One sunny afternoon I went down the steps into Erland's garden and wandered past the Ghost orchid to the ivy-covered embrasure with the stone carving of the mermaid.

For me, this was where it all began. The long-awaited holiday with my sister, which had changed into nightmare and murder.

The stone seat, so tranquil in sunshine, aroused terrifying memories of those hallucinations when I was knocked unconscious by Frank in the Troll's Cave. They do say your former life flashes before your eyes at the point of drowning, but mine was even more extraordinary, for I had been transported to another time.

The funeral procession of the Maid of Norway.

That would always remain vividly in my mind, despite all that had happened afterwards. And now as I looked around, I knew for certain that it was Hopescarth I had seen before Earl Patrick had built his palace here. The landscape and the sea were unaltered, this fragment of an ancient wall once part of the hermit's cell where the mourners had halted with their little queen –

To dig a grave.

Looking closer, I saw that this embrasure had not been intended a seat. And although the search for the Maid's dowry would continue, I had solved another mystery.

I looked up at the house and Erland was standing by his study window. He had been watching me and waved. I waved back and stayed where I was, certain he would come into the garden.

He did, made some preliminary remarks about being glad I was enjoying the sunshine on his little sheltered seat.

I shook my head, said quietly, 'It isn't a seat, Erland. It's a grave.'

'Now what makes you think that, Rose?' he asked cautiously, so I told him about the dream.

'This is where they laid her to rest. Am I right?'

Erland had listened silently. Now he nodded. 'My grandfather found it when he was working on the garden. Here deep in the earth and he told no one. The information was to remain a family secret passed from father to son. If we have a boy, then I'll tell him and he must swear to keep it secret in his turn.'

'Does Emily know?'

He shook his head. 'Not even a wife: wives are not always discreet,' he added wryly and I wondered if he was thinking about Thora. 'Otherwise we will have folk clamouring to dig up the lassie's bones to put them in a museum.'

He thought for a moment. 'There was something strange though. Her grave clothes had rotted but, after all those hundreds of years, her golden hair was still lustrous, long and beautiful as it had been in life.

'Grandfather Scarth replaced her reverently, exactly as he had found her. He took only one thing to keep and preserve in the family for ever.' His smile was a question.

'The Yesnaby locket? That can't be, Erland. It's not medieval.'

'I know that. Grandfather had it specially made. But it

has a secret. Inside is the one memento of the Maid. A lock of her hair.'

He looked at me and there were tears in his eyes. 'Will you keep our secret, Rose? You, who have, I suspect, to keep so many people's secrets in your chosen profession.'

'I will keep it, Erland.' And he took my hands, kissed them, his eyes closed for a moment. Then we walked back towards the house.

Conscious of being watched, I looked up at the window. There was someone there. A familiar figure.

I was having one of my hallucinations again, I thought. Don't be daft, Rose, it couldn't be – if wishes were horses, then beggars would ride.

In the kitchen, Emily and Gran were smiling, exchanged faintly conspiratorial looks. The door opened and—

'*Jack!!*'

I rushed forward, threw myself into his arms. We hugged and kissed oblivious of the rather embarrassed audience who quietly withdrew…

As he released me, I drew a deep breath.

'Jack Macmerry, what on earth are you doing here?'

He regarded me solemnly. 'I know you don't believe in coincidences, but this one was very strange. I've been working on a fraud case. Our man was last reported in Stromness and looking through the old newspapers, the headline: "Hopescarth peat-bog burial!" caught my eye. I was sure you'd be interested.

'Later that day I went to Solomon's Tower as usual to check that everything was all right and there was Thane sitting at the back door.'

Frowning, he seemed reluctant to continue. I panicked. 'He was all right, wasn't he?'

At that Jack smiled wryly. 'I don't know how to put this

to you – to describe it, but I got the impression that he was
– well, imploring me to do something. He started running
round me in circles. Thought he was just missing you,
hungry – but when I offered him some scraps, he just
turned up his nose.'

Jack stopped, bewildered. 'There was more than that,
Rose. If that dog could speak, the words he would have
used were that – you – were in danger.'

Pausing to let that sink in, he added: 'It has happened to
me before. Remember when that madman tried to kill you
and when you were in deadly danger in a fire. I hate to
admit to things I can't begin to explain or understand,
Rose, but Thane has a link with you somehow—'

'Can you tell me when this happened?' I interrupted.

'Oh yes. 30th August. About four in the afternoon.'

And that was when I was in the Troll's Cave,
unconscious, with my dream about the Maid of Norway
being laid to rest and Thane had appeared at my side,
urging me to wake up – that I'd drown.

Jack was saying: 'Anyway, I decided I'd come to
Stromness with the lads, my excuse to track down our
fraudster. So here I am.'

'Thane – how is he?' I had a sudden longing for my
deerhound as Jack said gently:

'Whatever forces move Thane, he'll know that I'm with
you and that you are all right.' He took my hands. 'I've got
a few days' holiday, don't need to rush back. I'd love to see
Orkney,' he added wistfully.

'First, I have someone else you have to meet.'

'Another member of the family?'

'Yes, Sibella, my great-grandmother. She's 102 and she's
a seal woman.'

As we walked to the door, he stopped: 'Wait a moment.

Seal women. They are sort of witches, aren't they?'

'Something like that.'

He groaned good-humouredly. 'I don't know that I'm strong enough for two witches in the family.'

'Oh, you'll like this one. She's fond of animals.'

In reply Jack kissed me and said approvingly: 'You are looking well, Rose. Obviously a good restful holiday away from crime has done you a power of good.'

And we walked down the road to meet Sibella.

Other titles available from Allison and Busby
by Alanna Knight

In the Rose McQuinn series:

The Inspector's Daughter

1894. In a desperate attempt to recover from the loss of her husband and her baby son, Rose McQuinn returns home to Edinburgh from the American Wild West. Before long she unwittingly steps into the shoes of her father, the legendary Detective Inspector Faro, by agreeing to investigate the strange behaviour of Matthew Bolton, husband to Rose's childhood friend Alice. Alice is convinced Matthew is having an affair but Rose suspects he may have been involved in something much more sinister – the brutal and still unsolved murder of a servant girl. From her isolated home at the foot of Arthur's Seat and aided by a wild deerhound who has befriended her, Rose starts to piece things together, until she gets too near the truth and puts her own life in danger.

Dangerous Pursuits

During a peaceful walk out on Arthur's Seat, high above the city of Edinburgh, Rose McQuinn stumbles across the body of a woman in the ruins of St Anthony's Chapel. Reporting her discovery to a nearby police constable, she assumes that the case is in safe hands. So she is shocked when she returns to the scene to find that both the body and the policeman have disappeared. Further complications ensue when a local woman is reported missing. Unshakeable in her belief that the two cases are linked, Rose determines to pursue a discreet investigation into the double mystery. But she soon finds herself in a terrifying situation, cast in the role of the murderer's second victim…

Ghost Walk

Since the disappearance and presumed death of her husband, Danny, three years ago, Rose McQuinn has managed to overcome her grief and begin her life afresh. She has fulfilled her ambition of becoming a 'Lady Investigator, Discretion Guaranteed' and is on the threshold of marrying her lover, Detective Inspector Jack Macmerry of the Edinburgh Police. But pre-wedding jitters become the least of her worries when a nun from the local convent claims to have received a letter from Danny. Is the elderly nun simply confused, or could Danny really still be alive? Unnerved and determined to find out the truth before her wedding, Rose begins to investigate. However, after two suspicious deaths, all the signs suggest that a ghost is about to walk back into her life...

In the Tam Eildor series:

The Gowrie Conspiracy

July 1600. After rescuing King James from a runaway horse, the enigmatic Tam Eildor finds himself in the monarch's favour, and the royal benevolence is furthered when Tam agrees to investigate the murder of Margaret Agnew, the Queen's midwife. As Tam and his good friend Tansy Scott set about discovering who could have attacked her and why, they come across rumours of a buried secret from the King's past – a secret that could put the King and members of the court in danger. With treacherous forces at work, the King is led away from the palace to Gowrie House in Perth, and into the heart of a mystery that still puzzles historians today...

The Stuart Sapphire

August 1811. George, Prince of Wales, has his own reasons for welcoming Tam Eildor to the Royal Pavilion. His latest mistress, Sarah, Marchioness of Creeve, has been murdered in the royal bed; strangled with her own string of pearls. Newly created Prince Regent, George realises that a sordid scandal must be avoided at all costs, and enlists Tam's services to quickly and – more importantly – quietly find the killer. But murder isn't the only crime Tam has to solve: on the same night as the Marchioness's death a priceless gemstone, the Stuart Sapphire, was stolen. With a double investigation on his hands and his own life in constant danger, Tam struggles to outwit the sinister forces that seem determined to prevent him from discovering the truth.